"I Won't Take No! You Don't Mean It, Maura, You Know That When I Touch You . . ."

Standing as he was, on the threshold, Neil looked like some magnificent golden god. For one moment neither he nor she moved or spoke as they stood eyeing one another, taking each other's measure. Then Neil broke the spell and stepped forward. He pulled her toward him with an urgency that surprised her. She staggered slightly as the weight of his body pressed against her, his mouth nestled in her hair, his hand caressing the curve of her cheek.

As he pulled her closer, tighter, her resistance fled. His tongue was hot and sweet like honey. He crushed her to him in a kiss more complete than any he'd ever given her. The sensation was as nothing she'd ever known. She thought she would die if he didn't stop; she thought she would die if he did.

FORTUNE'S BRIDE

Joy Gardner

A TAPESTRY BOOK
PUBLISHED BY POCKET BOOKS NEW YORK

This novel is a work of historical fiction. Names, characters, places and incidents relating to non-historical figures are either the product of the author's imagination or are used fictitiously. Any resemblance of such non-historical incidents, places or figures to actual events or locales or persons, living or dead, is entirely coincidental.

An *Original* publication of TAPESTRY BOOKS

A Tapestry Book published by
POCKET BOOKS, a Simon & Schuster division of
GULF & WESTERN CORPORATION
1230 Avenue of the Americas, New York, N.Y. 10020

ISBN: 0-671-46053-6

First Tapestry Books printing January, 1983

10 9 8 7 6 5 4 3 2 1

Printed in the U.S.A.

Prologue

MAURA PAUSED AT THE TOP OF THE WINDING marble staircase in the Fifth Avenue mansion. In the pier-glass by the window, she caught a glimpse of herself. Her gown was of satin and lace and rose-colored, a warm, vibrant rose that enhanced her white, creamy complexion and seemed to deepen the blue of her eyes, the burnished gold of her hair. Maura was pleased, and yet she felt a sudden pang of regret. She should have worn white. A bride, a virgin, wears white.

"He's a good fellow, a kind fellow, that's what's important," her Irish father would have said. And, as usual, he would have been right, Maura told herself. Immediately after the ceremony they were going to Saratoga, that famed playground of the rich, with its baths, its gambling casinos, its racing tracks. Peter—Peter Van Diver, heir to the railroad magnate's millions and one of the wealthiest men in New York City and, in fact, the world —had suggested to his soon-to-be wife it would be more practical for her to dress in a

1

gown she could travel in. Also, the ceremony would be brief; since Peter's wife had been dead barely a year, it would have been almost sacrilegious to do otherwise.

Maura's slender white hand gripped the bannister, resolutely. Head high, she started down the stairs. And then, stopped, abruptly.

"At the foot of the stairs stood a striking-looking man. He was tall, tan, with the sun-bleached hair of a Viking. She could not see what color his eyes were, but the way they were fixed and staring at her made her suddenly go crimson. She felt a sensation totally alien to her; she'd never known it in her young life and she could not, at the moment, put her finger on it. But whatever it was, it gave her a feeling of lightness, dizziness. Her fingers clutched the bannister for support. Who was he? she wondered. But at that moment, he turned abruptly and walked into the next room.

Recovering, Maura proceeded again down the stairs. Just as she reached the bottom, a short, plump man, slightly balding but with a wide smile on his round face, hurried toward her.

"Maura, darling! What a beautiful bride you make! Come!" Peter said.

He offered his arm. Together, they walked down the long marble hallway to the drawing room. Maura's blue eyes swept across the walls of red African marble, to the dark Flemish tapestries, to the floor of pale Nubian marble. A second Taj Mahal, one critic had called the brownstone, newly erected just two years before in 1888 on Fifth Avenue. Another critic, not quite so kind, had deemed it a mausoleum.

Maura agreed with the second critic. Certainly, it was as cold as a mausoleum. It was also as dark. Why were there so few windows? As they entered the drawing room she saw a profusion of flowers in white and gold, but even their loveliness could not shake the gloom from the house.

The gloom was reflected again on the faces of the three women standing grimly at attention as Peter and she walked in.

"My daughters," Peter said, cheerfully. "You remember, Maura? This is Anna." A dour, dark-faced woman nodded, glumly. "And Paula." A slightly younger, but equally dour-faced woman nodded now. "And my Gladys." This last was said with enthusiasm and the woman, younger by at least five years than her two sisters, seemed at first glance equal to that enthusiasm. For she was truly lovely, with a heart-shaped face and auburn ringlets framing that face in the latest and most flattering of styles. But her greeting to Maura was perhaps the coolest of all. "Oh, yes!" she said, with a small shrug, and turned to say something to her sisters.

Involuntarily, Maura shivered. How they hated her! She wished they could have been friends. But she took comfort again from one of her father's adages: "One is fortunate if one knows one's enemies. It is the ones who pretend to be friends and then stick a dagger in your back who are the most dangerous!"

"Here, now," Peter began, as three young men entered the room, "are my sons-in-law, George, Anna's husband, Albert, Paula's, and Thomas, Gladys's young man."

All three shook hands limply with Maura, while she murmured, with as much enthusiasm as she could muster, "How lovely to meet you."

She turned, as Peter's hand tugged at her sleeve. "Dear, there's one more person I want you to meet. . . ."

It was he! Standing by the fireplace now, those eyes were searching hers, again. Closer now, she was able to make out their color, black, with the pupils huge, dark, unfathomable. Again, she felt herself grow tremulous under his steady gaze.

"Neil," Peter was saying, "Neil Prescott, my right-hand man. You've heard me speak of him before, Maura?"

Of course. But then, everyone had heard of the illustrious Mr. Prescott who, after the railroad magnate Captain Van Diver's death, had become the driving force behind the Van Diver's millions.

Smiling, Maura offered her hand. For one moment, it lay in his, like a small bird's, pulsing in his larger, stronger one. Maura felt a tiny quiver, like an electric shock, go through her. . . .

"The minister is here, dear," Peter said.

Maura wrenched her hand away and took Peter's arm again.

"We are gathered here today . . ." the minister began.

Desperately, Maura tried to straighten her thoughts, her emotions. Born in the slums of the city and the lower East Side, Maura had, nevertheless, come from good stock. Her mother had been a willowy Irish beauty. Maura had inherited her good looks but perhaps more important, she'd inherited her father's proud Irish temperament and his canny good sense. She knew when she was acting foolishly, and she berated herself now. Peter was a fine man, a good man. Hadn't he eased her dying mother's last days? And if it hadn't been for him—

Maura shivered slightly. But she would not think of that now, the life she had escaped. She was safe now, she told herself. Safe . . .

"Do you take this woman to be your lawfully wedded wife?" the minister was saying.

Peter turned to her, smiling broadly. "I do."

Maura smiled warmly back. But as the minister turned to Maura and began: "Do you, Maura . . . ?"—she glanced away from Peter. It was something she would again berate herself for later but, at that moment, she couldn't help herself. It was as though he held a magnet and was making her turn. . . .

Suddenly, she was aware of a strained silence. They were waiting for her, she realized. She murmured: "I do. . . ."

But at that moment her eyes were fixed, not on Peter, but on him! For one dizzy, crazy moment, she thought I've married *him*, Neil Prescott!

She had not, of course. That fact was brought home to her only too quickly as the minister pronounced the final words: "Now you may kiss the bride." For it was solid, plump, but kindly Peter who moved forward then, beaming, to claim his first kiss from his lovely bride. . . .

Chapter One

WIDE-EYED, MAURA STOOD AT THE ENTRANCE
to the Van Diver's private rail car. With its
rich oak and mahogany paneling, plush crimson cushions, kerosene lamps in gilt and
silver and thick carpet, it was beyond her
wildest dreams.

Only once in her young life had she been
treated to a ride on the railroad. It had been
before her father's accident. He'd taken her
"uptown," as they called the area around
Fourteenth Street, to watch a matinee star-
ring some of his fellow performers. Maura,
who regularly attended her father's song-and-
dance shows, had been thrilled because this
time her father had chosen her, the baby, to
go with him, instead of one of her four brothers. The only black cloud had been the
thought of her brother Kevin's jealousy and
anger. Maura had dreaded going home, knowing that Kevin would have fixed some "pun-
ishment" for her. Once, when he'd been
angry, he'd overturned a bowl of scalding

soup on her. She still bore a faint scar on one leg from that soup. This time, she would come home to find Kevin had torn her schooldress, her only other dress, to shreds. But she'd enjoyed the matinee with Papa, watching the tumbling acts, the clowns and comics who took unexpected and ridiculous pratfalls on the stage. She and Papa had laughed till their sides ached. Then, the final treat: they'd taken the train home.

There was scant comparison between that train and this. Though her father, in his gentleness and concern, had tried to find the cleanest place for her, she couldn't help but be aware of the dirt, the filth. The hoodlums with unwashed faces and curious, glittering eyes staring at them. . . .

But this! This was a car for a prince—no, a king! She took one step inside and, with youthful exuberance, twirled around once, twice, in a small dance or *rinnce,* as the Irish called it.

"You like it, Maura?" Peter looked pleased.

"Oh, yes! It's beautiful!"

"I think so, too. Actually, it was my father's idea. He traveled so much up and down the lines, he needed a private place to sit and do his work. . . ." Peter's voice trailed off, remembering the old man, the Captain, and the times Peter had been forced to sit with him and go over the accounts. How he'd hated those accounts! He'd hated even more the way his father had picked at him.

"Of course," Peter went on now, "I've had it refurbished since then. . . ." Again, his voice

8

trailed off. His father, in the way of many self-made men who are never truly comfortable with their fortunes, had provided himself with only the bare necessities. He'd lived almost penuriously. It would never have entered his mind to have such lavish decorations in a railway car. "Who needs 'em?" he would have said. "Besides," he would have added, noting the cushions, "any fool knows a hard seat is better for the back than a soft cushion!"

He was probably right, Peter thought. God knows he had been right about almost everything else. But Peter, on the other hand, liked comfort and perhaps even more, beauty. . . .

He gazed admiringly at Maura's lush young beauty. That brief kiss at the wedding ceremony had been all he'd claimed from her so far. He squeezed her bare arm and watched a slight flush rise under her cheeks. It excited him, but he reminded himself hastily that they had a long ride ahead of them. . . .

"Ah—" he began. "We'll be leaving shortly. There are just one or two things I want to discuss with Neil when he comes back. Oh, here he is." He glanced back at Maura. "Perhaps you'd like to freshen up a bit?"

Maura's eyes were on the tall, strong figure striding down the railway platform toward them. She nodded and departed, hastily and gratefully.

The awkwardness she'd felt at her first meeting with Neil Prescott had not eased one bit. After the wedding ceremony, the three daughters and their husbands had said their goodbyes. Maura had been happy to bid them farewell, knowing that, unfortunately, it would only be a short respite. She and Peter would be in Saratoga for just a week before returning to New York. It had been a relief to leave, but at the doorway, Neil had surprised Maura by offering to ride with the couple to the station.

All three had sat side by side on the long back seat of the carriage. Maura, in the middle, had felt like a slice of mutton between two slices of rye. The thought had amused her at first, but very quickly she'd felt a flush of annoyance. Why, she might have been a pane of glass, they paid so little attention to her! Their talk was all of business, business. . . .

"We've bought up every available share of Erie stock on the market," Neil had informed Peter. "We now own approximately thirty per-cent."

"Good, good," Peter had nodded, while adjusting his tie.

"I believe," Neil had gone on, "it might be wise to start trading on the Ohio shares. It's my feeling they'll bring nothing but grief, if you hang on to them. You'll only get a profit of six or seven by selling now, but it's better than the three or maybe two you'll be stuck with if you hang on to them."

"Whatever you think," Peter had agreed.

As Maura had listened, a strange thing had happened. Almost in spite of herself, she'd found her interest quickening. It occurred to her that now that she was a part of the family, she should try to make sense of what they were talking about.

"Could you explain that, Mr. Prescott?" she heard herself asking.

She'd caught him off his guard. It had pleased her, curiously enough.

But Neil had recovered quickly. "But, of course, Mrs. Van Diver. The market is turning bearish. You know the bear. He walks with his head down, as opposed to the bull—heads up. It's my idea, we should get out—sell, that is—while we can."

"I think I see," Maura began.

But, at once, Peter cut in. "This is nothing you should concern your pretty head about, Maura," he said, touching her arm lightly.

Maura had nodded, then obediently fell silent. Had she done the wrong thing? "But if you have a curiosity, you must speak up." How many times had her father told her that? It was a fact that, about some things, Maura was shy. All during the trip, for example, she'd tried to avoid looking directly at Prescott. Whenever his eyes would meet hers, invariably she would feel flustered, embarrassed. She'd felt the same way when, accidentally, his arm would brush against hers in the carriage.

On matters of the mind, however, Maura was more secure. Her father, like many Irishmen, had been political by nature. He would sit for hours discussing politics with Maura and encouraging her opinions. She knew she had a good mind. She decided now, however, not to press the matter with Peter. Perhaps, first, she might find some books on business and finance. She would study them and surprise Peter. There was no reason, she decided, she shouldn't know, understand and be able to help him in his business.

After this conversation, a silence had fallen in the carriage. Maura's eyes had fixed uneasily on her hands, the gold-and-diamond band on her finger. She'd never worn anything on her hand before. It felt strange. She adjusted the band, uneasily.

She was well aware that jewelry was symbolic. A ring was as much a tie, as a king's crown. This particular ring, she realized, signified she was someone's wife. Peter's wife. It stood for all the rights that were now his, and to which she had pledged herself. . . .

Looking up suddenly, she'd caught Neil Prescott's eyes on her. Why? It had flashed through her mind that he'd been thinking the same strange thoughts. . . .

Quickly, his eyes had jerked away, and as they'd pulled into the station he'd hopped down from the carriage. "See you in a few minutes," he'd cried, leaving Maura and Peter to wend their way down the platform to the train alone.

In the small dressing room now, Maura brushed her long golden hair. She brushed slowly, delaying the moment when she would have to go out and face Neil Prescott again. But how silly! she scolded herself. She laid down the brush, then studied herself for one more moment: the fresh cheeks, the clear blue eyes, the pretty but strong chin. She raised that chin slightly now and, steeling herself, walked out.

"For you." Neil smiled and held out a bouquet of newly blossomed pink-and-white posies.

"How lovely!" she cried. She buried her nose in the flowers. She was visibly touched. It was her first wedding present. No one, not the daughters, not even Peter, had given her anything. She assumed Peter was waiting until tonight to give her a present. She was holding his until then, a leather pouch for his tobacco which she'd made herself. It had turned out well, reminding her of another pouch she'd made for her father. . . .

"The porter will bring a vase," Neil was saying. "I'll ring." He tugged at a long golden tassel by the window.

Like a genie summoned from a box, a porter in bright red livery appeared. He took the flowers from Maura. "Yes, ma'am, I'll take care of them. And the champagne, Mr. Van Diver? Shall I bring it in now, or will you wait until the train starts up?"

"Now," Peter ordered.

A few moments later, a cart bearing a silver bucket with a magnum of champagne, shimmering crystal plates and glasses, and trays of curiously shaped hors d'oeuvres was wheeled into the car.

"Try this." Peter layered something liver-colored onto a cracker and handed it to Maura.

She bit into it, and wrinkled her small nose.

The taste was strange but wonderful, she decided after a moment.

"It's *pâté*." Peter smiled.

"May I make the toast?" The question was asked of Peter, but the darkly piercing eyes were fixed on Maura. "To Maura and Peter," he toasted, in a voice that was rich and deeply vibrant. "To a long, happy wedded life."

Maura smiled, uneasily. Was it the sentiment? Or the way it was said? Unsure, she raised her glass with the others and drank.

"Oh, Mr. Van Diver?" It was the porter. "Can I see you for a moment? There's someone here with a message from your office."

"Oh Lord, I better see to this," Peter grumbled. "And I wanted to keep today private! Oh, well. I'll be right back."

As he shuffled off to the next car, Neil's eyes stayed fixed on Maura.

Again, she shifted uneasily. The way he was staring! "Is something the matter, Mr. Prescott?" Maura heard herself say suddenly. "Why are you looking at me like that?"

A half-smile hardened on his face. "Sorry if I'm making you uneasy, Mrs. Van Diver." The smiled broadened across that tan, handsome face. "I remember something the Captain used to say. 'If somebody's uneasy, there's usually a good reason. He's carrying something around with him—most likely a guilty conscience.'"

"What!" Maura couldn't believe her ears. "Are you saying I have a guilty conscience!"

He shrugged his broad shoulders slightly. "If the shoe fits—"

"You're full of phrases like that, aren't you?" she snapped back furiously. Out of the corner of her eye, she noticed the flowers. Just a few moments ago she'd been so touched by his gesture, and now—? "Really, Mr. Prescott," she began, her voice slightly calmer, "I had hoped we'd be friends."

"So had I. But Mr. Van Diver has the first claim on my friendship," he said, flatly.

It was like a slap in the face. How arrogant he was! she thought. An angry reply was on the tip of her lips when she heard footsteps— Peter Van Diver walking back. At the same time, the warning whistle blew.

"I'm glad you're still here, Neil," Peter said. "You'll keep in touch at Saratoga?"

"Certainly." Neil put down his glass and shook hands with Peter. Turning, he nodded gravely at Maura. In the glare of the train's lights, the dark pupils of his eyes lightened. The look she received was strange and unfathomable. There was suspicion, and something else she couldn't read. . . .

She managed a smile. "Goodbye, Mr. Prescott," she said, coolly.

"Goodbye, Mrs. Van Diver."

She watched as his slim, broad-shouldered figure slipped out the door and felt a mixture of relief and, strangely enough, disappointment. A moment later, she heard Peter's light, high-pitched voice.

"Sit, Maura dear," he said, "I have one or two things to attend to. But I'll be right back."

Slowly, the train began to make its way out of the dark tunnel. Maura tried to keep her mind on what lay ahead. Soon they would be coming out of the tunnel, into the fresh, open air, and soon also, she would be embarking on a new life. An exciting one. She would be discovering all sorts of new things, new, wonderful places! First, Saratoga, of which she'd heard so much about: the casinos, the baths, the races! She longed to see the horses; she had always loved animals so. And what a relief in this steamy August weather to be away from the city, and to be breathing that fresh country air! Yes, Saratoga was an ideal spot for a honeymoon. . . .

Honeymoon. The implications of that word impressed themselves upon her: the fact that she was a virgin, that, except for a few brief kisses, she had never been touched. She shrugged, and tried to brush the thoughts away.

Instead, she found herself thinking of Neil Prescott and that parting look in his eyes. How angry he had made her! Why should he be so suspicious? Yet she had seen something else in those dark eyes. It occurred to her suddenly that it was not unlike the pitying look the few visitors her father had had after his accident had given him.

She was suddenly more perplexed than ever. Could he be suspicious, and still pity her? *Oh, how foolish, Maura!* she told herself. She had misread him, that was obvious. Neil Prescott was a man of many moods, she could tell.

But he had made her uneasy. Without realizing it, she hugged her arms around herself, as she waited. . . .

Peter was making his way back into the car. "Ready for your long trip?" he asked.

"Yes," she said. There was a slight tremor in her voice that startled and annoyed her. "Yes, Peter," she repeated more firmly.

Chapter Two

MAURA SAT IMMERSED ALMOST TO HER CHIN IN a tub of hot perfumed water. The maid who'd drawn it for her—the first time anyone had drawn a bath for her!—had sprinkled the hot water liberally with salts scented like roses. Maura took a deep breath. She felt almost sinful.

The long day was finally coming to an end. She suspected that Peter, at this very moment, was sitting in his own tub of water. Shortly, very shortly, there would be a knock at the door. . . .

She sighed softly. An hour or so earlier she and Peter had checked into the United States Hotel. She'd been thrilled. For the hotel was magnificent, newly erected, taller than its older competitor, the Grand Union Hotel, which faced it, and far grander. It stood five stories high, and four or five street blocks in length. Jutting up toward the sky, majestically, eerily, were its twin arabesque towers sinking into a jungle of Victorian scrollwork,

18

cupolas and gargoyles, all supported by a dozen giant-sized, heavily ornamented pillows.

But the crowning touch was the veranda, which wound halfway around the hotel and on which several hundred people on wicker rockers rocked furiously!

Maura had been amused and proud as she'd walked past the people into the lobby with Peter. The desk clerk, half-asleep, had jumped to attention.

"Mr. Van Diver!" he'd cried. He'd slammed his palm on the buzzer. Half a dozen bellhops had come running.

"Everything is ready, Mr. Van Diver," the desk clerk had hurried on. "I'm sure the suite will meet with your approval. And yours, Mrs. Van Diver."

He'd stopped to look at her; all the bellhops had stopped to look too. At that instant it had seemed to Maura that everything stopped. The rocking chairs on the veranda were still; all conversation ceased. Maura had watched lorgnettes raised, earcups placed to the ear. And then, she'd heard: "Little golddigger! Well, she certainly got her hooks into him fast enough. Still, he's no lily. He might have had the decency to wait a little longer after his poor sainted wife's death!"

Maura had felt herself shrink inside. Had Peter heard also? She'd glanced at him but head down, he'd hurried her away, up to her suite, then gone on to his.

Alone, Maura had railed at the meanness,

the unfairness of the woman. Calling her a golddigger! But she was not! At least Peter knew that. Twice, she had refused to marry him. It was only after seeing how kind he'd been to her dying mother that Maura had become convinced Peter was a suitor worthy of consideration. Of course, Kevin's actions had forced her to make the decision quickly. . . .

There was a sharp rap on the outer door. Maura's dreaming was cut short. She started.

"May I come in, dear?"

"Yes, Peter," she said, flustered. "I'll be right out."

She raised herself out of the tub and hastily sponged herself with the thick towel. Her nightgown of pale blue silk had been carefully laid out on the chair by the maid.

As she dried herself, Maura studied her reflection in the mirror: the firm, high young breasts, the small waist that tapered down to hips slender as a young boy's, but curved as no young boy's ever were. She reached up and released a pin in her hair. Her long golden hair came tumbling down. It reached almost to her waist.

"You are a prize," her father had told her more than once. "Only the best man shall have you. I'll see to that!"

But her father, unfortunately, had died too soon to make good his promise. . . .

"Maura!" she heard now. There was a touch of impatience in that voice which puzzled her. She had not heard it before.

"Coming!" she called. Quickly, she slipped on the thin silk gown, which Peter had picked out for her on their one brief shopping expedition. But how low it was! Modestly, she looked about for a pin to fix it. Before she could find one, however, the door to the dressing room was flung open.

"Maura!"

Her husband stood in the doorway in a red silk dressing gown. The belt, hastily tied, was coming undone. A graying, hairy chest was revealed and, below that, an incipient paunch.

Maura swallowed hard. "I'm sorry," she apologized. "I didn't realize I was taking so long. . . ."

Had he heard her? He grabbed her arm and was pulling her toward the bed.

"Peter . . ." she began. "You're hurting me!"

Without answering, he dragged her to the foot of the bed, then stopped abruptly. With one quick movement, his hand reached out and tore the filmy nightgown to the waist.

Maura made a vain attempt to cover herself, but her arms were thrust aside as Peter flung her on the bed. He paused for one moment, to pull off his robe and to impatiently undo the bottom half of his pajamas.

Watching, waiting, Maura was not so much frightened as bewildered. Was this sweet, kind Peter? What had happened?

Her eyes traveled downward, below that paunch. Peter was the first man she had ever seen and she could not help but think—from that first sight—that a man was hardly a pretty thing. . . .

He leaped toward her now. Bold, ready, he began to push her legs apart.

"Peter, please!" she cried once more. Again, she had the feeling he had not heard, or had not wanted to hear. But suddenly, he surprised her, as he paused.

"You are a virgin?" he asked.

Why should he ask? The fact that he might have a doubt hurt her as much as his roughness. "Yes, of course," she murmured.

He smiled, the satisfied smile of a cat after a saucer of milk. For one moment, his eyes roamed over her—the pale perfection of her skin, her milky white breasts with their rosy tips. The loveliness of her long gold hair, strands of which fluttered across her breasts like a filmy coverlet and extended down past the belly to a matching but paler triangular patch of curly hair.

Lustfully, he wet his lips and, climbing on top of her, entered her.

Maura felt her insides being pummeled, so sharply, so intensely, she bit her lips to keep from crying out. But he kept on, on, until suddenly there came a stabbing pain she couldn't bear. She was sure she'd been ripped in half! She screamed.

Even then, he did not stop. But as he kept on, the pain blessedly eased and Maura felt a new sensation, something almost akin to pleasure. In her innocence, in her confusion, she did not understand but instinctively she moved her hips to prolong the feeling.

Peter stopped abruptly. As he pulled away from her, Maura saw a look of distaste on his face. But was it distaste or—something else? She could not know.

She looked down then and, for some reason, Peter did also. By the dim light of the ebbing fire in the fireplace, they saw drops of blood on the sheet.

"My poor child," Peter said, in the soft, kind voice she had known before. He patted her hair with a gentleness that surprised Maura. And suddenly, abruptly, he left.

Hot tears released themselves while Maura tried to think. Who was this strange man she'd married? What was the reason for his curious behavior? She could not believe it was typical of a wedding night, but then, how could she know?

She found no answers to her questions. She was simply too tired to fathom them out. She turned her face toward the fire which, at least, gave a small measure of comfort. With arms wrapped around herself, she slept.

Sunlight streaked through the room, dancing on the gold sconces on the wall, pirouetting on the ornate candlestick holders over the fireplace, resting for a moment on a gold-and-green tapestry, until at last, it made its way toward the four-poster bed.

Maura blinked and opened her eyes. For one moment, she lay there under the lovely delusion that she had died and gone to heaven. For surely heaven, if there was a heaven, would be all sunlight and gold and pale yellow roses in vases. . . .

Then, her eye caught the edge of the small, silver-wrapped package on the night table. The leather pouch, the wedding gift she'd forgotten to give Peter. She sighed and turned suddenly. As she moved, a sharp, stabbing pain shot through her.

Was it her arm? Yes, but her leg, also—no, both of them—hurt. It seemed to her that every part of her ached. Pulling the covers aside, she saw the blood spattered on the sheet. In that moment, she relived it all—the pain, Peter's brutality, his strange behavior afterward. . . .

There was a soft rap on the door. Hastily, she pulled up the sheet.

"Yes?" she asked.

A plump maid, with her stiff cap slightly askew, entered. She carried a silver tray with orange juice, coffee, fresh rolls and butter. "Mr. Van Diver was asking for you, ma'am," she said. "He sent you this." She handed Maura a note.

"Maura, darling," she read. "I've gone out for a short while, but I would like to take you for a drive or perhaps a walk along the Promenade when I return. I'll ring in about an hour."

It was signed: "Affectionately, your husband, Peter." Maura stared at the signature for a moment, then slipped the note back into its envelope and put it on the night table. She

24

poured some cream into her coffee and sipped it slowly while she puzzled over the note.

"Shall I draw a bath?" The maid interrupted her thoughts.

"Please. Thank you."

The hot tub soothed both her nerves and her aches. She closed her eyes and decided for the moment not to concern herself about the note. She would be seeing Peter shortly. His face and his actions would tell her soon enough what he'd meant.

She dressed carefully, choosing after much thought a light blue gown that brought out the deeper blue of her eyes. The waist was snug to show off her slenderness, the neckline square and décolleté, flattering her high, lovely breasts. It was a warm day, so she chose a white, filmy stole for her arms.

At the sound of the door, she nervously hurried out of the dressing room. She was on time today, at any rate. She had tried not to think about what he might say or how he might behave, but she couldn't help but be anxious now.

"Why, Maura, how lovely you look!" he cried. "I have a surprise for you! Turn around," he ordered, smiling. "And close your eyes."

Obediently, she turned and closed her eyes. She felt something cool around her neck, then Peter's hands fastening it.

"All right," he said cheerfully. "Open your eyes!"

She opened her eyes and gazed into the mirror. A necklace, shimmering and lovely, of lapis lazuli and pearls, had been fastened around her neck.

"Oh, it's beautiful! Thank you, Peter!" She turned to kiss him, but he stepped aside hastily, so that the kiss intended for his lips brushed off his cheek instead.

Puzzled and flushing, she walked to the night table. "I almost forgot," she said. "This is for you."

Peter opened the silver-wrapped package. "How sweet." He examined the pouch, then tucked it into his pocket. "Thank you, dear. It will be just the thing for my tobacco. Now, shall we go?"

In an ebony carriage, aptly termed a Victoria after the carriage favored by the Queen, they drove down Broadway, a wide tree-lined boulevard with its promenades alive with people. Handsome young men in Prince Albert coats, with white tie, boiled shirt and poke collars, were taking their pretty silk-gowned, bonneted ladies for a walk after the races, before dinner and the casinos. Arm in arm, the couples promenaded, past the elm-shaded, terraced lawns of Morrissey's famous Club House, past the new Fountain Hall splashing rainbows of color from its immense, stained-glass windows, and along Congress Spring Park, where the sounds of an oom-pah-pah band could be heard playing.

Delightedly, Maura looked to, fro, taking everything in. "Look at that, Peter!" she would cry. And, "What is that?" Or, "Do you know them?"

Patiently, he would tell her who the couple

was or explain about the bands or whatever it was she wanted to know. He was his sweet, kind self again, so much so that Maura wondered if she could have dreamed the night before. But she knew she had not.

Couldn't they talk about it? she wondered. But something told her a woman did not talk about things like that with her husband. It was a shame, she thought. A man and a woman should be more honest, more open, with one another. Still, she could not bring herself to bring up the subject with Peter, but neither could she make herself stop thinking about it. And wondering what would happen tonight. . . .

"And now, Maura," Peter said suddenly, "what about some dinner?"

They went to Granger's, the newest of the many fine restaurants and which, Peter informed her, boasted the best food in town. She'd thought she wasn't hungry but as she nibbled on the unfamiliar but delicious hot hors d'oeuvres, her appetite grew.

"I can see you're hungry, dear," Peter said. "Eat, please. How about some oysters? And some clams on the half-shell," he told the waiter.

"I never want to see you go hungry again," he said to Maura. He patted her arm and stood. "Will you excuse me, dear? I'll be back in a few minutes."

He left quickly, pausing at a table a few feet away to talk to a young couple, then walking on and pausing again, longer this time, at a table in the corner of the room where a young girl sat. The daughter of a friend? Maura wondered. He was talking animatedly. Then, all at once, he leaned over—to whisper something in her ear? To kiss her? Maura couldn't be sure. As she stared, Peter straightened up quickly, then strolled off and out of sight.

Again she was puzzled, but her attention was quickly claimed by the waiter. He had just served her oysters and clams; he was now replenishing the wine and the rolls.

"I never want to see you go hungry again," Peter had said. Slowly, Maura selected a roll and buttered it. As she did, she took a trip back, to a time when a meal such as this would have been beyond her wildest dreams. . . .

Chapter Three

She had been born Maura O'Rourke in a tenement on the lower East Side. Historically, the area between Canal and Fourteenth Street has been the melting pot for the Italians, the Irish, the Jews and all other nationalities who emigrated to the United States. In the early 1870s, however, when Maura was born, the area was still predominantly Irish. "Shanty Irish," as they were called and hated. The name came from the way they were forced to live, in the poorest, dirtiest of hovels, crowded together in buildings that were cold and drafty in winter, hot as the Sahara in summer and firetraps all year round.

Maura had grown up with the clang of the fire engines' bells in her ears. One might have thought she'd come to take those bells for granted, but she never did. The moment she heard them, she would stand quite still, straining her ears to discover where the engines were coming from and where they were headed. Only when she was sure it was not her street, her home, would she breathe a sigh of relief. Years later, when she tried to fathom why she had acted so, it occurred to her she'd only been repeating what her father used to do. From the time she was a little girl, she could remember walking with her father when an alarm sounded, then having him grab her arm and bring her to a halt, while he stood, biting and chewing his lower lip nervously. As a young boy, he'd seen his mother perish in a fire in Ireland, and he'd been helpless to save her. The fear of fire, instilled in him then, had never left him.

It was Sean O'Rourke's only fear. He'd left Ireland with nothing but the clothes on his back, bringing along with him a young wife, a small child, with another on the way. With nothing in his pocket, he had nothing to lose, he'd told his more pessimistic friends. In addition, Sean reasoned, he was young, he was strong; he also had a God-given talent. He was a performer: he could sing, he could dance after a fashion, he could tell a joke. He was also nimble, fortunately, for it was the fashion of the day for the vaudeville performer to do everything—sing, dance, joke and combine those talents with tumbling acts, and mock Punch and Judy shows. In Ireland, O'Rourke had been a popular favorite until hard times had forced the closing of half a dozen theaters. When people have no money to eat, they can't go to the theater. But there was no doubt in Sean's mind that in America, the land of opportunity, he would once again become a popular—and this time—well-heeled favorite.

Contrary to what he'd heard, however, he'd

found the streets were not paved with gold. Once in a while a small nugget would shine, but like as not, he'd find it was fool's gold rather than the real thing. Still, Sean made enough to provide for his family, an ever-growing brood of boys. The crowning achievement of his life was the day his tiny daughter was placed in his arms.

She had the beauty of his wife—her clear skin, her golden hair, her eyes as blue as a Dublin sky. He tried not to be immodest, but he could not help but think her spirit, fortunately, was his and not her mother's. Nora O'Rourke had been broken down over the years, defeated by childbirth, by sickness, disappointment, poverty. Watching this happen had hurt O'Rourke, but his own spirit was indefatigable. He was determined not to see it repeat itself with his daughter. For Maura had his love and feeling for life; she shared his gaiety, his courage. She would have fine things, his daughter, and a better life than he or her mother had had. So help him, he vowed.

So he pampered her in the few small ways he could. He bought cheap little trinkets to delight her; he took her for long walks in which he pointed out the sights and sounds of Manhattan Island. Perhaps even more important, he protected her from what he called the "ruffians" in the neighborhood. When he was at work and could not protect her, he instructed her four elder brothers to take his place. Which they did, grudgingly, and after a fashion.

All four were streetwise, tough. The neighborhood was a haven for gangsters and prostitutes as well as thieves and murderers. To grow up, to survive, a young boy had to be tough. Still, they'd inherited some of their father's amiability and generosity and, except for the next-to-eldest, Kevin, they were not bad boys.

Kevin was the black sheep. He kept the others in line, making them "do" for him. They fetched for him; they covered for him with alibis whenever needed; at times, they did special "favors," roughly translated as stealing for him. As far as his sister was concerned, instead of protecting her, he terrorized her, or at least he tried to. But Maura stood up to him bravely. Secretly, she was afraid, but she had the good sense to realize that if Kevin saw this fear, all was lost.

She did her best to ignore him. Most of the time, she succeeded and she was not, in fact, unhappy. She had a roof over her head; she had enough food—watery stew and stale bread perhaps—but better than that of many of her neighbors. She was learning her sums; she could read, write. At night, she would recite aloud to her father before he went off to work, usually selecting something from Dickens, very often from her favorite, *Great Expectations*.

The highlight of Maura's week, however, was Saturday. That was matinee day and almost every Saturday her father would take her with him to the theater to see the show.

The show had changed over the years. O'Rourke was now part of a five-man act, which called itself the Five Shamrocks. They made themselves up with red wigs, red noses and green whiskers, and did an act on ladders and scaffolds. It climaxed when the five of them tossed bricks at one another and fell into a mortar box, finishing it all off with a rousing song and dance.

The particular Saturday Maura would never forget—Patrick Rooney from Cork, the first in three generations of song-and-dance men (his grandson would make "Sweet Rosie O'Grady" famous one day) was the headliner on the bill. On the way to the theater, Maura and her father sang snatches of the tune Rooney had made popular, "Is That Mr. Riley?"

> I'd have nothing but Irishmen on the
>   police,
> Patrick's Day would be the Fourth of
>   July . . . !

"Shall I come backstage afterward?" Maura asked when they arrived at the theater.

"Sure, luv. Here's your ticket," he said, kissing her.

Maura sat in her balcony seat, waiting. Rooney, as the headliner, would come on last. But he was merely the icing on the cake. It was her father, as always, she'd come to see. She sat through the opening act, two Irishmen, Ryan and Kelly, who did their song and dance with scoop shovels. Then the Five Shamrocks came on.

Holding her breath, Maura leaned forward to watch her father. He was by far the funniest and most talented, she thought. She had memorized his act, so that she knew it as well as he. She repeated his lines softly to herself, then laughed, as though she was applauding herself. She held her breath sharply again at the end of the act when it was her father's turn to climb the ladder. . . .

It all came so fast then, she wasn't sure what had happened. One moment, Sean O'Rourke was standing on top of the ladder, the next he was lying flat on his back on the stage, while the audience laughed and applauded as though this was some strange new finale. But Maura knew it was not.

"Papa!" she screamed. She raced out of the theater, around the side to the stage door. She arrived just as they were carrying her father out, en route to the hospital.

It was not until the next day that Maura learned her father's fate. His back had been broken in the fall. The doctors could do little for him. He stayed in the hospital for two weeks, then was carried home, up five flights of stairs that he would never walk down again.

Maura's heart ached each time she came home and saw her father propped up by the back window that looked out to the alleyway and the next tenement. This was his view, his life. He grew silent and cool to everyone, rousing himself at times only for Maura. He would talk and joke with her, but even then only for a short while. Much of the time, he would beg her to get him a pint. If she refused, he would find some way of getting it anyway, so most of the time she gave in, selling her few trinkets to keep him content, at least for a short while. Drink eventually killed him, though as far as Maura was concerned, Sean O'Rourke had died the night of his fall. She was almost grateful when he was finally released. . . .

If his misery was over, however, her mother's had yet to begin. A month after Sean O'Rourke's accident, Nora had had a baby, a sickly girl who died in her second month. The baby had left Nora O'Rourke weak and unable to cope. Perhaps—if she'd had the proper food and nourishment? But she did not. At times, Maura's brothers managed to steal some food and bring it home. Maura was grieved that they should steal, but she cooked the food and gave it to her mother, saying nothing.

There were many more times when there was no food. Maura left school. She was old enough, she decided, to work. She would try and get a job at one of the sweatshops, sewing. Each day, she made the rounds of the local shops. It would just be a matter of time, she told herself.

One day, coming home, she heard the clang of the fire engines. Her heart skipped a beat. It seemed so close to home! She waited with dread till the engines passed by. Blessedly, they were not headed for her block.

But something drew her to the fire. Afterward, she regretted it. For it was horrible: the smell, the smoke, the cries of people in pain and separated from their families. Maura saw one young woman, her body racked with sobs as she held a small child. Someone tried to take the child from her, but the woman screamed and wouldn't let him go.

"Poor thing," a woman standing near Maura commented. "The child's dead. It's the landlord's fault. He's burning us all out, so he can collect the insurance. What does he care who he kills?"

Maura was shocked. But she had heard such stories before. It was said that landlords hired young boys to set the fires. With a sigh, she turned to leave, when a face in the crowd caught her eye. It was her brother, Kevin, wearing a small smirk on his face. . . .

Sick at heart, Maura went home. Over the next few days, she came to a decision. She would leave home; she could no longer tolerate Kevin's evilness. But before she could put her plans into action, Kevin came home with a plan of his own.

"I've got a fine mate for you, Maura," he said. "Joseph Cassidy."

"Cassidy?" she repeated. She knew the name. He ran a saloon on Water Street, with a gambling hall in the back. Sometimes he'd be standing outside while Maura was running home. Always, she felt his eyes on her, watching. And once, one terrible Saturday, when her father and she had been late for the matinee, Cassidy had driven them in his carriage. It was the one time her father had seemed insensitive to her feelings. He had chatted on and on, while Cassidy had leered at her. All Maura could think of during the ride were the women she'd seen at the saloon, with dyed red hair, breasts popping out of their dresses. Did he want to dye her hair, put her in a dress like that . . . ?"

She'd shivered. "You've made some kind of deal with him, haven't you, Kevin?" she guessed. "How much money do you owe him?"

An angry spot of red shone in Kevin's cheeks. He did not like being questioned; he particularly did not like being found out.

"None of your business!" he snapped. "I said, I've found a good mate for you. It'll be one less mouth to feed around here and you'll have your belly full, so why are you complainin'? You'll do what I say!"

"I will not!" she cried. "I won't go!"

"Oh, no?" He hauled off and slapped her then, so hard that she reeled back and fell against the wall.

From the next room, Nora O'Rourke cried out, weakly: "Maura?"

Shaking his fist, Kevin turned on his heel and left.

Maura splashed cold water on her face before she went into the next room. "It's all right, Mama," she soothed, turning her head so her mother wouldn't see the red mark on her cheek.

She plumped up the small pillow under her

mother's head. "Can I get you anything? A cup of tea?"

"No." Nora O'Rourke shook her head, dully. Lately, she had no appetite at all. She was the one reason Maura had hesitated about leaving. But she knew her brothers, even Kevin, would take care of her.

"I'm going out for a while, Mama," Maura said. Quickly, she slipped out the door and down the stairs.

The day was chilly; she could have used a wrap, but she did not go back. She started to walk. Where she was going she had no idea; she just wanted to get away—from the house, from Kevin. She knew Kevin: this would not be the end of it. He'd made a deal with Cassidy, and a little thing like her refusal would not stand in the way.

Maura kept walking until she found herself in the Wall Street area. She paused then, to look around.

Since the beginning of the century, Wall Street had been regarded as the financial center of the country. The name had come from the nine-foot palisade or wall erected by Peter Stuyvesant to ward off Indians. The wall had long since gone; the street was shadowed now by other "walls" of brick and steel. Other things had changed. The street, which had seen royal pageants pass by, and later, a triumphant Continental army, was now the scene of financial speculation.

Maura, who had once walked along this area with her father, listening as he pointed out historic points of interest, like Fraunces Tavern, once a favorite of George Washington's, was hardly aware of any of its famous landmarks now. She continued on her way, but wherever she went, all she seemed to see was Kevin—the evil look on his face, the way he'd shaken his fist. She was doomed if she walked back in that house, she knew. But where else could she go?

Oblivious to the people, the traffic, she started to cross the busy street.

"Watch it!" someone cried.

Who? she wondered. Were they talking to her? She glanced up, in time to see two horses rearing up, about to come down—on her!

She screamed, and fainted.

When she opened her eyes, she was in a dark, curtained carriage, resting on a soft leather cushion.

"Take another whiff of these smelling salts," someone suggested, holding a handkerchief to her nose.

The handkerchief was fine linen. Maura bent her head obediently, sniffed, then looked up.

The man holding the handkerchief to her nose had a round, plump face, with kind eyes.

"I always used to keep some on hand for my late wife. She often got dizzy spells," he explained. "But I'm glad you're feeling better. May I introduce myself?"

He held out a plump hand, with perfectly manicured nails. Maura, who'd never seen such nails, either on a man or woman, stared.

"I'm Peter Van Diver," he said.

Maura shook his manicured hand. "I'm Maura O'Rourke. You've been very kind, Mr. Van Diver. But I think I should go now."

She half stood, and reached for the door-knob.

A look of alarm came over his face. "Please! Don't go! I'd like very much to take you to dinner, if I may? Delmonico's is just a few blocks away."

"Well . . ." She hesitated. But he looked so distressed, and it occurred to her that she was hungry. "Yes," she said, after a moment. "I'd like that. . . ."

"Was that good, dear?"

Maura looked up, startled. Peter had just sat down again.

"Saratoga's noted for its fine food. I'm glad to see you've finished your plate."

Maura smiled. "It was delicious. But aren't you having anything?"

"Later, perhaps. I have some business to attend to now. If you'd like to go back to the hotel, I'll take you to the carriage. We can go to the casino later, if you like."

"Fine."

In her suite at the hotel, Maura found herself puzzling again over Peter. What "business" was he talking about? Wasn't Neil Prescott attending to everything in New York?

It was curious, certainly, but she had little time to worry over it. She'd been in the room just a few moments when there was a knock on the door.

"Come in," she said, expecting the maid.

Her back to the door, she heard a laugh—startling and familiar. She spun around and saw with alarm it was not the maid. Nor was it Peter.

It was him. . . .

Chapter Four

"KEVIN!" SHE CRIED. SHE STARED INTO HIS eyes. She had always thought it one of the more curious things of life that of her four brothers, it was Kevin she most resembled. He was four years her senior, but except for that, they might have been twins. They had the same golden hair and deep blue eyes, the same fair complexion and regular features. But on Kevin the features had been perverted somehow, so that the mouth, instead of being upturned and smiling like Maura's, pouted sulkily; the eyes looked inward, instead of out; the nostrils sneered with contempt and, very often, anger. "Kevin was born angry," his father used to say. What he had not said—perhaps because he hated to admit it even to himself, even though he knew it was true—was that Kevin had also been born mean. . . .

"How did you find me?" Maura asked, still slightly flustered.

"What makes you think it was that difficult?" He grinned.

"I—" she began, then stopped. Joey, her

youngest brother, must have told him, she realized suddenly. She'd met Joey on the street one day when she'd been with Peter. She'd mentioned the wedding then, but she'd been sparing about the details. Joey, the most gentle of her brothers, had seemed to understand. The less they—and particularly Kevin —knew of the details of her life, the better.

She watched now, as Kevin walked around the room, examining lamps, running a hand over the coverlet on the bed. He pocketed some matches, then an ashtray and a silver spoon the maid had forgotten.

"You can't stay!" Maura blurted out suddenly. All she could think of was what if Peter should come back and find him!

"Oh, no? And what kind of a welcome is that for big brother?"

Grinning, he lowered himself into the chair by the fireplace. He propped his boots on the coffee table. "Could you rouse the maid for some coffee? No"—he changed his mind— "make it a draft of beer. I'm thirsty."

"I told you, Kevin, you can't stay. Get out! Now!" she ordered.

"Nasty, ain't ya?" He jumped out of the chair, his face flushed and furious.

Maura tried to reason with him. "Please, Kevin. Maybe I can meet you later somewhere. But you can't stay here."

"Why should I want to meet you later?" he snapped. One boot smashed an ashtray off the coffee table. It went crashing against the wall.

Maura stared at it while he laughed.

43

"I'm no more fond of you than you are of me, dearie. But after comin' all the way here, I'd like a little somethin' for my trouble. A little green, if you don't mind." He held out his hand.

"I don't have any money, Kevin."

"What?" He laughed again, harshly this time. It hurt her ears.

"After just marryin' the richest stiff in town?" he snapped. "Don't tell me that!"

"It's the truth, Kevin." It was. Peter had either forgotten or else decided that she wouldn't need any money, at least at the moment. When they arrived back in New York, Maura assumed she'd be given a certain amount of household money. At the moment, however, she had no cause to buy anything and she never would have presumed to ask Peter for money.

With a firm step, she started toward the door. "I'm afraid you'll have to go now, Kevin."

The expression on his face was one of pure fury. "No money, eh?" He spotted her purse on the bureau. Grabbing it, he emptied it on the floor. A small comb, a compact and a single, souvenir coin fell out.

Frustrated, Kevin glanced up. His eyes, hot, piercing, seemed to relax for a moment. "What have you got there?"

Automatically, Maura's hand went to her throat and the necklace. She took a step backward.

"C'mere," Kevin said, starting after her.

"No—!"

She swung away from him, around the bed, but he raced after her and grabbed her. She tried to wriggle free, but she could not. His body pressed her against the wall, while his hands closed around her throat.

She felt him fumbling with the clasp, but she was powerless to move her head, or to prevent his taking the necklace. In another moment, it was free of her neck and in Kevin's pocket.

"Kevin, please!" she pleaded, gasping as he let go of her. "Anything but that!"

"What else do you have to offer, dearie? Nothin'," he guessed.

Grinning, he started for the door. As he pulled it open, he turned back.

"I almost forgot. Congratulations, sis!" Laughing, he slipped out.

Maura sank down on the bench in front of the vanity. Her throat ached. Around her neck was a red, raw circle where the necklace had been.

Her mind was racing. Any moment Peter would be back to take her to the casino. Would he notice the necklace was gone? Hopefully not. He might overlook it for the moment but it was inevitable, however, that he should find out. She could not postpone telling him indefinitely.

She covered her face with her hands. Until her marriage, she had rarely indulged in tears. But for the second time in less than twenty-four hours, she started to cry.

* * *

The question Maura dreaded did not come. Peter, it seemed, had forgotten the necklace almost immediately after he'd given it to her.

He had other things on his mind. Wherever he took Maura—to the races, the casinos, to dinner—he would disappear. His absences were sometimes as short as ten minutes, sometimes an hour or so. At times, Maura would be attended by another couple; more often, she was left alone.

She couldn't help but feel hurt. On the other hand, Peter made up for these lapses by being particularly attentive and considerate when he was with her. During the day, he took her shopping, replenishing her meager wardrobe with half a dozen gowns, myriad silk slips, lacy camisole tops. He bought her bonnets with ostrich feathers and wide, scalloped brims. He selected jewelry: an exquisite single strand of pearls, a gold and turquoise choker, an ivory pendant.

"Pick out anything you like," he told her generously. Maura was cautious at first, but she had faith in her own good taste and had to admit she did enjoy shopping. How wonderful to be able to afford the pretty gowns she used to stare at longingly in store windows!

Peter made the shopping even more fun, for he seemed to enjoy it even more than she. It occurred to her that he loved dressing her up so that he might show her off. And while a part of her rebelled against that—she was not a show-thing, a doll, after all, to be put on display—a part of her was touched that he should be so proud of her.

Only once on a shopping expedition did her heart stop for a moment. In a shop off the Promenade, while she was looking at dresses, she noticed him fingering the nightgowns. She held her breath as she watched. She was grateful to see he lost interest quickly, and made no attempt to buy her one.

Since that first night, he had not returned to her room. The first two nights, she had lain awake all night waiting for the knock that never came.

Was he embarrassed? Sorry? Disappointed? Again and again, she went over that night in her mind. It was strange to think Peter might fear her. On the other hand, she recalled quite a few times she'd gone forward to kiss him only to have him shrink back from her.

On the Promenade he took her arm and, in public, he always greeted her with a brief kiss on the cheek. Other than that, however, they had no physical contact. Young and perplexed, Maura wondered about it. She knew little of married life. In her own home, she had rarely seen any signs of affection between her father and mother. She could not know that, through the years, her mother, sick and worn, had finally refused to have anything more "to do," as she put it, with Sean O'Rourke.

Maura's nature was warm and loving, like her father's. But having no better experience of marriage than his loveless one to guide her, she could not help but believe that, though her own marriage was strange, weren't they all . . . ?

Chapter Five

NEIL PRESCOTT HAD DRIFTED IN AND OUT OF Maura's thoughts that entire week in Saratoga. Once Maura was back in New York and in the Fifth Avenue mansion, however, she found herself thinking of him more than ever.

She would pick up a paper or magazine and spot his name, his face. Often, a lovely-looking young woman—always, Maura noted, a different one—would be on his arm.

Then there was Peter. He was always talking about Neil. Hardly a conversation passed where his name did not crop up. In the evening, they would run into Neil at parties. Even in her own house, Maura could not be sure, going down the stairs, walking into the library, finishing her breakfast coffee, that Neil Prescott would not suddenly stroll in.

They were always polite to one another, if a trifle cool. Maura was quite happy to slip away from him. Whether he was still suspicious of her or not, she couldn't tell—though he still gave her those deep, searching looks that seemed to say I'm keeping an eye on you! For whatever reason, she wasn't sure. . . .

But he made her angry—furious, in fact. Yet despite the turmoil he caused her, she had to admit she was intrigued. Was it his blond good looks? Was it the way he carried himself, so arrogantly, proudly? Or was it simply a combination of everything, including his mind? A good mind had always intrigued her—her father had had one. Neil's, she could see, from what Peter told her, from what she read in the papers, was particularly fine. She had not given up the idea of questioning Neil further about the business. For the time being, however, she'd decided not to. She would put it off until she'd picked up some books on business and finance so she would know at least something about what she was talking about.

But before she picked up those books, before she did anything in fact, a dozen—no, more like a hundred!—things required her attention. Beginning with the house. Maura was determined to do something to make it more comfortable, to make it cozier, warmer. She studied each room; she conferred with decorators, designers. Carefully, she sifted through the advice they gave her and began to order. She selected comforters for the chairs, thick rugs for the cold marble floors, heavier drapes for the windows. She succeeded in taking a bit of the chill off, though, to be frank, not much.

The structure of the house itself defeated her. It lacked light because there were so few windows, and those windows were small and improperly fitted. If it lacked warmth, the fireplaces were to be blamed. They were not too small, but rather, too large. One might think that might make the house warmer. In actuality, it made it more drafty and the fires more difficult to light and to be kept lit.

Maura was also handicapped by Peter. He hated any kind of change in the house. "What are you doing?" he would say crossly. He would tear off a comforter, tug at a drape. "The finest designers furnished this house," he would tell Maura again and again. "It cost me a fortune!" He would point proudly to the dark, ugly armoire, which Maura secretly wished she could burn, and say: "Know how much that cost?"

She began to realize that it was money, not comfort, he appreciated. And since it was his house, she soon gave up all attempts at change.

She confined herself to her own suite of rooms. Here, however, she was at last truly successful. By concentrating on soft colors, using rugs and warm afghans and comforters, with huge bowls of flowers to brighten the dark corners, she succeeded in making her rooms a haven of privacy, comfort and delight.

It was a much-needed, necessary haven, as far as Maura was concerned. Only here was she away from the ever-critical eyes of Peter's daughters. They came to dinner twice a week for the sole purpose (or so it seemed to

Maura!) of staring at her, making several cutting remarks, and then virtually ignoring her.

The rooms also provided a haven for Maura from the servants, who observed her with the same critical looks, the same cool shrugs and lifted brows as did Peter's daughters.

Maura might have complained about the servants to Peter, but she did not. Only once, when her personal maid was truly insolent—bringing her cold coffee, then drawing her bath with lukewarm water and muttering under her breath that the first Mrs. Van Diver never took so many baths, nor washed her hair so many times!—did Maura go to Peter.

"I'd like to select my own personal maid," she told him. "I have nothing against Clara, but—"

"Clara's an old crow," Peter said, quickly. "Of course you may choose your own maid."

Maura interviewed several candidates and chose Abby, a shy girl only a year younger than herself, inexperienced but sweet and eager to please. Maura was never sorry she'd chosen Abby. She became a friend—at a time when Maura had no friends.

This fact was painfully brought home to Maura immediately after she and Peter returned from Saratoga. Directly after Labor Day, the social season in New York began. There were parties, galas, openings almost every night. Without fail, Peter and she would be there.

They went to Delmonico's, where they

dined and danced with the rest of the "Four Hundred." The famous listing of the "Four Hundred" had been compiled by Ward McAllister for Mrs. Caroline Astor, as a record of Who was Who in society.

As a Van Diver, Maura was now on the list, although she was rarely treated as such. Perhaps, if Gladys and the other daughters had been kinder, more ready to accept her, she might have. But the daughters' obvious snubs at parties and social gatherings only encouraged others to do the same. Maura would have preferred staying home, but Peter insisted they go out each night. And she could not refuse.

They went to Madison Square Garden, the elegant building at Madison Square and Twenty-eighth Street, which had been designed by Stanford White, with its tower copied from the Girelda in Spain and topped by Saint-Gaudens's statue of Diana. They saw several concerts at the Garden and once, a Wild West show, complete with cowboys and wild steers.

At the recently opened Metropolitan Opera House, Peter and Maura saw Christine Nilsson in *Faust*. The opera house was truly magnificent, Maura thought, with its gold-embossed walls, the gilt-and-maroon boxes—*baignoires*, they were called—of the Golden Horseshoe, where they were sitting.

The real show, however, was the people. Maura had never seen so many diamonds, so many tiaras. Gladys was wearing a particularly dazzling one as she held court in the *baignoire* next to Peter and her. Maura held her head high while the flow of visitors streamed in and out of Gladys's box, ignoring her completely.

"Tell Mr. Van Diver," Abby suggested once when Maura had come home, holding back tears. But Maura would not. It was a matter of pride, for one thing. She was her father's daughter, after all, and she would handle her own problems, fight her own battles. And if she had gone to Peter, what would he say? That they would not go out anymore? But that would be foolish. Or, perhaps, that he would speak to his daughters? But that would only make them resent her more. No, she would say nothing. . . .

In early October, they received an invitation to what promised to be the social event of the season.

"In commemoration of his services to the Union during the Civil War, a dinner dance is being held to honor Louis Philippe Albert, Comte de Paris, at the Plaza Hotel," the invitation read.

"You shall have a new gown," Peter said at once.

"I have so many I haven't even worn yet," Maura reminded him.

"No matter. You must have something special," he insisted.

To please him, Maura went to the dressmaker. She chose a green velvet material, which she had cut simply, with a square, low-cut neckline as was the fashion, a tucked-in bodice and a long, flowing skirt.

The night of the dance, Abby brushed Maura's hair until it shone, then placed a lovely, glittering tiara on top. Peter had surprised Maura with it that morning. So he *had* noticed at the Opera House, she realized.

When she'd finished dressing, she went downstairs to the drawing room to wait for Peter. After a while, she became concerned. Peter was taking a long time to dress, which was not like him. At last he came downstairs, but looking flushed and not well.

"Is anything the matter, Peter?" she asked, anxiously. "If you're not feeling well, perhaps we should stay home."

"Just a little indigestion," he said. "I'll be all right. Besides, I would not deprive you of the opportunity of meeting the duke."

"That's very kind," Maura said, "but I'm more concerned about your health."

He seemed genuinely surprised. "You are, aren't you?" he said. Then, surprising her, he seized her hand and kissed it warmly. "You are a sweet child. Shall we go, dear?"

The scent of twenty-five thousand red and white roses greeted them as they crossed the long red carpet into the Grand Ballroom of the Plaza Hotel. The ballroom was lit up like a fairy tale, with hundreds of stained-glass lamps on tables and not one but three dazzling crystal chandeliers aglow in the middle of the magnificent room.

More than five hundred guests had been

invited, and the room was awhirl with activity. Almost at once, however, the hostess, Mrs. Geoffrey Smythe, spotted Peter and Maura.

"Let me introduce you to the duke!" she cried.

He was a short, dark man with lively black eyes. The moment those eyes rested on Maura, they lit up as brightly as the crystal chandeliers.

"Would Mrs. Van Diver honor me with a dance?" he asked.

Maura glanced at Peter, who was beaming proudly.

"Of course," she said.

Heads turned as she walked onto the dancefloor with the duke. The other couples scattered, leaving her alone on the floor with him.

With just the two of them, the room seemed even larger. As the duke led Maura slowly around the Grand Ballroom, she wondered why the other couples did not join them. Was it protocol? Or perhaps the couples would join in later?

But they did not. The band played on and on, and she and the duke danced. Here, there, Maura picked out a familiar face on the sidelines. She saw Peter beaming, then a few feet away, Gladys with her husband, Thomas. Thomas seemed pleased, but Gladys's face was a blur of anger.

It seemed to Maura that the dance would never end, but at last she heard the final chords.

"Thank you." The duke bowed and kissed

her hand, and led her off the floor. "I would like to claim another dance later, if I might?"

"Yes, of course," she said, slightly flustered, as she looked around for Peter. But he'd disappeared again.

It was her hostess, not Peter, who found her.

"You and the duke made an enchanting couple," she gushed.

Maura winced slightly. She remembered all too well how the same Mrs. Smythe had snubbed her at the last dinner-dance.

"There's someone who's been wanting to meet you, my dear. Oh, here he is!"

He was tall, slimly built, with a small, clipped mustache and an attractive smile. He bowed low to kiss her hand as Mrs. Smythe introduced them.

"Mrs. Van Diver, Lord Parker. Lord Parker has just come from England. Mrs. Gladstone has gallantly released him from duty for the moment so we might have the pleasure of his company."

She tittered like a small noisy bird when she finished. As the music started again, Lord Parker bent toward Maura. "May I have the pleasure of this dance?"

Maura hesitated. Perhaps she should look for Peter. But she knew from past experience it was fruitless; Peter would appear when *he* felt like it. And why shouldn't she dance? She liked the frank look in Lord Parker's eye, as though he realized Mrs. Smythe was so much nonsense.

"I'd like to dance." She smiled.

His arms were strong, his conversation pleasant. He talked about his trip from England over a stormy Atlantic. He mentioned Mr. Gladstone, a name that was currently being mentioned as the man who would soon head up a new government in England.

Maura listened with interest. She was grateful the talk was focused on him, not her. For her own part, she found it pleasant just to waltz around the room, away from the eyes of the curious, and listen to this man. There was something about him that made her feel at ease.

After a time, however, she began to worry about Peter. "I think I should be getting back," she said after the second dance, when Lord Parker showed no inclination to stop. "My husband hasn't been feeling well."

"I'm sorry to hear that," he said. "Of course."

They came off the dancefloor. "Shall I stay with you until your husband returns?" he offered.

"That's sweet. But I really shouldn't keep you."

"It's my pleasure."

She was grateful for his company, though she found herself listening with only half an ear as she became more and more anxious about Peter.

Suddenly, someone brushed against her arm. She turned, expecting Peter. She found, instead, Neil Prescott.

In formal evening dress, he looked even

more striking, more handsome. His dark, deep-set eyes held her gaze.

"Ah—Lord Parker," she stammered slightly, remembering her manners. "I'd like to introduce Neil Prescott. He's my husband's—"

"Yes," Parker cut in quickly. "Everyone knows of Mr. Prescott and the wonders he's done for Van Diver Enterprises."

They shook hands, then Neil turned to Maura. "May I have this dance?"

She should have refused. She should have gone in search of Peter. But his dark eyes held her gaze so steadily she was mesmerized. "Yes," she murmured.

Dancing with him was unlike anything she'd ever imagined. They whirled around the floor at a pace so fast she was forced to simply cling to him. He was holding her so close, she was embarrassed. But then she forgot everything—her concern about Peter, or what people might think of her or say about her. If they were staring, gaping at her and the way she was dancing, she couldn't have cared less. All she cared was for the moment, the dance. She wished suddenly, crazily, that it would never end. That they would go on like this, arms around one another, on and on and on. . . .

"Are you enjoying yourself?" he asked abruptly, his dark eyes glittering under the gleaming chandeliers.

"Oh, yes! It's wonderful!" she murmured. The words were scarcely out of her mouth when she blushed. Why, she sounded like a schoolgirl! This was the man, she reminded herself, who'd been so suspicious of her, so rude.

But he was smiling now, a warm, open smile. "You're the belle of the ball," he said. "Everyone's eyes are on you. Let's give them something to watch!"

They whirled around the floor faster, faster. She closed her eyes for a moment, feeling like a bird in flight.

"Does this please you, Mrs. Van Diver?" His lips were warm against the tip of her ear.

She pulled away abruptly. "Why not?" She threw her head back, raising that strong, stubborn chin, so like her father's. It told him, at once, that she had spirit, that she would give back what she got.

He laughed. "Your husband's daughter, Gladys, has a face as long as a grandfather clock!"

Maura glanced toward the side where Gladys stood watching, her face, sure enough, long as a clock. In spite of herself, Maura began to laugh too. For the first time, she felt a kinship with this dark-eyed man who was whirling her around the floor. He had a sense of humor, at least. She liked that. She also appreciated that he could laugh at the conventional, the staid and stuffy customs. Perhaps they could be friends, after all . . . ?"

She was dizzy. The music had stopped, but she was not aware of it until she saw the other couples leaving the floor. Finally, Neil led her off, but he did not take her back to where she'd been waiting for Peter. Instead, arm still around her, he seemed to be leading her in a different direction.

Dazed, she questioned him. "Where are we going, Mr. Prescott?"

The "Mr. Prescott" sounded stiff, awkward. It brought a smile to his lips. "Neil, please. And don't worry so, Mrs. Van Diver."

The "Mrs. Van Diver" sounded absurd after his correction. But she didn't protest. Vaguely, it occurred to her that this use of her name was his only formality.

His arm was so tight around her! He was leading her as though they were still on the dance floor. And she followed as though drugged, dazed. She felt mesmerized. She could hear a small, warning voice cautioning her not to go. But that small voice was muffled by the louder, stronger one that said wherever he took her, wherever he went, she would go.

He led her out of the ballroom into a tiny room, an anteroom that resembled a storage room or pantry. Maura almost expected to see a butler, or in this case, several waiters bustling in and out. But, no, the room was empty of both people and supplies. It had a door with a lock on it and little else to distinguish it.

"Neil . . ." she began, puzzled.

"Wait," he said. Turning, he snapped the lock shut on the door.

For the moment it took to shut the door he'd released her. Away from his arms, she began to think more clearly. *Had* he mesmerized her? Was he some kind of witch—no, warlock? If not, she wondered how on earth she could have allowed him to lead her back here. She was another man's wife. . . .

But that moment of clearness was over almost at once, as turning, he gathered her into his arms again.

"Oh, Maura!" he whispered into her ear.

The last bit of restraint, of formality, was gone. He began to kiss her, not gently, but feverishly. Again she heard that warning voice, but again she could not resist. The only other man to have kissed her was her husband, but who could call those brief, perfunctory brushes across the cheek or her lips, kisses? These were neither brief nor perfunctory; these had the taste of nectar, the sweetness of honey.

The tip of his tongue danced on the edge of her lips. Her teeth, clenched at first, opened slowly but willingly as he probed further. His tongue plundered her small, sweet mouth, tasting what no man ever had. And she felt dizzier, more giddy than ever. The electricity she'd felt from that first touch of his hand on her wedding day was stronger now by tenfold, a hundredfold! She trembled as his hands pulled her closer. Strong fingers began to explore her bare, beautiful shoulders, so white, with the feel of silk. Then, those fingers slipped inside her gown. . . .

He shouldn't be doing this! I shouldn't be letting him do this! she told herself. But she was powerless to stop him. Even if she'd wanted to—and she did not want to! The weight of his body pinned her against the wall. She felt his hands now on the straps of her gown. The next moment, the straps were lowered, her breasts bared. They shone like marble.

"So beautiful!" she heard him murmur, as he cupped one full, perfect breast in his hand and began to kiss and caress the erect, rosebud nipple. She couldn't think at all. In back of her throat, she moaned softly.

There was a sudden, loud rap on the door.

In fright, Maura, using all her strength, broke away.

Neil put a finger to his lips.

"Mrs. Van Diver?" someone called.

Maura recognized Abby's plaintive voice. Hastily, she tugged at the straps on her gown. She managed to hoist them up, but without bothering to fasten the gown, she ran to the door.

"What is it, Abby?" she asked worriedly, opening the door just a crack.

"It's Mr. Van Diver," Abby explained quickly. "He's not feeling well, ma'am. He wants to go home."

"Of course," Maura cried at once. "I'll be right with you, Abby."

The maid hesitated, uncertain whether she should come in and help her mistress. But Maura decided that for her quickly enough by slamming the door.

Her back to the door, she fumbled with the buttons on her gown.

"Shall I do that?"

Maura looked up into Neil's grinning face. As much as he had mesmerized her before, he infuriated her now.

"Get away from me!" she cried, whirling away from his touch.

He stood just a few feet away, smiling as he watched her continuing to fumble with the buttons and the interminable hooks and eyes that fastened the gown. At last she succeeded and, pausing one more moment to straighten what she was sure was a crooked tiara, she turned back toward the door.

"Ah, Maura, wait! Please!" he called suddenly.

But Maura would not. All she wanted was to get away from this mesmerizer, this charmer, and go to her husband! She flung open the door and ran out.

She was frightened when she saw Peter. His face was the same bright shade of red as the plush velvet carpet that had lined their way into the ballroom. And Peter was panting so, as though he couldn't catch his breath.

"Oh, why didn't you listen, Peter?" she said anxiously. "I told you we shouldn't have come!"

"Yes, we should have," he insisted. "I'm glad. It was important for you to come. And you were the belle of the ball," he added proudly.

His words, echoing Neil's, sent a sharp pang of guilt through Maura. And the fact that he looked so proud and happy made her feel doubly guilty. She put a finger to his lips. "No more talking, please! Let's get you home!"

The moment they arrived she insisted on calling the family doctor.

"Such foolishness," Peter said, crossly. "I feel fine."

"I'm glad," she said. "But I'll feel a lot better if a doctor looks at you," she added firmly.

"You can thank God for two things," Dr. Brickman said after he examined Peter. "First, for having married not only a lovely but a very sensible young woman, and secondly, for coming home when you did. You're not a young boy anymore, you know. You can't work all day and go out all night. Now, I want you to be quiet for the next few days. Eat sensibly, stay calm, no aggravation and, above all, rest. No more of this burning the candle at both ends. I'll give you something to help you sleep tonight."

"Thank you for coming at such a bad hour, Doctor," Maura said. "I'm very grateful."

"Perfectly all right, Mrs. Van Diver. Please call me if there's any change."

After he left, Maura waited with Peter until he'd taken his pill.

"Would you like me to stay with you?" she asked a little shyly, awkwardly. She had never "stayed" in this room; in actuality, she'd scarcely been in this room other than to direct the servants about the cleaning of the drapes, the changing of the bedspread. She looked around the room and noticed the *chaise longue.* "I can sleep there if you like." Her cheeks flushed. "So I won't disturb you, that is," she added.

"There's no need, Maura. But I appreciate your offering. And thank you. You've been very good to me," he added as she turned and started toward the door.

Peter's parting words only served to make Maura feel even more guilty and abject. How could she have allowed what had happened tonight? What had gotten into her? And why, *why* had Neil Prescott behaved the way he did? They had been so cool, *cold,* to one another! Until tonight . . .

And what must Neil think of her? she wondered. For the first time it suddenly occurred to her: could anyone else have seen him slip into the room with her?

The questions kept her awake till dawn. Finally, exhausted from worrying, she drifted off to a troubled sleep. It was after ten when she woke. She heard rain on the windowpane as she rang for breakfast.

"How is Mr. Van Diver?" she asked Abby the moment she appeared with the breakfast tray.

Abby shrugged her small shoulders. "Fine, I think, ma'am. He's at work, you know."

"At work?" Maura sat up straight in bed. "No, I didn't know. Oh, how foolish! How could he?"

Abby shrugged again and ran to open the blinds.

Silently, Maura mused. How could Peter have defied the doctor's orders and gone to work? Although obviously, she told herself, he must be feeling better.

The thought made her feel a bit relieved. Still, she found herself gulping down her juice and coffee. She ate only two bites of her roll before flinging it down on the tray.

"Can you draw my bath, Abby, please?" she asked.

Quickly, she slipped out of bed, then out of her sheer gown. She would bathe, then dress and go downtown at once. Until now, she'd avoided the Van Diver offices. Once, when she'd asked Peter to take her with him to the office one day, he'd told her the first Mrs. Van Diver had never gone. Although he hadn't actually refused to take Maura, she'd realized it was his roundabout way of saying he'd rather she not come by, either. But today, Maura told herself, was different. She wanted to see for herself how well Peter was, but just as she was finishing dressing, Abby flew into the room.

"What is it?" Maura asked anxiously.

"It's—it's," Abby stammered, "Mr. Van Diver! Two men! They've just brought him home!"

Maura rushed past Abby to the hallway, in time to see two heavyset men half-walking, half-carrying Peter up the stairs.

"What is it? What happened?" she cried.

One of the men turned from Peter to regard her, briefly but kindly. "He collapsed at the office, ma'am."

"Oh, Peter!" She came a few steps closer. "Peter!" she repeated. How dreadful he looked! His eyes were half-closed, his face unhealthily ruddy. He blinked and tried to say something, but he choked, instead.

"Don't try to talk!" Maura said, frightened. "Everything will be fine, dear," she went on, trying to keep her voice low and not to show her panic.

"Has the doctor been called?" she asked the men.

"Yes, ma'am. He should be here any minute."

"Damn fool!" Dr. Brickman sputtered angrily, as he raced up the stairs a few minutes later. "Why on earth was he allowed out?"

"I didn't know he was going," Maura said, feeling miserable.

"I see. Well, it's not your fault, I'm sure, Mrs. Van Diver. I know him. He's a hardheaded fool. Well," he said, entering the room, "let me see what the damage is. Everybody out!"

Peter's door slammed shut behind the doctor. Maura had no recourse but to go back to her room.

"Let me know the minute the doctor comes out," she told Abby.

Half an hour later there was a knock on Maura's door.

"The doctor's just come out, ma'am," Abby informed her. "And the family and Mr. Prescott've just arrived."

Dr. Brickman's face was grave when Maura met him in the hall.

"Tell me, doctor. Will he be all right?" she asked.

"I'm afraid," he began slowly, "there's not much I can do. It's his heart, you see. It's a miracle to me that he's still breathing. Try to keep him quiet. Perhaps . . . perhaps . . ." He shrugged slightly, then started down the hall.

Maura hurried to her husband's room. As she reached the threshold, she paused.

Anna and Paula were at the foot of the bed. Near the head of the bed, Gladys stood. The way she was dressed—all in black—made Maura shiver. Her eyes focused on the other side of the bed now, where Neil Prescott, also in black—or was it dark gray?—stood.

Turning, Neil saw her. Maura flushed at once. Avoiding his eyes, she started toward her husband's bed. Grudgingly, Gladys made room for her.

"Oh, Peter!" Maura murmured. His face was no longer so flushed, but his eyes were closed. For one long moment, Maura thought: *I've come too late! He's dead!* But she reached for his hand and with her touch, his eyes opened.

She fought back tears. The doctor had warned her to keep him quiet, and she didn't want to upset him anymore than he was.

"Try to rest, Peter, please," she pleaded.

But Peter's eyes, so drowsy-looking, suddenly opened wide. Puzzled, it occurred to Maura all at once that he was staring at a point past her. She spun around.

He was looking at Gladys. She was holding up something that glittered and gleamed in the light. Maura blinked. It was a piece of jewelry, she realized, a necklace of lapis lazuli and pearls. Her necklace!

"Recognize this?" Gladys asked.

With a start, Peter struggled to sit up in bed.

"No!" Maura said, trying to push him back. Peter was struggling to say something, but he could not get the words out.

"It was mother's," Gladys added.

"No, no!" Peter stammered, and the words came out at last. "Maura's! It was Maura's!"

"Stop this!" Maura cried. "Can't you see you're upsetting him?"

In answer, Gladys's face hardened. Like a cold, hard rock, Maura thought. She whirled away from her, toward Neil. "Can't you stop her?" she pleaded.

But he only looked at her coldly, and remained silent.

"Don't you wonder," Gladys went on, "what I'm doing with the necklace, Daddy? She"— she pointed at Maura—"she pawned it! Mother's beautiful necklace! Pawned it, Daddy!"

"Maura?" There was a stricken look on Peter's face as he gazed first at the necklace, then at Maura. He half sat up again. His eyes stayed fixed on Maura, his lips moved, but no words came out. Then, suddenly, he fell back across the bed.

Anna and Paula let out a piercing shriek from the foot of the bed.

A moment later, Doctor Brickman rushed in. "What is it?" he cried. He laid his ear on

Peter's chest, his hand grasped for a pulse. But there was none. With a sigh, he stood and confirmed with a nod what they already knew.

As he walked out, Maura spun toward Gladys. "You! You've done this!" she cried. "You're evil! Evil!"

She whirled toward Neil. "Why didn't you stop her? You knew what she was going to do, didn't you? Didn't you!"

"You're the evil one," he said coldly.

His eyes were so dark, like black ice. Furious, hurt, she slapped him. She could see the red mark of her fingers on his face as he continued to stare at her icily.

"Get out!" she cried. "All of you! You're nothing but vultures! You have no right here! No right! He is my husband! *My* husband . . . !"

The daughters gave her a silent look of loathing as they backed out. Neil stared at her for one more moment, then turned on his heel and left.

She wanted to call after him: *Please don't go!* But she didn't. Instead she flung herself on the bed.

She reached for her husband's hand. It was already cool to the touch, but she continued to hold it, crying. She was crying for many things. For Peter, the strange way he'd died, the fact that it might not have happened if he'd stayed home, if he'd rested. She was crying for that, for the horror of the last few minutes of his life, for the terrible look of reproach he'd given her.

71

She was crying, also, for herself. She'd been hurt. She had not betrayed Peter, whatever he had thought. Her only unfaithfulness had been those few moments last night with Neil. Neil who hated her. She had seen that in his eyes. . . .

But she would not think of Neil now. She laid her cheek against Peter's hand. How cold that hand was! Peter, her husband.

If their marriage had been strange and loveless, still it had provided her with a measure of protection. Peter had been a shield, a buffer against the rest of the world. Now that he was gone, she wondered what would happen. What would become of her?

Chapter Six

THE NEXT FEW DAYS WERE AN AGONIZING TIME for Maura. She had a sudden urge to flee. But as the young widow she had certain obligations. It was the least she could do for Peter to fulfill them.

So she endured it, telling herself it would be over soon and she would be free. What she would do then, she wasn't sure. She'd have a certain amount of money, though how much she had no idea. Peter had altered his will after they'd married. She knew his daughters would inherit the bulk of his estate, but she was certain he'd made some provisions for her.

She would be able to live comfortably, most likely very well. Before settling down again, she might travel a bit. She would like that. Of course, a young woman didn't go off traveling by herself, but she could hire a companion. And she could take Abby along with her.

The idea of a trip was a consoling thought to keep in back of her mind while she shook hands and greeted the visitors—the senators and judges, the professors and tycoons, the wealthy and distinguished—who came to pay their respects.

The hours at the funeral home, the Frederick E. Pride Funeral Home, from which so many of the social New York families buried their dead, were long and trying. Maura had little support from the family. They stood apart from her, scarcely speaking to her unless it was absolutely necessary. As for Neil Prescott, Maura did her best to ignore him. He, she had to admit, at least, was polite as well as considerate. At one point, she felt he was going to apologize, but she cut him off.

The last evening, Lord Parker came to pay his respects.

"I'm so very sorry," he said, offering his hand. "I do wish my circumstances were different and I could stay a few days longer. I have the feeling you could use a friend, Mrs. Van Diver."

She was touched. How perceptive he was! "Thank you," she said as they shook hands. She was genuinely sorry to see him go.

Later that evening, the family went up, one by one, to view Peter's body for the final time.

Maura was the last. She steeled herself as she looked down at him. . . .

His face was glistening and polished. In his dark business suit, he looked very proper and solemn, as though he was going off to work. Maura tried to remember him as he had been that last night at the Plaza Hotel. How proud he'd been of her! Yes, she told herself, that is the way she would remember him. . . .

The day of the funeral it rained, a cold, bitter rain that went through to the bones. Maura dressed as warmly as she could, but she still felt the chill.

She was tired. The eulogy had been so long! The minister, then half a dozen of Peter's peers, had paid their respects. Afterward, Maura had sat alone in the black carriage on the long drive to the burial site. Now, as she stood in the rain by the grave, it seemed to be taking an eternity.

Peter was being buried in a huge stone crypt, with his father, the Captain, on one side, and the first Mrs. Van Diver on the other. The burial site and the crypt had, ironically enough, all been planned by Peter. It had been one of his father's last wishes that a proper burial site be found for all the members of the Van Diver family. Peter had searched and found what he'd thought was the perfect spot, on a hilltop in Long Island overlooking the water. It had been completed only recently, and the bodies of Peter's mother and father had been moved to the new site. The first Mrs. Van Diver had claimed the next grave. Peter had had no idea he would be following her so quickly. . . .

The chill rain beat down relentlessly. Maura sighed. She overheard two women standing near her.

"Well, she's made herself a pretty penny, hasn't she?" said one.

"And in less than two months' time!" said the other.

The first woman laughed, then hid her face in a handkerchief.

A few feet away, Maura shivered. The remark had been both cruel and unfair. She was angry with herself for letting it bother her, but it did. She could not stop shivering. Though the chilling rain was, no doubt, as much to blame as the remark. It was becoming more than she could bear.

She hugged her arms around herself. As the body was being placed in the crypt, she felt suddenly faint. As the symbolic handful of dirt was tossed, she felt herself sinking, also, into the earth. . . .

Strong hands grabbed her and held her. Dazed, she looked up into the dark eyes of Neil Prescott.

"Are you all right?" he asked anxiously.

"Yes, I'm fine. Thank you," she said, a little stiffly. She tried to pull away, but he kept his arm around her.

Silently, he walked back with her to her carriage. She was grateful for his supporting arm, though she never would have admitted it.

"May I ride back with you?" he asked, surprising her.

She nodded, and he helped her in.

Sitting beside him in the car on that long drive back to Manhattan, she became sorry she had agreed to ride with him. For the ride was as awkward, as uncomfortable, as that first one when he'd accompanied Peter and her to the station on their way to Saratoga. . . .

"There's something I want to say," she said, suddenly, surprising both him and herself. But all at once, it had occurred to her that this was the perfect opportunity. Chances are she would never have another. And she felt a sudden compulsion to set things straight.

"About the necklace," she began. "I didn't pawn it. I would never have done such a thing! I . . ." Here, she faltered; she couldn't bring herself to tell him about Kevin. "It," she went on after a moment, "was stolen, or lost. I was never sure which; that's why I never mentioned it to Peter."

She flushed slightly at the fib. But it was better to fib than to tell him about Kevin.

Neil's eyes fixed on her with burning intensity. "I understand, Maura. And I'm sorry if I misjudged you. The fact is, somewhere along the way, it occurred to me that something like that must have happened. After all, why should you pawn a necklace? It made no sense. I told Gladys Van Diver as much the other day. And I wanted to apologize to you. Actually, I tried to several times, but I got the feeling you were avoiding me. Well, I can't say that I blame you—"

He broke off suddenly. His dark eyes glanced away from her, toward the window. She followed his gaze.

They were crossing the river. Just at that moment, as the rain was easing up, the sun was making an effort to come out. The combination, etched faintly across the horizon, was a rainbow.

"How beautiful!" Maura cried. "I've never seen a rainbow so clearly before!"

"Haven't you? I have. But it's one of the reasons I love this city. There are always surprises. One moment it's gray and dingy with rain and smoke. Then, suddenly, there's a burst of sunshine and a rainbow. And—why are you smiling?"

"Why?" Maura shrugged. "I guess because I didn't realize you noticed things like that."

Again his eyes focused on her, taking her in slowly. "I notice many things," he said.

"I'm sure you do." She flushed at the significance of her words, then told herself she was being silly, once more. She fell silent and so did he. The silence remained like a curtain between them until the driver pulled up in front of the Fifth Avenue mansion.

"Well . . ." she began.

But Neil stopped her, by putting a staying hand on her arm. "Wait! There's one more thing I've noticed: you haven't been eating regularly. I'd like to take you to lunch, if I may. It'll do you good to get away from that house for a few hours."

"Well . . ." But she hesitated only a moment. "Yes, I'd like that."

"Good. I'll pick you up in an hour."

They drove to George's, a tiny restaurant on Tenth Street in the Village. Maura had never heard of it, but it was a pleasant surprise, elegant, tastefully decorated and softly lit.

The maitre d' seemed, at once, surprised and delighted to see Neil. "Come," he said, and ushered them to a table away from the others in the back of the room.

Maura sat, quiet and thoughtful, as Neil proceeded to order their lunch. She studied his profile, thrown into relief by the dim candlelight. It was a very fine profile, she thought: strong, handsome, with just that touch of arrogance that was one of the first things she'd noticed about him. It was that arrogance, she decided, that made her uneasy. Despite herself, she kept thinking of that night at the Plaza, of how he had whirled her around the ballroom floor, then whisked her off to the anteroom. And then . . .

But no, she would not think of that, not today of all days! Today, after all, was the day she had buried her husband!

Her eyes fell, almost in shame, to the white tablecloth. Oh, why had she come? she asked herself. She searched and came up with two reasons: as he'd suggested, she knew it would be a godsend just to get away from that mournful, empty house for a short time. Secondly, she'd hoped, after his apology, and particularly after that remark about the rainbow, that the two of them might become friends. It was a welcome thought—that they might be friends.

Neil had finished ordering. The maitre d' walked away and Neil turned his attention to her.

"Let's make a pact, shall we?" he proposed. "I know today and the last few days have been very trying, terrible days for you. But let's not talk about them. You need to get away from it for a little while."

He paused to break off a piece of roll and butter it. "Tell me about yourself, Maura," he said. "You know, I don't know anything at all about you."

For a moment, she was completely taken back. She was not used to talking about herself. Hardly. The fact was, in her entire lifetime, only one person—her father—had seemed at all interested in what her thoughts were, what she wanted, who she was. Other than he, not one person, not even Peter, had ever asked her about herself. Slowly, falteringly at first, she began to tell him about her beginnings on the lower East Side.

She told him about the neighborhood that was at once funny and sad, and about her family. She skipped over the details about her brothers, and found herself concentrating instead on the love of her life, her father. She talked about his act with the Five Shamrocks. She repeated the jokes, and in the way of someone who's grown up with a performer in the family, she began to mimic her father— his songs, his jokes, his peculiar Irish accent that won over the audiences every time and that had won her heart. . . .

Maura heard laughter.

"That's wonderful!" Neil laughed. "I'm sorry I didn't get the chance to see him."

"Yes, you would have loved him," she said, simply. "Everyone did."

"Did you want to go on stage, as a child?"

She shook her head. "I never thought of myself as a performer. I do like to recite, though." She told him about her love for Dickens. "And what about you?" she finished, quickly turning the tables on him. "I don't know anything about you."

"Well . . ." He hesitated, as the maitre d' poured the wine. It was a full-bodied burgundy. He took a sip, nodded approvingly. The maitre d' finished pouring and left.

"All right," Neil shrugged. "If you're sure you want to hear. . . ."

He'd been orphaned at the age of three. As a child, he put himself to sleep dreaming he could still hear his mother's voice, singing to him. If so, that faint recollection of her voice was all he remembered. In actuality, his first memories were of the home he'd been brought to, the Charles E. Cunningham Home.

"There was a boy's home in our neighborhood on the lower East Side," Maura interrupted. She shivered slightly as she remembered. "It was like something out of *Oliver Twist.*"

He laughed. "This was nothing like that. They were really quite decent to us. We ate regularly, if not all that well, and they kept us clean, particularly on Sundays, when the visitors came to look us over."

There were few visitors, however. It was the rare family in those days who wanted to adopt, and could afford to adopt, a child. Still, some children were accepted into families, though usually the younger ones.

Each Sunday, Neil would watch as the prospective parents made a fuss over the babies or the small youngsters. He would wish bitterly that someone would notice him, take him. But he was twelve years old before someone finally did.

He remembered the day well. He had almost not come down to the visiting room. He was now the eldest child at the home, and he had come to believe that he would never be adopted. Soon, as a matter of fact, he was to be released from the home and sent out to work.

And why hadn't he been adopted? He was the tallest, strongest, best-looking youth in the house. His hair was white-blond and suggested a Scandinavian heritage; his dark eyes, puzzling in such a fair face, were huge, with a thick fringe of black lashes. He was a handsome boy, so handsome he was almost beautiful.

Yet, perversely, whenever he was approached by an eager couple he would do something—make a sharp remark, "act up," as they called it at the home, by being unruly, tripping another young boy, perhaps—doing something, at any rate, that would make the couple think twice. And why did he act that way? He never stopped to think about it, but if he had he might have realized he did so simply out of fear. Though he did want to be adopted, how could he be sure that the couple who adopted him were the right couple, that they would be good to him, that they would know how to take care of him properly, to deal with him? At least, at the home, he knew what he had.

But on a certain day, a man came to the Cunningham Home who would not be put off by looks or unruly manners. This was a man who could deal with anything. Ironically enough, he had not come to the home looking for a child. In the previous five or six years, he'd grudgingly given money there. He had, in fact, almost been shamed into giving the money by one of his peers. He resented it. Giving money without its being earned was against his better judgment. To ease his mind, he'd come to the home to see how well that money was being put to use. But when he saw Neil, he began to get other ideas. . . .

Captain Van Diver was one of the most powerful men in the country. If one considered the growth potential of all of his investments ("My money is so well invested," he'd once told a business friend, "that I get twenty-five cents back on every dollar, if not more."), he was also the richest man in the country, and as rich, if not richer, than the Duke of Westminister, the richest man in the world.

With so much wealth, one might have thought he had had everything he wanted. But the one thing he wanted had been denied him.

For the Captain had wanted a son to follow in his footsteps. His wife, unfortunately, had been sickly. Thrice, she'd been pregnant, and thrice, she'd lost the child before her time was up. After fifteen years of marriage, when she became pregnant again, the Captain was almost delirious with happiness. He made sure she took care of herself—after the first few months she scarcely left her bed. At the end of nine months, she at last gave birth—to Peter. At times, while Peter was growing up, the Captain had fooled himself into thinking there might be a chance for him. But plodding, heavyset Peter was close to forty now. As far as the Captain was concerned, it was foolish to hope anymore.

That afternoon, as he strolled past the visitor's room, he suddenly spotted Neil. Heart beating wildly, he stopped short. The sunlight had fallen so on the boy, on his hair, his face, that the Captain was struck, at once, by the physical resemblance between Neil and the boy he himself had been. How strange, how uncanny, that Neil should resemble him so! And not only physically. The Captain sat down and had a long talk with Neil. Neil snapped back with one or two of his smart remarks, but the Captain, instead of being put off, roared. They were just the kind of thing he would have said himself when he was a boy. It convinced him (modesty was *not* one of the Captain's virtues) that the boy was more like him than he'd first suspected. Certainly he had the makings of a good mind. Here was the son he'd always wanted. That very night, he made plans to take Neil out of the home.

The Captain lived to see Neil put through the best of schools. During vacations and even holidays, Neil worked from sunup to sundown at the office and in the stock market. After Harvard, Neil was given his own private office, with orders to report directly to the Captain.

One might have thought that Peter would have resented Neil. But he did not. Neil was so much younger than he—just a child when Peter first met him. And since Peter had had no son, like his father, he came to look on Neil as his own child. If his father looked after Neil's mind, it was Peter who carefully supervised Neil's clothes and manners and later, inspected the girls Neil dated.

Peter was secretly relieved to find that, although the girls chased after Neil constantly, he did not seem particularly interested in any of them. His real enthusiasm, like the Captain, was for his work.

Perhaps the genuine reason Peter did not resent Neil was his realization that it had never been the Captain's intention to surplant his son. Blood was blood, after all. Everything would remain, in fact, in Peter's name, which was all he was concerned about. For his services, Neil would be generously rewarded with the best of incomes and, along with it, the personal satisfaction of knowing it was he, not Peter, who was running the business. . . .

Neil glanced up from his wine. Maura's head was bent slightly over the burgundy. Even in the dim candlelight, Neil could see how brightly her golden hair shone. How lovely she was!

It occurred to him that he'd told her more

about himself tonight than he'd ever told anyone. He hadn't intended to, but there was something about her that invited confidences.

Of course, he had hardly told all. Nothing about the women—the debutantes (and the debutantes' mothers!) who had chased after him in college, and who were still chasing after him. Nor about clever Sarah Montebello who even now was waiting for him. He had never intended to become involved with Sarah. He thought of her as his mistress. Suddenly, he grinned to himself. Sarah obviously didn't consider him to be her master!

Very few women were like Maura. No, not one, he thought. From her story, he realized that what he'd guessed about her was true: she was truly innocent. Peter had picked a rare one this time. He wondered, suddenly, if she'd guessed the truth about Peter. Somehow, he suspected she hadn't. No, she was truly innocent. Poor thing.

Impulsively, he leaned over and patted Maura's hand.

She started at his touch.

"Sorry," he said, quickly. "I didn't mean to startle you. But perhaps we should be starting back."

"It is late, isn't it?" she said, realizing all at once how quiet the restaurant had become. Everyone else had left long ago.

"I should be getting back to the office," he said. And Sarah, he thought. Hang Sarah. But he waved for the check.

There were no more silences on the way back. It was as though the curtain had been torn away and discarded. They talked about their lunch ("Marvelous!" Maura said, though in actuality she'd eaten little). They commented on the way the day had cleared up so suddenly.

They talked of many things, though neither said what they were thinking. But the undercurrent of their feelings was so strong that when the carriage stopped in front of the Fifth Avenue mansion, Maura's heart stopped with it.

When would she see him again? she wondered. Would it be too unladylike to ask? She flushed slightly. Her husband had just been buried. Still, she couldn't face the thought of being alone in that big, cold house.

"I wonder . . ." she began.

At the same time, he started: "I wonder . . ."

They both laughed.

"Would it be too rude," he went on, "if I invited myself to dinner?"

"Yes!" she laughed. "I mean, no. Yes, please come!"

"I have some things to attend to," he said. "Would nine be all right?"

"Fine," she said.

An hour later, as Maura was resting, there was a knock on her door.

"These just came, ma'am," Abby said. In her arms were a huge bouquet of long-stemmed red roses. Maura opened the note:

"Today was the first day we met. It's the first day, I hope, of a long, enduring friendship. Neil."

With all he'd given her, Peter had never sent flowers. And these were so beautiful! Maura's hand brushed one soft velvet petal. Finally, reluctantly, she handed the bouquet back to Abby to be placed in water.

She lay down again to nap. But she was much too excited to sleep. She began to wonder about him, the small orphan boy he had told her about, the man he had become. And what was he doing now, she wondered . . . ?

He was trying to work. His thoughts, however, kept straying to Maura. The way the light had played on her golden hair, the clearness of her complexion, those deep blue eyes. That delightful laugh . . .

It was fortunate he had no heavy decisions to make that day. The market had been particularly quiet, in deference to Peter, he suspected. The day the Captain had died the market had closed down completely, the first and only time it had happened.

Now, Neil suspected the bears and bulls were waiting to see what he would do. Well, let them wait, he thought. He'd learned that from the Captain. Let them get anxious while they were waiting, and they were sure to make mistakes. Year in, year out, the Van Divers had profited from those mistakes.

He grabbed his jacket and briefcase. He would call it a day.

"James, I'm leaving," he told his assistant. "I'll be in bright and early tomorrow morning."

James groaned. Bright and early, as he well

knew, meant seven A.M. "Fine, sir," he answered. "I'll be there."

Neil's first stop was Sarah Montebello's. It was a duty stop, but he consoled himself with the thought that it was on the way.

Sarah, like Maura, was a widow, and a young one. Unlike Maura, there'd been no children, however, to claim the estate. Sarah had been given full title to everything. And "everything" was considerable. Her husband's fortune, made in the stockyards out West, had not, however, brought him social acceptance. He'd been considered *nouveau riche* and when he'd thrown his hat into the social whirl he'd been snubbed.

Sarah's social fortunes had improved considerably after his death. Sarah, who had the wiles and tricks of a snake charmer, had endeared herself to Caroline Astor. She had helped with the planning of many of Mrs. Astor's dinner-dances and balls, in both New York and Newport. It was rumored it had been Sarah's idea that Mrs. Astor should give a ball in—of all places—the stables of her "cottage" at Newport. Instead of the usual hothouse orchids and roses, Mrs. Astor had been persuaded to decorate with red peppers, pumpkins, turnips and eggplants.

"Such an amusing idea!" everyone had said. "And how brilliant Sarah is!"

Sarah was, in her way, Neil had to admit. He had met her at one of Mrs. Astor's parties. Her dark hair and eyes, almost as black as his, had intrigued him. What had intrigued him even more was her lack of coyness.

Bed with Sarah had been more than agreeable. Their bodies understood each other and had continued to do so, even after Neil came to realize that Sarah was too moody, too temperamental for his tastes. She was a woman he could never fully trust, and once he'd realized that his passion had slackened.

Unfortunately, hers had seemed to grow more fierce with time. It seemed to Neil that Sarah was constantly chasing after him, leaving messages all over town, wherever he went. He'd found two at the office that day when he'd arrived. Well, no more, he vowed.

The carriage pulled in front of the upper Fifth Avenue mansion, designed in red-brick, Georgian style. Quickly, Neil jumped out and raced up the stairs.

He found her in the drawing room. It was an exotically decorated room, with a leopard rug in front of the fireplace. The leopard had been shot by Sarah's husband, and still looked as though it were about to pounce. On one side of the rug stood a huge palm tree, bearing a long chain of orchids. Beneath the tree was a purple velvet *chaise longue*. On it, Sarah sat, clad in a white satin dressing gown, a white feathery boa around her shoulders.

There was also a pout on her olive-skinned face. "You're late," she said.

"I'm sorry," Neil said, briskly. "But it couldn't be helped. And, unfortunately, I can't stay now."

"You can't?" she cried. "Why not?"

From the sound of her voice, he realized she was on the verge of a tantrum. "I've told you before, Sarah," he said sharply, "I don't like scenes."

"It's that young widow, isn't it?" she hurried on regardless. "It *is* her, isn't it?" she guessed.

"It has nothing to do with her," he snapped angrily. "In case you've forgotten, I'm a businessman. I have work to do. Now, good night!"

They ate by candlelight in the oversized dining room at the Old English table which, when all its leaves were in, seated a hundred. Peter and she had rarely used it.

Yet, from the few evenings she and Peter had dined at home, Maura remembered how Peter's plump face had looked at the other end of the table. Where Neil was sitting now. . . .

"Were you busy at the office?" she asked.

"Not too."

"You know," she began a little hesitantly, then went on, "I'd thought, once or twice, about coming down to the office. But Peter didn't seem to like the idea. I understand his first wife never set foot in the office. Still, it seems to me that it doesn't hurt to know a little about the business that's putting the bread on your table. Don't you agree?" She paused. "Of course, that was before . . ." She fell silent, and dipped her spoon into her consommé.

"You're thinking of the will, aren't you? The reading's tomorrow afternoon, isn't it?"

"Yes." She was thinking it would be senseless for her to learn anything about the business now. She glanced up. He was staring down the long table at her.

"What will you do, Maura?" he asked. "Do you have any plans?"

"I'm not sure. . . ." She paused as the maid removed the soup plates and the butler served the veal.

"Perhaps," she went on, as the servants left, "I'll travel a little. I've always wanted to do that. Though I haven't really made up my mind. . . ." She drifted off.

He sipped his wine thoughtfully, then put down the glass. "There's plenty of time to make plans," he said. "But they should be made at leisure, *your* leisure. You must not feel pressured, Maura."

He did not say it but she realized he meant by the family. She was grateful for his concern.

They had coffee and brandy in the smaller of the two downstairs drawing rooms. It was the one Maura felt more at ease in, particularly so tonight since the butler had laid a cozy fire.

They warmed their brandy in front of the fire, while Neil amused Maura with talk of some of the parties he'd been to. He told her of the hostesses who wrapped cigars and bread rolls in $100 bills with the hostess's initials on them in gilt, all to lure people to their parties.

Maura laughed out loud when he described Mrs. Astor and her jewels. She wore so many and such heavy ones! She had one diamond necklace of forty-four huge stones, another of two hundred eighty-two smaller ones. It was said, truthfully enough, that even if you saw Mrs. Astor from the rear, you could not mistake her for she often wore jewelry all the way down her spine. That was why she always sat bolt upright in her chair. It was too painful for her to lean against anything!

All too soon, the evening came to an end.

Neil stood. They were both uneasy for a moment and silent, their eyes saying what their lips could not. It would have been unthinkable on this day, of all days.

Instead, Neil stepped forward and, taking her hand, brushed his lips against it gently. "Sleep well, sweet lady."

Maura's step was light as she walked up the steps to her bedroom. She felt slightly guilty that she should feel this way when Peter, poor Peter, was still fresh in his grave. All evening she'd been aware of the cutting looks of the servants. Yet Maura knew in her heart it had been an innocent evening.

Only Abby was happy for her young mistress. She said nothing, but as she took down Maura's hair and plaited it into a long braid for the night, she sang to herself cheerfully.

Maura felt like singing also. She hummed an air her father used to sing to her when she was a child:

> Sleep, baby, sleep,
> The father watches the sheep,
> Sleep, baby, sleep . . .

When Maura lay down to sleep at last, she found herself, however, eyes wide open, staring at the ceiling. If she stared hard enough, she could imagine Neil's face across the dining-room table. Word for word, she repeated their conversation in her mind. It delighted her. Only the talk about the will troubled her, but that would soon be over. After tomorrow . . .

Chapter Seven

AT ONE P.M. THE FOLLOWING DAY, MR. J. C. Ross, personal attorney for Peter Van Diver, came to the house to read the will. The family, all three daughters and their husbands, with the addition of Maura and Neil, received him in the library.

"I'll make this as brief as possible," Ross said. Adjusting his glasses, he began to rattle down a long list of charities: "To the Domestic and Foreign Missionary Society of the Protestant Episcopal Church, to Saint Luke's Hospital, to the Young Men's Christian Association, to the Protestant Episcopal Mission Society of New York, a donation of $100,000 each. To the General Theological Seminary, to the New York Bible and Common Prayer Book Society, to the Home for Incurables, to the Mission Society for Seamen and to the American Museum of Natural History, a donation of $50,000 each. . . ."

Ross raised his glasses. "And now, we'll go on to the main portion of the will. The estate, including both houses in Newport and on

Fifth Avenue, with all the paintings, furnishings, boats, carriages, stables, etc., and with the addition, of course, of all cash and securities other than that which is made reference to in this will shall be equally divided between my three daughters.

"To my good friend and valued business associate, Neil Prescott, the sum of $30,000.

"And finally, to my wife, the former Maura O'Rourke: a bequest of $20,000 a year, plus the additional sum of $5,000 a year to be paid each year at the first of the year, unless she remarries, at which time the $5,000 annual bequest will be discontinued. . . ."

There was a flutter of silk skirts and a few coughs. The daughters were getting restless.

"There is one more provision," Mr. Ross said. "May I read it?"

There were a few impatient nods. Mr. Ross propped up his glasses again, and read on: "In the event that my marriage with Maura O'Rourke is blessed with a male heir, the above will will be rendered null and void. The entire estate will then revert to my heir. In this case, each of my daughters will receive a bequest of $20,000 each. The provisions for Neil Prescott and Mrs. Van Diver will remain the same. . . ."

Maura heard a few gasps around the room. She was surprised to discover that she was holding her breath. She'd been startled. How strange! she thought. But, after a moment or so, it occurred to her that perhaps it was not so strange. If Peter had lived, perhaps things might have changed between them. Who knows? There might have been an heir. . . .

There was a tiny tinkle of laughter. Maura turned toward Gladys Van Diver, who was stage-whispering to her husband: "Well, that's *one* thing we won't have to worry about!"

Thomas laughed then glanced, embarrassed, at Maura as his wife stood. Clutching her sable stole around her shoulders, Gladys headed toward the doors. She was followed, in rapid succession, by Thomas, her two sisters and their husbands and Mr. Ross.

Only Neil lingered. "I must get back to the office," he told her. "But I wondered—could we have dinner tonight?"

"Yes, I'll tell the housekeeper."

"Don't bother. I'll take you out. To some place quiet," he added quickly. "Not Delmonico's."

She shuddered slightly at the thought of gay, overcrowded Delmonico's, where they would be sure to see and be seen by everyone.

"No," she said, "I think it might be quieter here. And we can dine in that small drawing room, if you like."

"Fine." He smiled, a sunny smile that lightened her heart, before he turned toward the door. When he reached it, he turned back. "Today didn't go too badly, did it?"

"No." She shook her head, smiling. She watched him go, wishing he could stay to talk. But she knew he was busy and she was grateful he was coming tonight. They could talk then. Oh, there was so much to talk about! But first, she would see about dinner.

She ran to find the housekeeper. "Nothing elaborate," Maura told her. "Just some soup, and something light, perhaps chicken. I'll leave that to you. But I would like it served in the small drawing room."

"The drawing room?" Mrs. Green, the housekeeper, repeated. If Maura had mentioned the Sahara, she could not have been more shocked.

"Yes, the drawing room," Maura repeated firmly. "As I said, it needn't be too elaborate."

She walked off, leaving Mrs. Green to mutter to herself. Mentally, Maura began to make a list of what she would need. She would want fresh flowers for the drawing room, and she would have to make certain the butler was aware so he would light a fire. Also . . .

She stopped herself. She was behaving like a schoolgirl! She reminded herself that Neil was being very sweet and attentive, but possibly he considered his attentions a part of his duty and something he ought to do out of consideration for Peter's widow. Except—

She kept coming back to that night at the Plaza, when he'd taken her to the anteroom and taken the straps of her gown down. . . .

She flushed. He hadn't thought of Peter that night. Unless—could he have been drunk? But she didn't think so.

With a sigh, she sat down in front of the vanity mirror. Abby began to brush her hair. She closed her eyes.

"You're looking better, ma'am," Abby said, a little smugly.

"I am?" Maura opened her eyes and stared at herself in the mirror.

"Yes. You'd gotten so pale. But now there's some color in your cheeks again."

Maura could see the fresh color herself. She knew who had put it there.

"He's a handsome man." Abby smiled.

"Oh, Abby, do you think it's wrong?" Maura blurted out.

"Oh, no, ma'am!" Abby shook her head, vigorously. "No!"

"But the way the servants look at me. And Mrs. Green—"

"Oh, don't pay any attention to her. She's an old crow."

Abby shrugged her young shoulders. She started to sing "The Irish Servant Girls" song, which always made the two of them giggle.

And so for a while, Maura was soothed, and forgot. . . .

"Have you come to any decision?" Neil asked. "What will you do?"

"Well . . ." Maura sat back on the green velvet couch. They had just finished what Mrs. Green called a "light meal" and what Maura called elaborate. It had begun with a thick cream soup, then a fish course, followed by a mutton chop, with a pudding for dessert. But Neil had seemed to enjoy everything and for that Maura was pleased.

She raised her glass of brandy to the fire,

toasting it as she spoke. "I assume I'll be given a certain amount of time to move. There's no great hurry, but I think I'll begin to look for a traveling companion. I'll be taking Abby along, of course. We'll go to all the places I've been longing to see."

"Like what?" he asked, curious.

"Oh, Ireland. I want to see where my father came from. All those stories I've heard! I think a few of the halls he played are still there. And I want to see if the grass is as green as he claimed." She smiled, remembering.

She took a sip of brandy. "Maybe then," she went on, "I'll go to London. I've read so much Dickens. I think I'd like to make up my own tour, going through each one of his books and seeing if I could pick out the houses. I'd like to see Covent Garden Market at sunrise, with all the flowers. And the Old Curiosity Shop—and oh." She paused suddenly, her eyes shining at the thoughts she'd just expressed.

"What about me?" he said softly.

"What?" She spun toward him, puzzled.

"I said, what about me," he repeated. "As the traveling companion."

He saw confusion on her face and at once, regretted what he'd said. "Oh, Maura, forgive me! It's much too soon for me to say anything! I understand that and I'm sorry. It's just that—" He paused.

Her face was a perfect white oval in the dim light of the fire. She looked so lovely, though her pale brows, knitted together, told him again how confused she was.

"I wouldn't be able to get away for a while

now, anyway," he went on, half to himself. "And, of course, people would talk, if you make any kind of a commitment. . . ." He broke off again. "Are you offended, Maura?"

It seemed to Maura that her senses were not functioning. She could not speak; she was not even sure of what she had just heard. Had she, perhaps, misunderstood him? Had he said what she hadn't dared to dream—that he wanted to go with her, to *be* with her?

"It *is* my fault," he was saying now, gently. "This is absurdly soon for me to speak of anything. It's unfair to you, Maura. Can you forgive me?"

She choked as she started to speak, and finally found her voice. "Oh, Neil—" It was the first time she'd spoken his name and she drew it out so that it sounded to her, and to him also, like music.

"Don't apologize, please!" she went on. "If you're guilty, I am also. You"—she flushed, then went on hastily—"you've said all the things I've wanted to say."

"Shh." In an instant, he had moved from his end of the long couch to hers. He pulled her toward him, stopping her lips with his.

She tasted the brandy at the edges of his mouth. She sighed and closed her eyes. But as quickly as he'd moved toward her, he pulled away and moved back again to the other end of the couch.

"Neil, why—?" She opened her eyes, puzzled. Then she stopped as she realized.

"It's too soon. You understand that, don't you, darling? Ah, you're smiling."

"At the darling. You've never called me that before. No one has."

"Well, you are. My darling." He gave her one long look that made her flush again. But she held his steady gaze as he stood.

"If it's nice tomorrow night, we'll go out. I'd like to take you for a long drive."

"That would be lovely."

The dark eyes that had seemed so black and unfathomable only a short time ago burned warmly into hers as he reached for her hand and kissed it gently.

"No, you are lovely," he said. "So lovely, Maura." He released her hand. "Until tomorrow, darling."

How could she sleep? After Abby had plaited her hair and she'd changed to her thin chemise, she lay down, convinced that she would never sleep. She could hear her heart beating wildly. Her biggest fear was that perhaps she *had* been asleep, dreaming. It did not seem possible that this had actually happened, that he had really said all those incredible, wonderful things!

She drifted off to sleep, at last. And now, she did dream, of the deep, burning look in his eyes the moment before he'd said goodbye. . . .

"Hello!" He helped her into the carriage. He'd been sitting with his briefcase, working. He had not come in, sending his driver instead to tell her of his arrival.

It was just as well, Maura thought. The servants were muttering and Mrs. Green had come to her early that morning to give her notice.

"But I will be leaving very soon myself," Maura had said, perplexed.

"It makes no difference," Mrs. Green had snapped back. "I cannot stay in a household with such goings-on!"

Her words stung. For one moment, Maura, angered, had felt like slapping the woman. How could she say, how could she even suggest such a thing? Except for that brief kiss last night, she and Neil had done nothing to be ashamed of. Yet here was this woman judging and condemning.

"What is it, now?" Neil asked, concerned. "You have problems written all over that lovely face."

"Do I? Well, it's Mrs. Green," she began, telling him about their talk.

"It's probably all for the best," Maura finished. "I thought, at first, I might also interview housekeepers along with traveling companions. But that doesn't seem practical. Mrs. Green will be leaving at the end of two weeks. Perhaps I should simply be ready to leave myself, then. . . ."

She paused. Neil was frowning. He sat back in the deep recesses of the black carriage and crossed his long legs.

"So you will be interviewing companions, then?" he said, after a moment.

"Well, yes," she said. Actually, she was uncertain what to do. In the bright light of morning, she wondered what it was that Neil had really said. She had to make some plans.

She hated the thought of leaving him and yet, did she have an alternative?

She turned to look out the window and saw that the shades were drawn. Well, it was a cold evening.

"You're shivering, darling."

It was the darling. She spun around toward him, wide-eyed, and looking so vulnerable, so delicious, he could not resist. He had made promises to himself all that day. He would not place any more of a burden on her, not at the moment. He would take her to dinner, but as the perfect gentleman. He would not lay a hand on her. . . .

But all his resolve went out the shuttered window when she looked at him that way.

"My darling," he said again, pulling her toward him. There was a heavy wool blanket which he kept expressly for cold nights. He pulled it over her now, while his hands began feverishly to fumble with the buttons on her dress, all the while kissing her and murmuring her name. "Maura, oh Maura!"

All day, after that interview with Mrs. Green, Maura had felt like a wanton woman. Now, dazed and past caring beyond the fact that it was he, really *he!* she helped unbutton the buttons that seemed to have multiplied a hundredfold. She sighed as he brushed his lips against hers. She clung hungrily to him, tasting the sweetness of his tongue, his mouth.

At last, the dress which she'd donned so carefully but which had become so cumbersome slipped off to the floor. His hands under her chemise caressed each full breast. She felt her nipples spring to meet his touch.

She shivered as his hand moved downward to her belly, her buttocks. In the cold night air, she felt warm, almost feverish. All she knew was she wanted him so!

Suddenly, he paused. "My darling," he whispered, "it shouldn't be like this. If you want, I'll stop."

But they both knew they were beyond the point of stopping. She shook her head, and he quickly undid his trousers. Then, lifting her chemise, in one quick movement, he pulled her on top of him.

Maura gasped in surprise. He'd done it so quickly, so expertly, she hadn't realized what he was doing. But as she felt him now, erect and hard, move inside her, she gave a deep moan of pleasure.

"Move, darling," he instructed. His hands helped teach her what Peter never had, lifting her, then releasing her, quickly, smoothly. Her body caught the rhythm at once, and she started to move, slowly at first, then faster as she gained more confidence.

Suddenly, she felt his strong arms around her, lifting her again, rolling her onto her back and moving inside in one deep, final thrust that made Maura cry out as they both exploded in a single, blinding flash.

She had buried her head on his smooth chest. She lifted her chin now, and looked into his shining dark eyes.

He smiled, then frowned slightly. "You're shivering again." He pulled the heavy blanket over her legs. "Are you all right? Was I too rough?"

"Yes and no!" she said, and at that moment, the carriage went over a huge bump and they collided together. They both laughed at the thought of what *might* have happened if they'd reached the bump a little earlier.

Then Maura, flushing, suddenly remembered the driver. "Could he have heard us?" she asked, anxiously.

Neil laughed again. "Don't worry about Myers."

Why? she wondered suddenly with a flash of jealousy. Was Myers used to this? Had Neil done this with others?

But even as the thought flashed through her mind, Neil guessed and hugged her to him, tightly.

"I've never done this with anyone, darling," he whispered, "not here. I think you'll agree it's not the most comfortable place in the world to make love. And there never seemed to be the necessity before. . . ."

Nor the urgency. But he had not been able to stop himself, to control his urge. Even now, looking at her, feeling her loveliness beside him, he was scarcely able to control himself. He wanted her again, desperately, but he did not want to frighten her.

"Here." He wrapped the blanket around her more securely. "You're not cold, are you?"

She shook her head.

"Hungry?"

"A little."

"We'll have something shortly. I'll tell the driver."

As he pulled down the mouthpiece to speak to Myers, Maura began to struggle into her clothes. She managed it fairly well, considering the close quarters, but she was having difficulty with the buttons again when he turned back to her.

"Here, I'll help." More than ever, he wanted to take the gown down again, but he fought against his own passions and helped fasten the buttons.

"Let's have some food, Maura," he told her. "Then there are a few things we should talk about."

They returned to the same little restaurant, George's, that they'd had lunch at the other day. Yesterday, Maura thought. Had it just been yesterday? It seemed as though a lifetime had passed since then.

The maitre d', delighted again to see Neil, found the same quiet table in the corner for them, out of sight of everyone else. This time, the maitre d' also served them, bringing first some wonderful hot hors d'oeuvres, then a thick vegetable soup, followed by fragrant, herb-scented chicken.

They were both ravenous. Maura finished everything on her plate, including a steamy, delicious serving of plum pudding. Neil waited until the coffee was served to talk.

"I've been thinking about what you should

do, Maura," he began slowly. "I think, perhaps, your first impulse was right. You should travel."

She felt a dull thud in the place where her heart was. Was he saying he wanted her to go away from him? To leave him? Was that it?

"There can be no question of your making a commitment so soon," he went on hastily, sensing her confusion. "Or of us marrying—" He seized her hand, suddenly. "I haven't even asked you. . . ."

He paused only for an instant, giving her no chance to respond. But all the answer he wanted he saw in her eyes.

"But if it can't be so, not now at any rate, I still can't bear the thought of our being separated for very long," he went on. "If you were traveling, it's very possible I might be able to join you at stops along the way. I go to Europe on business trips quite frequently, and it would be easier to see each other there. At least, till your mourning period is over.

"Of course," he finished, "it's up to you, darling. If it's what you want."

How could he think, even for an instant, she could not want it? "Oh, yes!" she cried. "It sounds wonderful! I could find out all the little out-of-the-way places to see in Ireland and England before you come and then save them to show to you . . . !"

"Yes, Maura." He did not say that all he would want to see was her. He simply held her hand.

Maura looked down at the strong, bronzed

hand holding hers. All at once, she was reminded of Peter's soft, plump hands and she found herself contrasting the way Peter had taken her with the way Neil had made love.

"There is one more thing. . . ." He hesitated. Was now the time to bring it up? he wondered. But he plunged on. "Despite my feelings for you, I want you to know, Maura, I would have controlled them. . . ." He paused. Would he? he wondered.

"At least," he continued, "I would have made more of an effort to do so, if I hadn't suspected that your life with Peter had been less than ideal. Knowing Peter . . ." He hesitated once again. But it had to be said, after all.

"I'd known about Peter for years, even while I was growing up. At one point, he even requested me to help secure young girls for him. I did it for a short time, then I put my foot down. My concern was the business; I wanted no part of any other monkey business."

"Young girls?" Maura repeated. It began to fall into place: the young girls at Saratoga, the girls at various parties in the city.

"Yes, Peter had a taste for young girls," he went on gently. "For—well, virgins, to be specific. Once they were deflowered, he lost all interest in them, poor things. Sorry, darling," he said hastily, as he saw her shudder and draw back, "but I thought you should know. For several reasons. As I've said, if I'd thought your relationship with Peter had been different, I would never have spoken so soon."

"Buy why," Maura said, after a moment, still puzzling, "if that was the case, did he marry me?"

"I've thought about that and I've come up with two reasons. First, I think he knew he couldn't have you any other way. And secondly, I think he realized at once what a rare, lovely thing you are. He was fond of you—no, more than that. I'm sure he loved you, in his way."

"Are you?" But even as Maura asked the question, she realized Neil's words rang true. She'd known Peter was proud of her and fond of her. Recognizing that fact softened the blow about the other revelation. . . .

"I'm sorry I had to tell you," Neil apologized.

"No, I'm glad you did."

"Good. We needn't talk about it ever again." He seized her hand again, and raised it to his lips. She felt the roughness of his sideburns against her hand and she had the sudden urge to be back in the carriage with him, in the shuttered darkness. Or up in her room, or —anywhere—so long as they could be alone. She flushed as she looked up at him, feeling sure he must be able to read her desire in her eyes.

Had he? "Shall we go?" he asked, smiling.

She was elated. But her elation was, unfortunately, short-lived. For once inside the carriage, he did not undress her as she'd desired, but only held her close, kissing her and murmuring into her ear.

"Not now, darling. It's late and cold. Anyway, the next time I want to lie properly in a bed with you. Maybe in my apartment. I'll see if I can make arrangements for tomorrow night."

She was disappointed, though she realized he was right. The carriage was hardly the most comfortable of places.

The ride was swift and, as far as Maura was concerned, over much too soon.

"Till tomorrow," Neil said, kissing her briefly.

The lingering taste of his sweet mouth stayed on her lips as he left her at the door. She walked inside, past the grim-mouthed housekeeper. As a fact, she hardly saw Mrs. Green. She was already dreaming of tomorrow night and Neil's apartment.

Tomorrow. It would be busy; she would begin interviewing. Quickly, she climbed the stairs to her room.

It was all working out as she'd dreamed it would. Despite this, however, a tiny, persistent Cassandra voice kept warning her something was about to happen. Something, she could not be sure what, but *something*. . . .

Foolish, she told herself. Nothing would happen; there was nothing to worry about any longer. But she could not hush that voice.

Chapter Eight

MAURA SPENT THE ENTIRE DAY INTERVIEW-
ing. It was a disappointing day, on the whole.
She interviewed ten women, each one looking
very much like the other. They all seemed to
be tall: angular and bony, with faint and, in
some cases, not so faint, little mustaches
sprouting on their upper lips. They were all
fortyish spinsters and each, at one time or
another, had been employed as a household
governess. Many still bore the telltale signs of
the governess. Maura recognized it in the stiff
way they held their hands, the grim tightness
around their mouths. She had the feeling they
would scold her sharply if they caught her
doing anything they considered naughty.

And since she might very well be doing
things the former governesses would consider
naughty, she began to wonder for the first
time about the necessity of having a companion.

If only she and Abby could just go off alone!
But that was clearly impossible. Abby was
much too young. There would be talk.

On the other hand, Maura would not have wanted to go to the corner with any of the applicants who'd presented themselves that day. She consoled herself with the thought that perhaps the following day she would find a fresher, more attractive candidate.

"You haven't eaten anything all day," Abby scolded her when she came up to dress for dinner.

"I'm not hungry," she shrugged. "But I had a huge supper last night."

Abby looked at her skeptically. She knew her mistress's habits. Even if Maura had eaten well the night before, she had a good appetite. She would have eaten something during the day, even if just a light meal of tea, an egg, some toast.

Maura shrugged. Until Abby had mentioned it, she'd scarcely thought about food. She had, in fact, sat down twice at the table that day, though she hadn't eaten. For some reason, she hadn't been able to take more than the tea, and only a mouthful of that. The sight of food had sickened her. It occurred to her now that perhaps she only had an appetite when she was with Neil.

The thought amused her. She laughed suddenly, heartily.

Abby looked relieved. "That's better," she smiled.

She started to take the pins out of her mistress's hair. "Those were some old crows you were talkin' to this mornin'," she ventured. "I hope none of them is comin' along with us?"

"No, Abby," Maura assured her. "We'll find

someone nice, I promise you." At least I hope so, she added to herself.

Neil came by early to pick her up that evening, but she was ready and anxious to see him.

They sat together in the back of the carriage, content, happy. Maura nestled her head on his shoulder, hardly saying a word. She wanted to be alone with him before they talked. And she was excited and curious about seeing his apartment.

The idea of living in an "apartment" was relatively new in Manhattan. For years, real-estate developers had argued that the city, squeezed between two rivers and with a limited amount of space, was the ideal place for apartments or multiple-unit dwellings. The earliest apartments, or "French Flats," as they were called, were built in 1869. But the first large, luxury apartment house began construction in 1880 by Edward S. Clark, heir to the Singer sewing machine fortune.

Clark had acquired a plot of land on Central Park West, between Seventy-second and Seventy-third Streets. According to a popular story, friends of Clark's told him he was crazy to make such a sizable investment way out in the country, in the middle of rundown farms and shanties. He might just as well be building "out in the Dakota, in Indian territory," they said. Thus, the name "Dakota" was given to the sprawling Renaissance building, with its gables, its dormers, its bay windows, balconies and turrets, that overlooked Central

Park with the grandeur of a large European château.

Maura was enchanted at first sight. It seemed so lovely, especially when compared to the rather plain and forbidding brownstone face of the Van Diver residence.

When she entered Neil's apartment, she was even more enchanted. The mahogany wainscoting and paneling, the shining parquet floors and warm red-thick fireplaces gave the apartment the cozy, comfortable feeling so utterly lacking in her own home.

"It's beautiful, Neil!" she cried.

"You like it?" he asked, pleased.

A valet soundlessly slipped forward to take her coat.

Maura, startled, stepped back.

"What is it?" Neil said, puzzled. "Here, let me take that." He helped her with the coat, then handed it to the valet.

"Thank you, William."

"Yes, sir. The supper is ready."

"Good. You may go for the evening."

As the valet left, Neil turned to Maura. "Now, what was that all about? I know William has a way of coming up behind you. . . ."

"No, it wasn't that. He reminds me of someone." She paused. "Cassidy," she said, as she placed the face with the name.

"Who?" Neil asked.

"Oh." She shrugged, sorry she'd said it. Both the name and face brought back bad memories. "Just a man from my old neighborhood." She did not go any further. She shrugged again almost as though she was trying to shake off the feeling of unrest, of evil that Cassidy conjured up.

"I see," Neil said. He did not see but he did not press her. "Shall we go inside?" he said instead.

He led her into a candlelit room, where a small round table sat in front of the wide window, overlooking the park. The view was glorious. The star-studded sky was darkly mysterious and mesmerizing over the wooded park.

"What would you like, darling?" Neil asked as he helped her into her chair.

The table was groaning under several steaming platters. Maura saw a thick, creamy soup and several kinds of fragrant stew. There was cheese off to the side of the table and pâté.

"I . . ." She hesitated, glancing up at him. The full moon shining in the window lit up his handsome, rugged face, those dark, narrowly slanted eyes.

In the foyer, there was the soft click of the front door. Maura realized, at once, that was what Neil had been waiting for.

He half lifted her off the chair into his arms. "I'm more hungry for you, darling. Unless—"

"I am, too," she said, quickly.

She felt his lips brush against her cheek, nuzzle against her hair. Then he took her by the hand and led her into the bedroom, to the bed.

This time she had taken care to select a dress with fewer buttons. Quickly, he undressed her. He slipped off his shirt, his trousers and, for the first time, she saw him naked.

And how beautiful he was! His body was golden all over and strong, like a young prince, with wide, powerful shoulders, a muscular chest that tapered down to a flat, hard stomach.

Slowly, Maura's eyes traveled downward. She had felt his manhood the night before, but now she watched, curious and excited as he grew erect and hard and ready for her.

And now, he took her in his arms again and laid her gently down on the bed.

"Maura, Maura . . ." he whispered feverishly as he pressed her close. The firm, smooth muscles of his chest were hard against Maura's soft nakedness. She loved the way he looked and felt, and the wonderful smell of him. Like a hungry animal, she sniffed his hair, the crook of his neck, his chest.

They were both so hungry, so ravenous for one another! Neil ran his tongue along the fine skin of Maura's throat to the high, pointed breasts. He wanted to devour her. He felt her nibbling on the fingers of one hand, and realized she felt the same. . . .

They could never have enough of one another, Maura thought. Don't stop! she cried silently to herself, as he climbed on top of her and began to thrust inside, slowly at first, then faster, faster, till she felt dizzy and half out of her mind.

"Don't stop!" she heard herself saying

aloud. The last word was drowned out by a moan, high-pitched and strangely familiar. It was a moment before she recognized it was her own voice. . . .

When it was over, they lay back on the bed, exhausted but gloriously content and happy, watching the stars outside the window.

"How beautiful," Maura murmured, and at the same time, Neil gathered her close to him and began to make love to her again.

It seemed to Maura that there was nothing in the world but their bodies. Nothing. She wished they might lie here forever. She had never been so completely, utterly happy in her life.

"I love you so much," he said, when he finally released her.

"I love you," she told him, almost shyly. She had never said it before, never once to Peter or anyone. Had Neil said it? she wondered.

But the question lay unasked on her lips as he lowered his head and, cupping one perfect breast in his hand, began to kiss and caress it. She closed her eyes. If life should stop at this moment, she thought, she would be perfectly happy.

Drowsy, content, she fell asleep, one leg entangled with his, with his face buried in her long, golden hair.

A golden band of sunlight, streaming in the wide window, woke her. She turned to find Neil, his head propped up on one elbow, smiling down at her.

"This is the way I want to wake up every

day," he said. "You're so beautiful when you sleep. You were smiling, you know."

"No wonder," she said, and then flushed furiously as he laughed.

"Come here," he said. He pulled her toward him gently, and kissed her—eyes, lips, the tip of her nose. She clung to him for one long moment. Gently, he undid her hands.

"We have to get up, darling. I wish I didn't, but I have a full day ahead of me . . ." His voice trailed off as he swung his long legs out of bed.

Watching him, Maura wished it were night again. Or that he might stay longer. But she knew he was speaking the truth: he had work. As for herself, they were sending over a new batch of prospective companions today to be interviewed. She sighed and, slipping out of bed, began to dress.

Neil had gone to wash. He called to her from the next room. "Neither of us had anything to eat last night. But William's laid out a breakfast in the dining room. Why don't you begin, darling?"

She walked into the small dining-room area. The table, which had been groaning under the weight of soup and stews the night before, was now freshly laid with a huge urn of coffee, platters of eggs, smoked salmon, porridge and sweet rolls.

She started again, as she noticed William/ Cassidy. Silly! she scolded herself as she sat down.

"May I help you, ma'am?" William asked politely.

He poured coffee and dished out a small bowl of porridge. "Would you like eggs? Some salmon?" he asked.

Maura shook her head. The smells were making her faintly nauseous. Even the bland porridge disturbed her. She pushed the bowl away and took a sip of coffee. Not even that went down smoothly.

"What is it, darling?" Neil asked when he entered. "You look so pale."

"It's nothing," she told him.

"It must be something," he said, concerned.

But she managed a smile. "I'm fine, really. But I do think I'd better be getting back."

Neil arranged for the carriage. "Go slowly," he warned Myers. "The roads are rough," he explained to Maura. "The less you're jostled, the better. And perhaps you should see a doctor when you're home."

"But I'm fine," she insisted. She was happy, however, that Myers followed Neil's instructions and drove slowly. Even so, Maura felt wretched. A wave of dizziness and nausea had come over her. She couldn't wait to get home.

The moment they arrived, she ran up to her room and flung herself on the bed.

"What is it?" Abby cried, frightened.

Maura could not speak. But after a few more moments, the sick feeling seemed to pass.

"I just feel a little weak," she told Abby.

"Let me bring you some tea and toast," Abby insisted. "You'll feel better."

Maura sat up in bed and forced herself to eat a little bit of the dry toast and to drink the tea. It did seem to make her feel better. The nausea and dizziness had passed and she could feel herself gaining strength and energy again.

But how strange! she thought. She was so rarely ill. It reminded her of something. . . .

She sat bolt upright in bed as it came to her. Her mother, the last time she'd carried a child, had been sick in the mornings. For almost three months, Nora O'Rourke had not been able to bear the sight of food. Maura had prepared the early meals for the family. Once the morning was over, however, Nora O'Rourke had recovered, and after three months time, the sickness had disappeared completely. By this time, Nora O'Rourke had begun to show, by her swelling belly, more visible signs that she was with child. . . .

There was a crash, as Maura dropped teacup, tray and everything to the floor.

Abby came flying in. "What is it, ma'am?" she cried, alarmed.

"I don't know," Maura said, near tears. "No, stay!" She grabbed the young girl's strong hand to give her support. Her mind was working, frantically. If that *was* the reason, it would change everything. Everything!

But, perhaps, she was mistaken. There was always that chance. Yes. . . .

She began to breathe more easily again. A doctor would know. Yes, she thought, that's it. She would have to go to a doctor. But whom?

She could not bear the thought of approaching Dr. Brickman. But if not Brickman, then whom?

Abby was still holding her hand. "Abby," Maura began, hesitantly, "would any of your friends have told you of a woman who knows . . ."

"About babies?" Abby finished.

"You guessed?"

"Yes," Abby nodded.

"Oh, Abby!" Maura sighed and released the young girl's hand. "Do you think it might be possible that I—" She could not finish.

"You won't know for sure until you see the woman," Abby said, practically. "I have a friend who knows someone. I'll see if she can come by."

"Please. And hurry!"

"Yes." Abby started toward the door, then stopped. "There's a woman downstairs about the position, ma'am. Will you see her now?"

Maura shook her head. "No. Tell her I'm sorry, but I can't see anyone."

It was late afternoon when a strong-featured, heavyset woman, with her hair pulled back in a gray bun, arrived at the house. Alice Hecker had made her living for the past twenty-five years as a midwife. She boasted to one and all that she knew more about babies than any doctor in Manhattan. "I can tell just from the look on a lass's face, whether she's with child or not," she insisted.

She swiftly examined Maura. From the moment she entered the room and had seen

Maura's pale face she had known what the verdict would be.

"Well?" Maura asked, anxiously.

"You're with child, ma'am," Alice Hecker told her. "About two months gone, I'd say. You'll have him maybe in early summer."

Silently, Maura opened her purse and paid the woman. As Abby came in to show her out, Maura told her she wanted to rest.

Abby shut the door behind her, and Maura lay back in bed. She wanted to be alone, not to rest but to think. Two months on the way, Alice Hecker had said. But, of course, the baby had to be Peter's. On that first, that only night. . . .

How cruel! She felt like beating her fist against the wall in frustration. This would change everything. The one fortunate part, she thought ironically, was that she had not yet chosen a traveling companion. For she could not possibly travel now.

All her plans! All *their* plans! she thought. The ones she and Neil had made together, to meet in Europe, to share the sights, to steal at least some quiet precious moments together until the time when they might be together for good! Everything was changed, finished.

Unless—? For one brief moment, she entertained the thought of not telling Neil. Of going on with her plans to choose a traveling companion and to leave. It would be some time, of course, before there were any visible signs she was carrying a child. She could deal with the problem of explaining it to Neil later.

It would have been perfect—except she couldn't do it. Neil was clever, for one thing. He might very well suspect. Even if he didn't, it would not be honest, not to anyone. Least of all, she realized, to Peter.

For this was Peter's child, his heir. "*He* will be born . . ." Alice Hecker had said, almost as though she was sure it would be a boy. In that case, all of this would be his—the estate, with all the houses, furnishings, artwork, antiques. Everything . . .

No, she could not run off. The lawyer must be notified, and Peter's daughters. Oh, how they would hate her when they found out! But there was no way she could help it. She could not change what had happened. Much as she wanted to, she could not.

What would Neil say? The rest of the long afternoon and into early evening Maura was plagued by that thought.

Over and over, in her mind, she saw herself telling him, trying to explain. She searched for different ways to put it to him, but in her mind's eye, the result was always the same: a disappointed, hurt look on his face. Then, invariably, he would turn and walk out.

She was tortured for hours until finally, at the stroke of nine, he rang the front bell.

"I'm sorry, darling," he apologized. "I wanted to get here earlier, but I couldn't. How are you feeling? Better, I hope?"

He took a long look at her. For the first time, she had used a touch of rouge on her cheeks to disguise their paleness. In the dimly lit drawing room, she seemed glowing and healthy again.

Only her manner puzzled him. She was strangely quiet and reticent. His first instinct was not to question her. But he was too worried to follow that instinct.

"Please tell me what's bothering you, darling," he said, sitting down next to her on the green velvet couch. He took her hand. "Whatever it is, we can talk about it, and it won't seem so bad. Nothing is worth having you worried, Maura."

His words gave her a slight ray of hope. "You're sure?" she asked.

"Of course."

"It won't change the way you feel about me?" she persisted.

"Nothing could change that," he swore.

She hesitated another moment.

"Well," he said, squeezing her hand, "are you going to tell me, Maura?"

He glanced up suddenly as a servant passed in the hallway. He frowned. How infinitely annoying and tedious it was to be in this house, he thought. He had never liked it when Peter was alive, but now it was even more loathsome. All these servants walking in, out. He longed to be alone with Maura. He had planned for the two of them to go back to his apartment. But first, he wanted to settle whatever it was that was bothering Maura.

"Well?" he asked again, with just a touch of impatience. "Tell me, Maura."

Maura heard the impatience at once, but misread it. Slightly flustered, she began to confess what had happened.

"I am with child," she said, using the words of Alice Hecker. "By two months. He," she added, for in her mind's eye it was definitely a boy, "will come sometime in early summer."

If she had slapped him—no, beat him—she would not have been more surprised at his reaction.

He dropped her hand and stood with such immediacy and urgency she jumped up, afraid that he would bolt suddenly, without even saying a word.

Instead, however, he stood perfectly still for a moment, his back to the fireplace. His dark eyes burned like coals and focused on her with such intensity, that almost without realizing it, she took a small frightened step backward.

But his voice, when he spoke, was calm, collected, as though in those brief moments he'd thought everything out: "This doesn't have to change things, Maura. We can still go on as we'd planned. . . ."

He paused. She waited, anxiously. It seemed as though he was saying what she wanted him to say. And yet, she had the strangest feeling. . . .

"You understand, Maura. It doesn't have to change," he repeated, "if you give up the inheritance."

"What?" she blurted out. She could not believe he'd said this.

Neil started to pace back and forth. Like a

tiger, she thought. A tiger who'd been threatened.

"But you won't need his money, Maura," he told her. "Don't you see? I have money; you must know that. As my wife, you'll never want for anything."

"But the inheritance! Really, Neil! You can't mean you want me to give it up. . . ." She sank down on the couch again. Her eyes focused on the fire. She was thinking of her father. How he had longed to give them something, to give *her* something to hold onto in life. More than wealth, a dry roof over their heads, the proper food—what he had wanted for them was position, a place in society. As a poor immigrant boy, he had never gotten it. But now, his grandson had a chance. . . .

"No," Maura said, firmly. "It's for my son, Neil. Try to understand. It's his place in life! I don't have the right to turn that down."

"Nonsense. I would take care of him. And that's not the point. The point is you, as my wife. Don't you see, Maura? I will not have my wife living on another man's money! I've seen too many marriages like that. . . ." He paused again.

He had stopped pacing, but the image Maura had had of the tiger at bay, the tiger threatened, was there in his eyes. Was it his pride that was threatened?

Suddenly, abruptly, he hurried toward her and seized both her hands. "Maura . . ." He pulled her up off the couch. "Sweet Maura, perhaps it's you who doesn't understand. We can marry now! Even if you are in mourning, hang it! We want to marry, we shall!"

"Neil . . ." The note in her voice stopped him. He was saying everything she wanted to hear, but the timing was all wrong. All wrong . . .

"Really, Neil," she went on, "how could we? How could I? It would place a taint on my child's name that could never be removed."

"Maura . . ." he began, protesting.

"Oh, yes, it would!" she went on, hotly. "You know it would! That is one reason—and the second we've already discussed. I cannot throw away my child's position in life. I can't, Neil! You must understand!"

His dark eyes glared at her. He shook his head. "There is nothing to understand, Maura. Either we can be together on my money," he reiterated stubbornly, "or we will go our separate ways!"

"I see," she said, softly, disappointed.

He reached for his hat. "If you'd like to think about it, Maura?"

She faced him, studying him for a long moment. His chin was set and determined; she knew he would not change his mind. But she was equally determined. She would not change hers, either. She could not. . . .

"No, Neil," she said, in a whisper of a voice. "I can't."

He spun away then and, brushing past her without so much as a look, without even a goodbye, he headed toward the door.

"Oh, Neil!" The words burst forth from her on their own, as though she had no control.

They were a plea, a plaintive cry, but he paid no heed.

She covered her mouth with her hand. A part of her wanted to get up, to race after him, bring him back with her. She might have in spite of everything that had happened, but she could not. Her feet were grounded into the floor. She couldn't move. And, if she could have, if she had managed to run out after him, she doubted it would have done any good.

His mind was made up; she had seen that on his face. He'd made the proposal she'd dreamed of, and she had turned him down. How cruel fate was! But there was nothing she could do now but accept her fate and the new, irrevocable change in her life.

Chapter Nine

SARAH MONTEBELLO SAT ON THE EDGE OF THE red velvet *chaise longue,* a contented cat's smile on her face. Her body—slim, long legged, with surprisingly full, voluptuous breasts —was nude. Stretched out before her on the *chaise longue,* also nude, was her lover—or *former* lover? But she did not like to think that. Men did not leave her; if anyone left, it was Sarah, and even then she liked to think that the man was always available to her. A simple crook of her little finger would bring him running. So, as far as Sarah was concerned, Neil Prescott had not left her. He'd only strayed for a short time. Sarah had known all the while he would be back. And here he was . . . !

She laughed, and ran her hand playfully over his tan, muscular chest. "Tired so soon?" she teased.

Neil's dark eyes narrowed, frowning, as he looked at her. He was slightly disgusted with himself for coming here. But this whole thing with Maura had sickened him so. He had started going to parties and dinner-dances again. It was inevitable, of course, that he should run into Sarah at one of them. He'd tried to avoid her, but it was not that easy. Also, he had to admit, she did attract him. She was not a beauty like Maura; she had none of Maura's sweetness or her finer qualities. She was, however, attractive and passionate. Perhaps the best thing he could say for Sarah was that when he was with her, he was able to forget Maura for a short while at least. . . .

"Ah, you're not *that* tired!" she cried triumphantly, as the results of her prodding and teasing became acutely visible. She raised herself on top of him and, with a sigh, began to direct him now for her pleasure, with a swivel of her hips, a cry. She could be insatiable at times, Neil knew from experience, but this time he heard her cry out quickly with pleasure and so he took his own quickly too.

He stood abruptly the moment he was finished, so abruptly she almost fell.

"Well," she said, slightly miffed. "What's the hurry? Is it that young widow? But that's over, isn't it?"

She laughed harshly, stopping as Neil gave her a black look. He picked up his trousers and began to don them hastily. Now that it was over, he felt slightly hollow inside. He had to leave.

"When will I see you again?" she demanded.

"When you see me," he said, shortly. At that moment, he was determined never to see her again.

But she knew better. She lit one of the long thin cigars she often affected and puffed on it slowly, contentedly, as she watched him hurry out the door. . . .

A door had slammed shut in Maura's life also. Her life had changed that abruptly. Another door, she thought. She'd had so many doors, so many changes in her young life. Her father's untimely accident. His death. Her strange marriage, then Peter's abrupt death. She had had a brief respite of happiness with Neil and then that, too, had ended.

She felt as though she were in limbo now. Her body, her life itself, seemed to be concentrated on one thing: waiting for Peter's child. There were times when she thought of what might have been and she found herself hating the child. Then she would feel guilty. The child was innocent, after all. It had not asked to come into this world.

But, neither had she! And, oh, if only she were not pregnant! *If.* She might have been in Europe now, enjoying the sights, waiting for Neil to come. For that matter, Neil might have been with her. They might have been married. . . . If she weren't pregnant. *If,* again . . . Oh, why had it happened? Why?

Over and over, she kept asking herself the same question. Somewhere along the way, she found a single ray of hope. All along—was it because of Alice?—she'd assumed the child would be a boy. But what if it were a girl? Then there would be no inheritance, no problems. She would be reconciled with Neil. They could go on with everything, as they'd planned. . . .

The thought cheered her as she went through her day. Her new life was a quiet one. With the exception of Alice Hecker, who dropped by occasionally to check on Maura's progress, she had few visitors. She went out for walks ("Good for your health and the baby's," Alice insisted), usually with Abby by her side; she read and reread her Dickens; she began to knit a blanket for the baby. For the color, she chose, after much thought, yellow. Though secretly she prayed for a girl, she would never have chosen pink. It would have tempted the fates too much. No, yellow was safer.

And so she went about her day. The phone was quiet; the mail ever quieter. She received a sprinkling of invitations—to a luncheon, a tea, but that was all. Of course, everyone knew she was in mourning, she told herself; she would not have been able to accept invitations even if they had come pouring in.

She was surprised that the family made no attempt to get in touch with her. Though perhaps she should not have been too surprised. She'd gleaned, from a few remarks Mr. Ross, the lawyer, had made, that Peter's three daughters were furious. The prospect of losing their inheritance had done nothing to sweeten their dispositions. Wouldn't they be surprised if they knew that Maura was also praying for a girl!

If Maura was surprised at not hearing from the family, she also was surprised at not hearing from Neil. She'd hoped that after the first shock, the first disappointment had worn off, he might come around, if only to see how she was faring. But she had heard nothing at all from him and after a time, she came to realize that she would not. At least, not until the baby came. Her daughter—she hoped . . . !

All she knew of Neil Prescott was what she read in the newspapers. He obviously had no regrets. He was frequently shown in photographs with a lovely young woman on his arm and was attending all the parties, galas and balls.

Their smiles and particularly those of the beautifully turned-out, smug young women on his arm twisted her heart. She studied the photographs, read and reread the captions, curious to know just who these young women were. At one point, she grew so jealous she gave up reading the papers entirely. She told herself it was foolish to torture herself like that; if reading the papers made her miserable, well, then perhaps it was better not to read.

Yet after only a few days of abstinence, she found herself picking up the papers again. It was no use. She *had* to see him. If the only way she had of keeping in touch with him was the papers, well then, she would read them.

Her time grew nearer. The days grew longer and warmer. She was heavy now, and walking became more difficult. She found herself spending even more time at home alone.

In the papers, she saw references now to Newport, where the Astors, the Fishes, the Belmonts had their summer homes or "cottages," as they called them. If the papers were to be believed, the entire island of Manhattan became deserted sometime in June when society's playground moved from the city to Newport.

As Maura read on, she thought of Peter's Newport cottage. Peter had described it briefly to her once, calling it glorious. Both the cottage and the colony of Newport excited Maura's curiosity, but it was out of the question for her to go up to Newport this year. In the first place, she was not in any condition to travel. Nor was she up to supervising the opening and refurbishing of the Van Diver cottage. Also, since she was still in mourning, she would not have been able to attend any of the parties—if, indeed, she were invited to any.

At times, going to parties with Peter, she'd wished she might have stayed home. Yet some of the parties had been fun. She remembered most vividly the one at the Plaza Hotel, her long solo dance with the duke. Then, dancing with the Englishman—what was his name?— oh yes, Lord Parker. The thought of the Plaza brought Neil to mind again, but she pushed that thought away. . . .

She thought, instead, of Peter's face after that ball. How proud he'd been of her. And yes, she had to admit that it *had* been fun. She was still a young girl, after all. Her life, so far, had been composed of few pleasures and a great deal of tragedy. She couldn't help wishing she were able to go to Newport, to see the sights, the people. To join in the fun. But that was impossible, now.

In early June, Alice Hecker stopped in to see her. The corners of her mouth lifted in a broad smile as she examined Maura.

"He's gettin' impatient! I have an idea he'll be joinin' us shortly!"

"Don't!" Maura said, a little crossly. She had told Alice more than once not to keep calling the baby a boy. But somehow, Alice always forgot.

"Sorry," Alice said.

"Anyway," Maura went on, a little anxiously. "Isn't it a little early?"

"Not too early. Don't worry. He knows what he's doin'. . . ." Alice paused, a slightly stricken look on her face. She'd done it again.

Alice left soon afterward, and Abby hurried in to Maura's surprise, carrying a huge bouquet of flowers, long-stemmed red roses.

"These just came, ma'am," Abby said.

Maura's heart leaped. There was only one person who sent her flowers. And roses! Eagerly, she tore open the card.

My dear Mrs. Van Diver:
   I expect you've forgotten me, after all this time. I can't say that I blame you, if you have. I must apologize. I had meant to write you after your husband's death.

But the hectic, frantic political pace here in London has kept me constantly on the go, with little time to relax and do the things one should and would like to do.

I will be coming to New York shortly, at which time I hope to make up for my negligence. Until then, please accept these flowers as a small token of my esteem and admiration for you.

Your servant,
Harold Parker, Lord of Lennox

Maura stared at the note for a long moment, then laid it on her night table. She was surprised and also a little disappointed. But, at once, she chided herself. How foolish to think Neil had sent them. And how sweet of Lord Parker.

She closed her eyes, trying to conjure up a picture of what he looked like. But after a few minutes she gave up. If his face was lost to her memory, however, she did recall his kindness. She also remembered how comfortable and secure she'd felt with him.

She opened her eyes. Abby had placed the vase of flowers directly in front of the window. The breeze lifted their scent and carried it to her. She smiled, softly. There was nothing quite comparable, neither so delicate nor so sweet as roses.

Her eyes still on the flowers, she thought how nice that Lord Parker was coming to New

York. It was something to look forward to, after all. . . .

The following week, Maura awoke in the middle of the night with the strangest sensation. Something had just burst. She felt wet, soaked to the skin. And deep down inside of her, she felt a sudden, painful contraction, then a release.

Frightened, she rang the bell for Abby.

"Is it your time, ma'am?" Abby guessed when she ran in.

"Yes," Maura nodded, biting her lip. She'd just felt another contraction.

"But what can we do?" she said, her eyes wide. Capable Abby suddenly looked like a frightened child.

"Why, we'll have to get Alice Hecker."

"But how?" Abby's brows knit together, perplexed. "I don't think she has a phone."

"Send one of the servants then, to fetch her! And quickly!"

Abby flushed. Maura was sorry, but it was obvious to her that the girl wasn't functioning. For a moment she forgot her own pain. "Have you ever seen anyone—your mother, perhaps?—have a baby, Abby?"

Abby shook her head. "No, ma'am."

Maura remembered now that Abby had been raised not by her mother but by a penurious, spinster aunt. The fact that Abby was really just a child was suddenly, painfully brought home to Maura.

But at what a time! For Maura was frightened herself. She needed someone to lean on.

She lay back against the pillow and felt its dampness. She could smell her own fear and anxiety in that pillow. As she saw Abby cowering, she realized, however, that she would have to take hold of herself. She would have to be the strong one.

"Abby!" she ordered. "I told you—send one of the servants to fetch Alice! And get me some ice. Hurry! My throat is parched!"

Abby ran off, grateful to be released.

Alone again in the room, Maura was almost sorry she'd sent her. Suddenly, she recalled her mother when she'd had her last child. How her mother had screamed, cursing everything, everyone—Maura's father, her brothers, even Maura who was trying to help!

Maura had been terrified that her mother would die, but surely she was stronger than her mother had been. . . .

As the pain grew stronger, the contractions faster, deeper, Maura grew even more frightened and less able to cope. Maybe she *would* die; she felt as though she was going to die. If so, she wanted just one thing: she wanted to see Neil again. . . .

She closed her eyes and, half out of her mind, she thought she saw him. He was standing, looking tan and handsome at the side of her bed. He leaned toward her and placed his strong, cool hand on her feverish brow, all the while murmuring sweet things to her. "Nothing has changed," he was saying. "Nothing, my darling. Darling Maura . . ."

"Maura . . ."

Maura opened her eyes, dreamily. At her bedside she saw not Neil but Alice Hecker.

"There. You're finally comin' around. You were out of your head for a while," Alice said.

"The baby? Is it here yet?" Maura said, hopefully. But, no, she felt the contractions again, stronger, more painful than ever.

"Almost. But you've got to help him. Now, push. Push!" Alice ordered.

"Alice, I told you—"

"Sorry, ma'am. I forgot. But you've got to push. Now try!"

She tried.

"Harder!" Alice urged.

"I'm trying, but it's so hot!"

"Give 'er some more ice to chew on, Abby. And push. Push!"

Maura chewed the ice and pushed, pushed till she was sure she could push no more. She gave one final push and then, suddenly, it came: the most agonizing, excruciating pain of all. It felt like her insides, everything, was being torn apart.

She was sure she was dying. Surely, no one could survive anything like this. And what about the child, she thought suddenly, panicking. Would it live? She had not gone through all this to have it die! It had to live!

And then, one final maddening fear: what if Alice were right? If—could it be possible—it would be a boy? But no, it couldn't be. It couldn't. . . .

But at that moment, she heard Alice's rough voice: "Yes, ma'am! There he is!"

He. Oh, no! Not a boy! she thought. She opened her eyes and saw a bald head, a red, angry face as he screamed in indignation at being slapped on his bottom.

"Look at how bonny he is!" Alice held him a little closer.

Maura glared. Why wasn't he a girl? Why? Yet as Alice held him, he seemed to stare at Maura. Maura told herself he couldn't possibly be staring; she knew from what she'd read that babies can't really see for a few weeks after birth. But she could have sworn he was staring at her, with such a pitiful look that she was strangely touched.

For one long moment, she stared back at him. Then her head dropped back on the pillow and she lost consciousness once more.

Chapter Ten

SHE CALLED HIM PETER, AFTER HIS FATHER.
His smile was somewhat reminiscent of his
father's, but other than that, he looked nothing at all like her husband (and for this, the
poor child should be grateful!). He did, in fact,
look very much like Maura. Even in his expressions, she could see herself in her son's
face.

Her son. She'd been so convinced she would
hate him and yet, almost despite herself, she
found she'd fallen in love with him. Once,
twice, she'd murmured to him—oh why
weren't you a girl? It would have made everything so much easier! But then she'd laughed.
Now that he was here, she couldn't imagine
him as anyone else. He was himself. Though
she saw parts of herself in him and, even
more so, points of similarity with her father—
his eyes, his nose, the way he held his small
head at times and looked about, curiously—he
had his own small but distinctive personality.
He was his own person.

At the moment, of course, he was just a

baby, though an adorable one. After two days of interviewing and checking references, Maura had hired an English nanny. The woman had come with the finest of references, but she had a grim set to her mouth that Maura hadn't noticed when she'd hired her. The stern-faced nanny often ignored young Peter's cries. Maura found herself, more often than not, disobeying the nanny's orders and running in to pick up the baby if she heard him crying—and often, when he wasn't; it was a good excuse.

"You will spoil that baby, Mrs. Van Diver," the nanny told her sternly.

"Babies are not ham or cheese. They don't spoil that easily. Anyway, I would rather see him laugh any day than cry," Maura told her.

The nanny stormed out indignantly. And Maura, after going through another series of interviewing, hired a different nanny with not quite such marvelous references but who was, fortunately, more tolerant and tender-hearted. Now Maura rarely heard the baby crying, but she continued, nevertheless, to run into the nursery whenever she wanted to pick him up.

She would hold him for long periods of time, crooning to him, singing little Irish ditties her father had once sang to her, talking to him. She would whisper the secrets of her heart to him, while he smiled and gooed back in baby talk. When he reached out and grabbed her finger for the first time with his chubby hand, it was as though he had clutched her heart. It was little wonder, perhaps, that she who had

so little love in her life should be so thoroughly captivated, so delighted, with her child.

How wonderful if she could have shared her
joy about her baby, who had become her love,
indeed, her life. But other than young Abby,
who was as charmed by tiny Peter as Maura
was, there was no one. Mr. Ross had been
notified, of course, of Peter's birth and he, in
turn, had duly notified the members of the
family. But Maura had heard nothing at all
from them—no phone calls, no letters, no
message of congratulations, not even one of
good health to their small brother. The small
brother they must resent—if not hate.

The family had all gone to Newport. Techni-
cally, they were still in mourning as she was,
but the rules were not quite so rigid as far as
they were concerned. Parties were forbidden
to her. Occasionally, Maura would see a mention of Gladys or Anna or Paula in the paper,
or a photograph of them at a small luncheon
or tea. On the list for parties or balls, however,
the family remained discreetly absent. It was
too soon, even for them.

On those same party lists, Maura noted,
from time to time, Neil's name. So he was
also at Newport. She had thought that since
she had delivered her child, she might hear
from him. Even if just a line. Even though the
child had been a boy. . . .

But Maura heard nothing. She resigned herself, at last, to no news and the weather. It
was a hot, steamy summer, the most humid
and uncomfortable in years. She regretted, at
times, not having gone to Newport, if only to

escape the city. But it was too late to even think of opening up the house. Perhaps next year, she told herself. In the meantime, she tried to make the best of it for herself and her small son. Then one day, Lord Harold Parker arrived.

A second bouquet of long-stemmed red roses announced his arrival. The accompanying note read: "Arrived in New York last night. I wondered if you might be free to join me for dinner this evening at the Plaza? Since it was the scene of our first meeting, it would be pleasant to revisit it again with you." It was signed: "Your servant and friend, Harold Parker."

Maura dressed for the evening carefully and, since the evening was warm, as coolly as possible. Her gown was black, of course, but of a light voile, which fitted her body tightly about the bodice, then swelled into a soft, flaring skirt. Above the simple and flattering neckline, Maura fastened a necklace of gold and emeralds. It was one of the many costly jewels that had belonged to the estate and which Mr. Ross had recently turned over to her.

While she finished dressing, Maura found herself wondering again about Lord Parker. She recalled how he'd come to the funeral services for her husband. There was no doubt in her mind that he was a sincere, kind man—and yet she wondered if she should be going out with him tonight. After all, she was still in mourning. Though if anyone saw her (and this she doubted; the whole world seemed to be in Newport), they obviously were just having a quiet dinner. So that was all right, but afterward—what then? she asked herself. The last thing she wanted was a flirtation. And was that what he was looking for—expected, perhaps?

She might have been tempted to turn down the invitation, but it was too late. Nervously, she sat awaiting him in the small drawing room. She wondered idly if she would even recognize him.

At the stroke of eight, the bell rang. She jumped up expectantly.

He strode into the room, smiling. He was tall and handsome, she noted at once. His hair was dark and curling; he boasted a small clipped mustache and a ready smile. She remembered him now, and she was glad she had not refused him.

"I've looked forward so much to seeing you again, Mrs. Van Diver," he said, taking her hand.

"How sweet," she said, flushing slightly. "Your flowers were lovely."

"It pleases me that you enjoyed them. And that reminds me." He reached into his side pocket and took out a small, gaily wrapped package. "For your son," he said, giving it to her.

She unwrapped it and found a tiny, delicately wrought baby's spoon in sterling silver. It bore her son's initials: PVD.

"The proverbial spoon." Harold Parker smiled.

She laughed. "It's his first gift! Oh, I wish

you'd come a little earlier! The nanny's just put him to bed. But perhaps?" She glanced at the staircase.

"No, I know what nannys are like," he said, quickly.

They both laughed.

"The next time," he added, "I'll come earlier. I'd like very much to meet him. Now, shall we go?"

The Plaza was quiet but pleasant. They dined by candlelight on Maryland terrapin, squab on points of toast, with champagne and ripe red strawberries with heavy cream for dessert.

Maura ate with enthusiasm. It was the first time she'd dined out in ages. The first time, she realized, she'd dined out with anyone but Neil. . . . She pushed the thought out of her mind, and turned her attention to Lord Parker —"Harold," as he insisted she call him.

All through dinner, Harold entertained her with stories of "Tum-Tum." "Tum-Tum" was the irreverent nickname bestowed upon his Royal Highness, Albert Edward, Prince of Wales. It was said that his appetite for food was surpassed only by his appetite for women. It was also said that his infidelities to his Danish wife, Alexandra, were a source of great sorrow to his mother, Queen Victoria.

Harold, as the discreet gentleman, skipped lightly over Tum-Tum's infidelities, focusing instead on the Prince's fondness for raffish company and his enormous appetite.

"They say Tum-Tum can put away half a ham and even a turkey at one sitting," Harold recounted. "And he's been known to totally annihilate a trifle—you know, the custardy English pudding? His friends are all gambling-house cronies and dance-hall Johnnies." He gave an amused little shrug. "And yet, in spite of it all, the people love him. They call him a Toff, which to an Englishman is a regular gent. Actually, who can blame the poor Prince? He's spent the best years of his life twiddling his thumbs, waiting for Queen Victoria to abdicate. She's well into her seventies now, and it doesn't look as though she's any closer to retirement than she was twenty years ago."

Maura laughed.

Abruptly, Harold put down his knife and fork. There was a broad smile on his face. "Ah, it's good to hear you laugh. I have a feeling you haven't been doing too much of it lately."

"Well—" Maura flushed slightly. It was the truth, but the man's prescience caught her off guard.

"Of course, you've had a hard time," Harold added, hastily. "I understand. Carrying a child all those months without your husband by your side. You're to be applauded for your courage!"

"Oh, really!" Now she was really flushing. "You know," she said hastily, changing the subject, "I had been planning a trip to Europe, before—before. . . ." She shrugged, and went on, "Anyway, the first place I wanted to see was England. I longed so much to see all the places Dickens wrote about. . . ." Maura paused again, her eyes gleaming as she dreamed.

"Such a shame you didn't manage it," Harold commiserated. "Still, there's no reason you can't come. We're planning a huge celebration for Queen Victoria's Diamond Jubilee."

"But that's not for several more years!" Maura exclaimed.

"We like to plan ahead in London." Harold smiled.

Maura laughed.

"So you should reinstate those plans. It could be a wonderful trip! And you needn't wait for the Jubilee. You could come over—oh, any time. I'd be on hand to give you the deluxe escorted tour. Oh, I realize that's impossible now," he went on quickly, seeing confusion in her eyes. "Still, it's something to think about."

Ah, haven't I? Maura thought.

"Shall we go for a drive before I take you back?" he asked. "I think the air might do us both good."

Their drive led them along Fifth Avenue.

"So this is the famous Millionaire's Row," Harold commented, looking at the rows of brownstones that lined the avenue, inside of which were housed some of the most famous and costly European treasures. They drove up and down the avenue, from A. T. Stewart, the merchant king's palace on Thirty-fourth Street, grandiose, opulent and covering almost an entire block, to the stately Darius Ogden Mills mansion on Forty-third Street, and on down.

At Madison and Fiftieth, they detoured to examine the neo-Italian Renaissance mansion which McKim, Mead and White, designers of Madison Square Garden, had built for journalist Henry Villard.

"They say the design was lifted almost brick for brick from the Piazzo della Cancelleria in Rome, you know," Harold told Maura.

"Whether it is or not, it's lovely," she said admiringly.

They drove on toward the river to catch the cool breeze. As they parked, Harold turned to her. "I'll be in New York for about ten days. I'd like to be able to call on you again."

His eyes were wide-set and pale gray. Honest and sincere eyes, Maura thought. The eyes of a man who did not lie. Still, it seemed to her she saw something in those eyes that made her slightly uneasy: obvious interest.

"I don't know," she smiled, nervously. "Perhaps. I am busy. . . ."

She watched his shoulders grow slack. But he was not so easily defeated.

"I understand, Maura," he said quickly. "It's much too soon for you. Your husband's death and now the birth of your son. I wouldn't dream of pressing you, Maura. I'm sincere when I say I would like only to be your friend. I realize how dull it must be for you with all of your friends away at Newport. I'd like to try to relieve some of that boredom."

"That's very kind," she said. And how misled he is, she thought, if he believes they're my friends!

But he was waiting for an answer. She smiled. "I would like to see you again," she said simply.

He took her home shortly afterward. On the following night, and almost every night until Harold sailed for England, they dined and went for drives.

As he had been that first evening, Harold Parker continued to be the perfect gentleman, though, Maura had the feeling at times that he ached to touch her. Curious and lonely herself, there were moments when she almost reached out to him, but each time, she stopped herself. She wasn't sure why, but she was afraid if she did allow a kiss, an arm around the waist, she wouldn't be able to stop.

She was desperately lonely, but though she liked Harold, she hesitated.

She knew that the real reason she could not commit herself was Neil Prescott. She was convinced that he would not return, still she could not dispel her memories of him.

When the time came to say goodbye to Harold, she was genuinely sad.

"I'll be back sometime next month," he told her. "It will be a long month for me," he added.

"And for me," she said, surprising him and herself.

For the first time then, she raised her head and he bent his to kiss her.

The kiss was warm and sweet and held a promise of things to come. When he released her, Maura was more confused than ever.

"Till October then," he said.

"Yes . . ." She watched him go, with his kiss still dewy on her lips. It had aroused her. She wondered if he were the reason or if he had simply acted as a surrogate.

For, eyes closed, she had dreamed that someone else was kissing her. . . .

Chapter Eleven

NEIL PRESCOTT'S SUMMER HAD BEEN AN UN-satisfying one in every respect. Certainly as far as business was concerned. In the summer of 1891, the flag of big business flew at half-mast. It was the time of the antitrust, when government was beginning to clamp down on monopolists such as John D. Rockefeller. "Unfair practices!" "Trust-buster!"—those were the terms being bandied about town.

It was a far different climate than the one Captain Van Diver and the other robber barons had known. Businessmen grumbled that had Van Diver and Gould lived in this era not half so many fortunes would have been made. Having known the Captain, Neil guessed that the hard-headed, aggressive opportunist would have made his millions in any era.

Van Diver had made his first fortune on the railroads, but very quickly realized it was necessary to diversify. At the time of his death, he'd been heavily invested in the market. In his role as manager for the Van Divers,

Neil had continued the Captain's heavy investment, and he'd also continued to diversify. The Van Divers now had interests in dozens of businesses from pharmaceuticals to the new up-and-coming electrical appliances.

But even the market was not the market of the Captain's days. People spoke in whispers of dire things to come. There were men around who still remembered the crash of '73, when unrestrained speculation had brought about the worst depression the nation had experienced to date. The Stock Exchange had been closed by President Grant. It had remained closed for ten days, but even that had not halted the resultant failure of more than 18,000 businesses.

Neil, more optimistic than some of his peers, felt that such a depression could never happen again. Still, he was wary and ever on the outlook for signs. He exercised prudence in all purchases and had bought little that summer. The market had been sluggish, as it usually was then. This year, however, he'd felt it was even more depressed and bearish than usual. Yes, it was a bad summer. . . .

That was business. For his social life, he'd spent much of the summer, again as he usually did, on long weekends up at Newport. As a bachelor and a much sought-after one, he was always very much in demand on the weekends, a feather in any hostess's cap. In years past, he'd enjoyed the hectic social pace and the Newport beauties who'd chased after him. But not this year. Not at all.

About the only woman he'd seen was his mistress, Sarah Montebello, and she had grown more impossible, more demanding than ever. He wished he'd kept his word and had stayed away from her. He'd managed it for two weeks, but there had come a night when he'd been so distraught, so disturbed about Maura, he'd been half out of his mind. He'd gone out walking, stopping off at pubs along the way until finally, about three in the morning, drunk and disheveled, he'd stumbled into Sarah's apartment. He'd hated himself the next morning. . . .

Damn Sarah! Damn everything, everyone! He was completely, totally soured on life. He began to turn down invitations. The last two weeks of summer, he didn't even bother to make the trip up to Newport. He stayed in the city, not even seeing Sarah.

After Labor Day, the market picked up. Neil welcomed the increased activity. Perhaps what he needed, he thought, was work. Yes, he would bury himself in work.

And that's exactly what he did, until one morning he had a visitor. . . .

Now that the baby was here and the cooler weather had come, Maura found she had more time on her hands and more energy. She remembered the promise she'd made to herself a while back and visited the bookstore. She picked up, along with a book on railroads and another on finance, a short history recently published on the Van Divers.

155

She read it cover to cover that night. She was fascinated. Why hadn't Peter told her more about the Captain?

The books on finance and business would also one day be part of Peter's heritage, along with the Van Diver business, and Maura studied them carefully, as she had once, as a young girl, sat down and studied her father's lines. When she was satisfied there was nothing more to be learned from the books, she thought for a week and finally came to a decision: she would go downtown.

She dressed carefully the next morning, wearing a simple black dress, with a single strand of pearls at the high neckline as her only jewels.

The Van Diver offices on Wall Street had been decorated by one of the city's most famous designers, Stanford Platt, in shades of pale blue and gray, with gold sconces on the walls and plush velvet sofas in the waiting room. It resembled more a drawing room than an office and as Maura sat, waiting, she was pleasantly surprised by her surroundings.

She was also, suddenly, alarmingly, anxious. Why had she come? Did she really want to know more about the business? she asked herself. Or was it just a ploy, a ruse, to see Neil? And whatever the answer, what would Neil think?

She held her breath and considered, for one brief moment, bolting.

But it was too late. Down the long corridor, she saw Neil approaching, his cheeks strangely flushed as she knew hers must be. But his voice remained calm and correct as he greeted her.

"Well, how very nice to see you, Mrs. Van Diver. I understand you'd like to see the offices?"

"Yes, thank you." She was surprised to hear her own voice, calm and correct, also. She stood, and they faced each other for a brief moment as two strangers. Then he lead the way as they walked through the long jumble of offices where supervisors and checkers for the railroad sat and mumbled about figures and schedules.

Neil introduced her to a few of the men. "John Thomas. He works the Boston run. And Albert. He's on the Hudson line."

The men nodded, politely. Maura returned their nods and tried her best to digest what Neil was saying.

"These are our schedules. This is a miniature model of a new railway car. Here are some more sketches—oh, and here's a breakdown on the market at the present time. See this line?"

He pointed to a zigzag line which apparently represented the Van Diver interests at the moment. It was confusing, she thought—one thing to read about in books and quite another to see in action.

"I think that's about it," Neil was saying, as they circled around the office. "Unless there's something else you had in mind?"

"No." For the first time, she looked him squarely in the eye. Those dark eyes. It was a mistake. The blood rushed to her cheeks so furiously she felt, for a moment, dizzy. She had the sense of his reaching out to grasp her hand. Or was it simply her imagination?

Quickly, she said: "I think I'd better be going." She didn't wait for his answer. Head high, she spun away from him toward the door. . . .

Leaving him puzzled. He'd been so shocked to see her—he'd just been thinking about her!—that he hadn't noticed her confusion. All he'd seen was her coolness. He'd admired that. He'd also admired the quick way she'd seemed to grasp things, much faster than many men.

But why had she come? And why had she left so abruptly? Simply to torture him? He did not understand. . . .

As for Maura, she berated herself. He must think her a fool. Later, as she calmed down a bit, she began to think—oh, what did it matter? If they were no longer lovers, they still had a common interest in the business. Why shouldn't she have come to the office? Why shouldn't she know more about the business? Why shouldn't there be some form of communication between them? It was the civilized thing, after all.

Feeling justified, she told the driver to stop at the bookstore. She purchased a half-dozen more books on finance and business. Then she proceeded home.

More than books began to claim Maura's attention, however. It was fall and invitations began to arrive. She received nothing like the basketful of invitations that had arrived the previous year when Peter was alive. Still, she was Mrs. Van Diver, after all, and, as a matter of form, she received certain invitations.

But she could not go unescorted. On one occasion, Mr. Ross, the lawyer who'd also become her friend, accompanied her to the opera. Maura was grateful for the opportunity to see *Faust* again, and the magnificent Opera House, which she had since learned from her books had been the inspiration of Captain Van Diver and Jay Gould. The reason: the Van Divers had been prohibited from buying boxes for the opera in the Golden Circle of the Academy of Music. The Captain had flown into a rage. When he'd calmed down he'd decided that, if he was being shut out of one ballgame, his only alternative was to start his own. . . .

Maura's evening with Mr. Ross had been a quiet one, and her only evening out until she'd heard from Harold. He wrote, apologizing for having been delayed. He would be arriving in the city shortly.

For Maura, this precipitated another problem: her gowns. She would have to have some new ones. From Abby, who'd become friendly with a few girls from other houses, she learned that Mrs. Klein was a favorite dressmaker. Maura made an appointment.

She was not disappointed. Mrs. Klein was skillful and eager to please. Moreover, her shop boasted a selection of fabrics—silks from Italy, velvets from the Orient, cottons and fine laces from Ireland—that was dazzling.

Maura made her selections and had a first fitting. Mrs. Klein promised she would rush two dresses, a purple silk and a rich, ruby velvet, one of which Maura would wear to the Baker's Winter Ball.

Harold arrived the week before the ball. Their first evening out, he took her to dinner, and then to the Opera. It was quite a change from her quiet evening with Mr. Ross. Lord Parker commanded attention. Dozens of Anglophiles flocked around him, eager to hear the latest news from Great Britain on the customs, the dress, the politics, and Queen and, of course, "Tum-Tum."

Within this coterie of Anglophiles, Maura was accepted at once, as she had never been before, not even with her husband. Perhaps that had been because Peter had a habit of wandering off, leaving her alone. But Harold never left her side, for which she was grateful.

It was an exciting, marvelous evening. Only during the drive home in the carriage did Maura begin to feel uneasy.

At the Opera House, she had realized again how very handsome Harold Parker was, and how attractive he was to women. No wonder; in addition to his looks, there was his position. She imagined he was popular in England as well. Harold Parker was a catch and no one with any sense or foresight would throw such a catch away.

All evening, in fact from the moment she'd received Harold's letter telling her he was coming, Maura had questioned herself. How did she feel about seeing him again? The answer she'd come up with was she did not want a romantic attachment. It wouldn't be fair to kiss Harold and think of Neil, to dream at night of a man she could never have. But, did this mean she couldn't see Harold? Would he be content to be her friend?

She needn't have worried. That first evening, Harold's goodnight kiss was brief, sweet and almost brotherly. The next evening, on the drive home, he ordered the carriage parked by the river. Hastily, however, Maura said something about a headache. Harold took the hint and ordered the driver to go on.

Maura felt guilty but relieved. Though she realized she could not continue to put Harold off indefinitely, she was grateful, for the moment, not to be pressured.

For the Baker's Winter Ball, she chose the ruby-red velvet gown. Close-fitting and cut low over her breasts, it had been trimmed with white ermine. Maura wore the diamond tiara Peter had given her and fastened a small chain of gold and diamonds around her neck.

There was an obvious look of admiration in Harold's gray eyes when he saw her. Gently, he took her arm and led her to the carriage. "I intend to stay close by your side all evening," he said.

"Because of the anarchist, you mean?" she asked, with a nervous smile. A month ago, an anarchist, expressing his disapproval of high society, had exploded a stick of dynamite at a dinner-dance at the Farber's. Miraculously, no one had been hurt, though part of the roof had blown off the mansion. Since then, it had become the style to joke about the anarchist, though, in truth, Maura did not think it was funny.

"No anarchist would dare show up to-night," Harold said. "We're going to have a lovely evening," he assured her.

Certainly it began that way. Baskets and urns brimming over with hothouse roses and pale, beautiful orchids were strewn along the way to greet guests, as they entered the Baker's lavish marble vestibule and hall. Maura went off to powder her nose at a magnificently appointed green-and-gold powder room, attended by four young women. Then she joined Harold in the huge ballroom.

The room was glittering; the chandeliers ablaze with light and the guests equally dazzling and gleaming in their finery. It was the trend, at the moment, for women to wear not simply a necklace or a tiara as Maura had, but to display *all* of their jewels at once. Under the weight, the women stooped slightly, like beasts of burden. But they bore their burden proudly.

"Look at her!" Paul Baker pointed a finger at his wife. "Half a million on her back!"

Mrs. Baker, their hostess, smiled a little wearily, while Paul Baker bowed and asked Maura to dance.

It was a *coup* to be asked to dance the first dance with her host. Gracefully, Maura began the quadrille in the squares or formation of the dance. Then suddenly, she drew in her breath sharply.

Across the room, dancing in another set of

four, was Neil Prescott. Looking very handsome in dark dinner dress, he held out his arm to his partner, an attractive dark-haired woman, with gold hoops for earrings and a print gown that made her resemble, faintly, a gypsy.

Maura whirled through the rest of the dance in a daze.

"I'll take you back to Lord Parker," Baker said politely as he led the way.

Harold claimed the next dance. He chatted easily, but Maura spent most of the dance looking over his shoulder for Neil. But he was nowhere in sight.

"Is anything the matter?" Harold asked.

She shook her head, embarrassed and guilty. Why was she behaving like this? She was not being fair to Harold.

"Are you enjoying yourself?" he asked, concerned.

"Oh, yes!" This time she managed a smile. Angry with herself, she determined now to enjoy herself and forget Neil and that woman, whoever she was.

She was her father's daughter, after all, and by sheer strength of will, she managed to put Neil out of her mind. She danced gaily with Harold, then with several of his friends. After that, surprisingly, Gladys Van Diver's husband claimed a dance.

"I'm sorry if the family has been neglectful," Thomas apologized as they went around the floor. "Gladys will probably tell you so herself, when she has a free moment."

It was a polite overture, though Maura suspected it had come solely from Gladys's husband, not Gladys. She was sorry. It seemed as though the family would never be reconciled, and she wanted that reconciliation for her son. She must take her place in society so that he, when the time was ready, would be able to claim his.

She danced till her feet ached, and the smile on her face felt as though it had been fixed there by some genie. She was grateful when Harold asked: "Do you think it's time we left? I have to be up early. Unless, of course, you care to stay a little longer?"

"Oh, no," she said, quickly. "Let's go."

It was after they'd said their goodbyes to their host and hostess and were on their way down the long marble hall to the cloakroom and exit that she saw them.

The woman, the dark, gypsy-type woman, was standing at the entrance to the cloakroom. The woman shot Maura a look, then threw an arm around Neil's neck and kissed him.

A pain shot through Maura's breast, as though she'd been stabbed. For one moment, she stood still, unable to move a muscle. Then she became aware of Harold at her side.

"I'll get your wrap, dear," he was saying.

"Yes," she murmured.

The next instant there was a thundering explosion.

"A bomb!" someone shouted.

Maura felt herself shoved to the floor, half-covered by someone's body.

"Are you hurt? Maura!"

Dazed, she recognized Harold's voice. "No," she murmured, untangling herself and sitting up. Harold, looking relieved, offered his hand to help her up. She took it, although her eyes were not on Harold but on the man at his side.

It was Neil. He'd thrown himself on top of her, like a shield. He was standing now, his dark eyes blazing into hers. She felt her heart leap, but she said nothing and neither did he.

Harold did the talking for all three. "Thank you—Mr. Prescott, is it?" He offered his hand, and Neil shook it briefly.

"I think you should see about your friend," Harold suggested. "Happily, the explosion was slight. I don't think anyone was hurt, but there has been some damage to the house—"

He paused abruptly, and turned, as they all did.

All eyes were on Sarah Montebello. She stood, off to the side of the damaged cloakroom. Her dress was covered with soot and there was a dark smudge down the side of her nose that made her look more like an Indian than a gypsy. She looked as though she'd been cleaning out a chimney, and she wasn't very happy about it. She glared angrily at Neil.

Maura spun away.

"Thank you, again," Harold said. Maura felt his arm around her now, guiding her out the doorway toward the carriage. As they started down the stairs, Maura was aware of a sudden movement in the darkness away from the lamppost that made her start. She saw a patch of pale blond hair as a youth scurried away. For the first time in a long while she thought of Kevin.

Could that have been him? Could *he* have done this? But Kevin was not an anarchist. He would never have risked himself for an idea or a cause. Money was his sole objective. Of course, someone might have paid him to do it.

Maura shivered slightly. Kevin, if it had been Kevin, was gone. She stepped into the carriage eagerly, happy to be on her way home.

The trip home was delayed, however, as the carriage swung westward toward the river. Harold turned to her. "It's late, I know, and we both could use our rest, but I must ask you one question, Maura."

He paused. The horses had come to a halt by the river. The moonlight, shining into the carriage, seemed to shine directly into his pale gray eyes as he looked at her. "Is he the reason?" he asked quietly.

"Oh, Harold!" she began. What could she say? But he deserved an honest answer.

"I honestly don't know," she went on. "I thought it was all over, really. But whenever I see him, it's . . ."—how could she describe it?—". . . so painful," she finished.

There was a moment of silence. Then Harold shrugged. "It's too soon, perhaps."

"I think so," she said quietly.

"Are you telling me there's a chance, Maura?" Harold's eyes, more than his voice, questioned her.

Maura shook her head. "I'm sorry, Harold,"

she began, slowly. "You deserve the truth. The answer is simply that I don't want another romantic attachment. The fact is—if it were anyone, or were to be anyone, I wish it were you. But it can't be. I know it, and it's not fair to you to let you believe there might be. I do like you very much, however, and I hope we can remain friends—" She broke off. Somehow, her words seemed to be coming out awkwardly. She hoped she hadn't hurt him.

But he managed a brief smile. "Thank you for being so honest with me, Maura." He raised her hand to his lips and kissed the palm gently. "Now, shall we go?"

An incredible weariness came over Maura on the way home. The dancing, the shock of seeing Neil, the sudden, terrible explosion and, finally, the talk with Harold had simply been too much for her.

"Did you have a nice time?" Abby asked, curious, as she helped Maura get ready for bed.

"Oh, very nice."

"He's a fine gentleman, isn't he?" Abby persisted.

"Very fine."

He was, Maura thought, as she slipped between the silk sheets. She was relieved, in a way, that she'd finally told him how she felt. Though she couldn't help wondering if they would remain friends or not.

As she drifted off to sleep, her thoughts wandered from Harold to Neil. In spite of herself. But she could not forget that brief moment when his body had covered hers to protect her. She had almost forgotten how wonderful the weight of his body could feel. . . .

Oh, what's the matter with me! she thought angrily. He had another woman. Even if he didn't, it was over between them, she reminded herself. *Over*. Life goes on, she told herself. It must. And turning her head to one side, she fell swiftly, exhaustedly, to sleep.

Chapter Twelve

THE BABY WAS HER PRIDE, HER JOY. HE WAS growing bigger and more curious. He was crawling now, which delighted Maura and terrified her at the same time. She was so afraid he would poke himself on the edges of the furniture. Worse yet were the stairs. She had nightmares about him falling down the stairs. She wondered how other parents dealt with all the mysterious, unmentionable fates that could befall their children. At last logic took over. You did the best you could, under the circumstances, she told herself. Regarding the stairs, she had James, the handyman, fit an extremely ugly but practical gate at the top of each tier of stairs. Maura gave orders that the gates were to be kept closed at all times—each time anyone passed by he would have to open and then secure the gates. The servants grumbled, but Maura didn't care. At least that was one less thing she would have to worry about.

"A fine child," Harold said. He was playing

with Peter in the drawing room, before he and Maura went out to dinner. The game he played and the one Peter enjoyed most was catch. He tossed the baby in the air, then caught him. Maura held her breath each time Harold tossed her son. But Peter squealed with glee each time, and Maura didn't have the heart to stop Harold. They enjoyed each other so much. There was also the fact that Peter, surrounded by a harem of women, needed a man to play with. He needed, though Maura was loath to admit it, a father. . . .

She sighed. The thought had popped into her mind more than once. Watching Harold now, she couldn't help thinking that he would make a good father.

Harold. Such a shame, she thought, but her feelings about him hadn't changed. She liked him as a friend, but that was all. Happily, he seemed content. Harold took her out in the evenings, but instead of parking, dallying along the way, he took her directly home. There were times, however, and in spite of the fact that she had been explicit with him, she wondered if Harold had accepted her answer. From a look he gave her at times, from the way he pressed her hand, she had the feeling that if Harold had been spending more time in the States, he might have put his question to her again.

Harold, however, had little time for himself. His was an able, very fine mind, particularly when it came to matters of finance, and it was because of this that he was needed in London.

He'd been traveling back and forth between America and London for the past four months.

"I understand my friends have been kept busy escorting you." He smiled.

"Yes, they've been very kind." The problem with escorts had passed. Harold's friends had been only too happy to escort her—the "future Lady Parker," as one of his friends had called her. Maura flushed now as she remembered. She had let the remark slip by at the time, but it was just this sort of thing that warned her that Harold had not taken her at her word. She had made up her mind at the time to talk to him about it, but as yet, she had not. . . .

"What is it?" Harold asked.

Maura shrugged. "I was thinking it's time Peter went to bed. Miss Richards?" she called. Even as she did, she realized she was being silly. Miss Richards would be in on the dot of eight, Peter's bedtime. Miss Richards was as punctual as a grandfather clock. Most of the time Maura was sorry the nanny was so punctual; she always hated to part with Peter. At the moment, however, Maura would have welcomed the distraction. Her instinct told her Harold had something on his mind.

She was right.

"And how is Mr. Prescott?" Harold asked suddenly.

Maura started. It was not quite the question she'd expected. It was the first time, in fact, Harold had ever questioned her directly about Neil. She shrugged slightly. "Nothing has changed, Harold," she said softly.

"I realize that, Maura. I was just curious. You've been seeing Neil, I take it, at dances and other social events?" he went on.

"Once or twice—" Maura broke off. Each time, Neil had seemed startled to see her. Though not quite so startled as she was. Fortunately, there had been so many people at each affair and she and Neil had been so far apart from each other that it had not seemed strange that he, who was running the Van Diver estate, and she, ostensibly the head of it until her son was older, were not greeting one another. Maura had noted, with a certain sense of satisfaction, that the gypsy woman had not been there.

"And?" Harold was looking at her, waiting.

"Please don't, Harold," she said quickly. "I told you there's been no change."

"But you are still troubled when you see him?" he persisted.

She lowered her eyes and looked away. "Yes," she said, after a moment. "I wish I weren't, but I am."

He said nothing for a moment, then she felt his hand stroking her hair gently. "It will pass," he said kindly. "With time. You are very young."

"Really?" She looked up at him. "You know, my father used to say that to me. 'It will pass, Maura,' he would say. 'It's going to be all right.' Somehow, I was always skeptical. . . ." She sighed softly. And look what happened to him, she thought—dying a broken, penniless man.

"But this will," Harold insisted. "Believe me, Maura."

She smiled faintly. She wanted to believe. "I hope so." She turned as Miss Richards, the sturdy English nanny she'd hired, came in.

"It's time for Peter's bath," she said cheerfully.

"Give us a kiss," Harold said, and Peter obliged with a hug and kiss.

"What about me?" Maura said, a little jealously, and he laughed and kissed his mother.

"Shall we?" Harold held her wrap. As he helped her into it, she found herself shivering slightly.

Peter's words had made her think of her father. She remembered the premonition she'd had about his accident. For days, no, several weeks before the accident, she had awakened each night, in the middle of the night, shaking. She'd known *something* was going to happen, though she hadn't been sure quite what. And now, it seemed to her, that the same feeling, the premonition of evil, was returning. . . .

"What is it, dear?" Peter was studying her anxiously.

She managed a smile. "Nothing. I'm fine."

"Good. I want you to enjoy yourself this evening," he said.

"I will," she promised.

She did enjoy herself, or at least she did enjoy Harold's company. The party itself was a little disconcerting.

It was at Caroline Astor's, in her famous "art gallery ballroom" at 350 Fifth Avenue, amid masses of flowers and French and Italian paintings. Mrs. Astor greeted everyone from her "throne," a divan on a dais covered with red silk. If you were invited to sit with her, it was tantamout to a royal audience. Maura and Harold were greeted perfunctorily by the "queen." Maura, very pointedly, however, was not asked to sit. Shortly after, Gladys Van Diver entered and Mrs. Astor coyly patted the seat next to her. There was a look of triumph on Gladys's face as she caught Maura's eye.

Silly women, Maura thought. Yet, she couldn't brush it off that easily. After Harold took her home, she lay awake in bed, staring at the ceiling.

It was all very well and good to say that she didn't care whether or not she was snubbed by the Astors, but the fact was, it was important to her child. It was her duty, her responsibility, to carve a spot for Peter in society. And at the top. To do that, she would have to establish herself as a leader.

There was one way to do that: to throw a ball herself, a grand ball. But the thought of a ball in this house, so cold, so funereal, put her off. No, she couldn't hold it here. . . .

It came to her suddenly. Why, she would hold it at Newport, of course! She had yet to see the house, but from all she had read and heard, that was the place! She could hold a glorious ball there, one that people would talk about for ages! Then she stopped. Of course, she might fail, the party might be a disaster, no one might come. How Gladys Van Diver would love that! Maura sighed to herself. But she was her father's daughter, wasn't she? She wouldn't think of the possibility of failure. Turning on her side, she went to sleep.

Abby woke her with a tray a little earlier than usual. Harold had asked her to come to the pier to see him off. It was a glorious April day, the twenty-third—Shakespeare's birthday. The thought cheered her; she would take Peter along.

On the way to the pier, she pointed out the sights to Peter and his nanny. To a ten-month-old, even a very bright ten-month-old, the sights couldn't mean very much, but to Miss Richards, recently arrived from England, and herself, they meant much more. Maura had lived in the city all of her young life, but there were times, when the air was crisp and the sky a Dutchman's blue, that she fell in love with it all over again.

In the park, she pointed out Cleopatra's needle, the tall, magnificent obelisk which the Egyptian government had presented as a gift to the city in 1881. On Broadway, she pointed out the Booth Theater, where Sarah Bernhardt had made her American debut in 1880; not too far away was Wallach's, where Lily Langtry had appeared two years later.

The streets were busy with carriages and bicycles, many of them bicycles built for two made famous by Diamond Jim Brady and his sweetheart, Lillian Russell. As they passed by, the couples, very often, were singing their song:

Daisy, Daisy, give me your answer,
  true . . . !

Maura sang along with them, delighted because it made Peter smile and coo. But she stopped abruptly as they reached the dock at Twelfth Street and the Hudson River, where Harold's ship would be embarking from. She did not want to give Harold any ideas. . . .

"I wish I weren't going," he said as he took her hand. "The worst of it is, I'm not sure when I can get back. I expect to be pretty busy."

"Perhaps I'll be in Newport when you return," Maura said. "I intend to open it up this year."

"By yourself?" He looked dubious. "It's a big job for a woman."

"I can do it," she said firmly.

"Well . . ." He shrugged slightly, then, pulling her toward him, kissed her. On the cheek. It was a sweet, brotherly kiss.

Maura smiled up at him, relieved.

"Will you miss me?" he asked.

"Yes," she said simply. It was the truth. She would miss him.

They stayed on the dock, waving, till the ship pulled out. When it was out of sight, Maura spun around toward the carriage. "We'd better get back," she said. "I have a lot of work to do."

She spent the afternoon drawing up a plan. The first task would be to hire a staff. Of course, she might take part of the staff at the Fifth Avenue house, but surely not all would want to come and she would need replacements. The following day and every day that week she interviewed until the staff was complete. It included: a butler, first and second chefs, a kitchen maid and a second maid, three laundresses, two footmen, three chambermaids, a housekeeper, and Abby, her personal maid.

After the staff was selected, Maura still had a few personal arrangements to make. She had several new gowns made, she bought some new suits for little Peter, and she made arrangements for the Fifth Avenue house to be closed. She was closing it earlier than her neighbors, but for a reason. She had no idea what to expect when she arrived at Newport. She was sure, however, that it would take a while before the house was in any kind of shape for entertaining.

So why not go earlier? It would be lovely to be in the country; it would be good for Peter; and she could get to work. It occurred to her that it would be quiet, perhaps even desolate with no neighbors around. But she was anxious to get going. And there was nothing to hold her in New York. She thought fleetingly of Neil, then shook her head. No, nothing . . . She would make her plans to leave, the earlier the better. . . .

On a quiet morning in early May, Maura, the servants and small Peter and his nanny set off for Newport. It was a bright lovely morning and the three stately black carriages proceeded at a quick pace.

Around one, they stopped for a picnic lunch. The cook had packed huge wicker baskets with ham, cheese, freshly baked rolls and cookies. There was milk for Peter, iced tea for everyone else. Maura found a spot under a large shady elm that looked out onto a rolling green meadowland. It was restful, and she might have lingered longer, playing with the baby, except that she spotted a few dark clouds in the formerly cloudless sky. Not wishing to get caught in bad weather, they started quickly back to the carriages.

The rain clouds broke just as they reached the outskirts of Newport. Maura was disappointed. She'd looked forward so much to seeing the city, and now to see it like this! She tried not to think of it as a bad omen.

She pressed her nose to the window, like a child at a sweet shop. On her lap was the guidebook and history of Newport.

According to the map, it looked to Maura like a crumpled old boot, with its toe pointing westward into Narragansett Bay, and its sole and rear to the Atlantic Ocean. The center of the city, Newport Harbor, was at the ankle of the boot. And the famous Ten-Mile Drive that Maura had heard so much about, connecting all the great estates along the shore, ran along the tie of the boot south from the center, west along the sole, then winding back over the toe to the center again.

The city was named for Newport, the capital of the Isle of Wight. It was founded in 1639 by a small band of men under the leadership of John Clarke and William Coddington, both of Boston and both under disfavor with Massachusetts authorities.

As Maura skimmed over its history, it seemed that Newport had originally been a haven for those who had left the Mother Country or other American colonies for freedom's sake. The Quakers and an early group of Jewish settlers fled from Holland and another from Portugal because of religious persecution. With the influx of immigrants, the city quickly became a commercial center, marketing in rum and molasses; it was also a center for farming, fishing and shipbuilding. After the Revolutionary War and the British occupation, however, the city's industries were almost totally destroyed. Commerce turned to New York, and the population dwindled away.

Slowly, Newport recovered. About 1820, it began to come into some notice as a summer resort. Accommodations were then meager, but the visitors, principally from the southern states and Cuba, enjoyed the wholesome air and fine bathing. By 1836, some far-sighted men realized Newport could become a great watering-place. One man who could not get hotel accommodations went out and bought a piece of land, contracted for a cottage—and was living in it a fortnight later. He liked the cottage idea so well he recommended it to his friends, who soon followed his example. The early cottages were cheaply made, built to last only a season, but even the more elaborate, luxurious ones that Maura passed on her way to the Van Diver's estates were called, fondly, cottages.

Maura held her breath suddenly as the carriage came to an abrupt stop. "This is it!" the driver called out to the others.

This? Maura peered out. "Oh!" she sighed. For even in the rain, she could not help but see how magnificent the Van Diver cottage was. While the driver jumped out to open the ten-foot, black wrought-iron gate that surrounded the estate, Maura took a closer look.

It looked like a castle—no! It resembled photographs she'd seen of French châteaux and Italian palazzi. It had, indeed, been designed by the famed architect Richard Morris Hunt, who built in the neo-American classic style. It was said of Hunt that everything he built was in some way reminiscent of the Parthenon, the Baths of Caracella or the Colosseum.

Maura had seen only their photographs in books but she immediately recognized the similarities. Those gleaming white columns, the domes, the terraces and balustrades! She had never seen anything in real life to compare!

As the driver proceeded up the winding path, she was, at once, excited and frightened. How could she ever live here? When she thought that home used to mean one tiny closet of a room, and now this! But she had made her decision.

And perhaps a wrong one, she suspected, when she entered. Though not because of the size or the grandeur. It was simply that the house, closed for more than two years, was in such disarray that, had a hotel been open and had she not been so exhausted (not to mention the weather!), she might have been tempted to walk out again.

But the new housekeeper, Mrs. George, took over quickly, practically.

"I want Mrs. Van Diver's quarters straightened immediately!" she ordered the chambermaids. "Air them and see that the linens are spankin' clean!"

"Now, Robert." She walked with the footman into what seemed, at first glance, an immense room, but which Maura later realized was actually the smaller of the two drawing rooms. "If you can lay a fire here to take the chill off of things, Mrs. Van Diver and the baby can rest until their quarters are ready."

Maura had been informed that there were some seventy-odd rooms in the mansion. Outside she'd spotted several small dwellings— for guests, she assumed, and also to house the servants. There was also a stable on the eleven-acre estate, a bird sanctuary and a shooting range. She would see all of it in time, but for the moment, she decided, she would take Mrs. George's advice and rest.

The baby slept blissfully. Maura, curled up in front of the fire, also began to nod off. But her nap was interrupted by Abby, bearing a tray.

"Soup and some biscuits," she said. "It was the best the cook could do. He's in there grumblin' about the stove. He can't work it."

"This is fine," Maura said tiredly. She managed a few spoonfuls of soup, then went upstairs. Her room was clean but spartan. Pictures, wall hangings, drapes, rugs—all had been put away.

The nanny took Peter off to his room, and Maura lay down. It was late, and after traveling all day she was exhausted. But she could not sleep. Perhaps it was the excitement of finally being here after dreaming about it all these months. Or—was it something else? These premonitions she kept having. . . .

She sat up, abruptly. It had struck her suddenly—the feeling that something, something evil, was going to happen, *here,* in this house!

Oh, Maura! she told herself. She was being silly. Foolish. She made herself lie down again. It was the rain, she thought. She had always hated rain. It had rained the day her father died. It had rained again, when her mother had passed away. . . .

The rain had grown heavier in the last few hours; from a shower, it was now a full-fledged storm. It bombarded her windows with the force of sharp, piercing pebbles.

Maura turned her face toward the pillow. She must sleep, she told herself; she had so much to do in the morning. By sheer effort of will, she put everything—her worries about herself and her child, her premonitions and even the rain, the damaging, punishing rain —out of her mind. And slept.

Chapter Thirteen

THE MORNING DAWNED FRESH AND CLEAR, THE loveliest of May mornings, with scarcely a hint of the terrible storm the night before. From her window, Maura could see the sea, glorious and a deep blue, just a shade bluer than the sky. From Peter's window, she saw the edges of the celebrated Cliff Walk, that linked the great estates along the shore. It was all breathtakingly beautiful.

"The servants are airing the house and fixing up their own quarters, ma'am," Abby informed her when she saw her. "And Mrs. George would like to see you when you have a moment."

Maura dressed quickly and started toward the stairs. But when she reached them, she paused. Like a sleeping, magnificent butterfly, the house was beginning to emerge from its cocoon. It would be days, probably weeks before it was restored to what it had been, but at least now she could see the beginnings. And how thrilling! How magnificent! The pale, pink marble staircase. The huge, crystal chandeliers, hung in tiers, from one floor to the next. There were the thick gold carpets, the mahogany wainscoting, the tapestries—the ones that had not been taken down and were now in the process of being dusted and steamed and restored to new freshness.

Slowly, she walked down the stairs, thinking that this is the way I might walk down at a ball. And what a perfect place for a ball!

"Mrs. Van Diver?" It was Mrs. George, looking perplexed.

"Yes?"

"I have some things to show you. If you'll follow me?"

Mrs. George led her through the long hallway that wound around toward the back of the house. Along the way, Maura glanced into the rooms. Each boasted a period fireplace; she saw antique Old English chimney-pieces. The Van Diver coat of arms, a majestic lion seated amidst oak leaves, was everywhere. A billiard room, two drawing rooms, a library. It seemed to Maura a labyrinth which she might never figure out.

"Here we are." Mrs. George flung the door open on a giant-sized room. Other houses might have linen closets but this, Maura realized, was an entire room devoted to linens, draperies.

"I wondered," Mrs. George said, fingering a pale blue drapery, "if you might like this for your room? There's so many, I wasn't sure. And about linens, what about this?"

Maura spent half of the morning with the

housekeeper and then excused herself. "I'll leave the rest to your good judgment," she said. She was anxious to see the rest of the house and perhaps take a walk out of doors. But first she wanted to see her son.

She was starting toward the great hall and the staircase, when Abby approached her. There was a look of disapproval on her face. "There's someone to see you, ma'am," she said. "Wouldn't say who he was, just said you'd see him. I showed him 'im in here." She pointed toward the drawing room Maura had rested in the night before.

"Thank you." Curious, she walked toward the room. But she'd taken only a few steps in when she stopped, startled. Kevin, his feet up on the antique coffee table, a cigar in his mouth, turned toward her, grinning.

"How are ya, sis? Nice place you've got here. Must have cost a pretty penny." He laughed. "Or two. Or three . . ."

"What are you doing here?" she said sharply.

"Oh, c'mon!" There was a wheedling tone in his voice. "Why are you always so sharp with me? Sit down—" He patted the velvet sofa, indicating a place next to him.

Maura ignored him. How could he do this? she thought. She tried to control her temper. "I told you, Kevin," she said, evenly, "I didn't want to see you anymore."

"And I told you I ain't that fond of you, either. But we're still blood, sis. And if one person needs somethin' that the other one's got, well?" He shrugged, smiling.

"I know what you're leading up to, Kevin," she began.

"Do you?" he cut in. "Good. That'll save us both a lot of trouble. I could use—oh, a coupla hundred, if you've got that much cash on you. If not—oh, whatever you've got. I can stop in around the middle of the week. . . ."

"No," she said.

"What's that?"

"I said no," she repeated firmly. His eyes that were so much like hers—but looked inward instead of out—were hard to fix with a stare, a glare, but Maura did the best she could. She would not give him the satisfaction of seeing fear. Nor would she give him any money. She did have some in her purse upstairs; she might have given it to him if she'd thought that would be the end of it, that he would disappear and she'd never see him again. But she knew that was just wishful thinking. . . .

"It's the gambling, isn't it?" she guessed. "You're in debt again."

"None of your business what it is," he roared. "You're my sis; you made good. It's your duty to do a good turn for me, you hear?"

"If I thought you would go, Kevin—" She paused. She'd been thinking aloud and, for one moment, she wavered. Why not? she thought. She had plenty; why not give him some? But at that moment, Kevin, seeing her hesitation, grinned. And she suddenly realized she could not. If she gave him money, he would be back again and again. There would never be an end. What frightened her more

than anything else was the thought that some-
day Peter might be forced to face this
monster. . . .

"No," she said again, backing away. "And
now, get out. Quickly. Before I call one of the
footmen. Or the butler."

She stood in the doorway now, so he could
see her threat was not an idle one.

A look so black passed over his face that
Maura felt her skin crawl. He jumped up,
tossing his cigar in the ashtray. "But you'll
be sorry for this. You'll see!" He started
toward her, his hand raised as though
to swat her, as he might have any irri-
tant.

But Maura never felt a blow. At that moment, Miss Richards entered with the baby.

"I'm sorry to disturb you, ma'am," the
nanny said. "I didn't know anyone was
here—"

"That's all right," Maura murmured. Peter
was holding out his arms to her. "Ma, ma!" he
cried. It was his new trick, his first words.
Maura had been thrilled the first time she
heard them, but now she was only anxious.
And Kevin, at once, saw this anxiety.

"Well, ain't he cute?" he grinned, walking
toward the baby. "Say hello to your uncle." He
chucked Peter under the chin.

Don't touch him! Maura wanted to cry. But
she held her breath.

"Looks like a healthy kid," Kevin went on,
grinning. "Let's hope he stays that way."

"Get out of here!" Maura cried suddenly,
furiously. "Get out!"

Kevin gave a small, insolent shrug and slipped out the door.

Maura gathered the baby to her. If anything had happened to him! If anything *did* happen. . . . Was this the premonition she kept having?

"Ma'am, shall I take the baby? You're shaking," Miss Richards told her.

"Am I? I'm sorry. Yes. Please." She gave the baby to the nanny.

"Goodbye, Peter." She waved at him as he left with Miss Richards for his airing. Thinking about it, Maura decided the fresh air might also do her some good. She would need a shawl, however. She rang the bell for Abby, but as she did, Abby walked in.

"Ma'am, there's someone else to see you. . . ." She paused. The someone was right behind her. . . .

Neil Prescott stood in the doorway. He wore a long black cape, his pale hair hatless and curled from the wind.

If Maura had been stunned to see Kevin, she was quite speechless now. Standing as he was on the threshold, Neil looked like some magnificent golden God. For one moment, neither he nor she moved or spoke; the single sound in the room was the crackle of the fire. And to Maura's mind, her own sharp intake of breath.

Then Neil broke the spell and stepped forward. "I was surprised to find you'd left the city. I have a few papers that need signing."

Maura was puzzled. "But I told John Ross.

He said not to worry. He would take care of everything."

"Yes, but there are still some papers that need signing," Neil repeated. He reached into a black leather case, plucked out some papers and held them out to her.

As Maura reached for them, she found herself caught, instead, by his eyes. She had seen desire in them before. And now, she saw it again.

"Why did you come?" she asked softly, as the papers fluttered to the floor.

He stepped forward, with complete disregard for the papers that crunched under his boots. He stopped abruptly, just inches away from her. . . .

They were standing so close—and yet he did not touch her. She saw a half-smile playing around his lips, as though he was amused by her question.

"I was concerned about you," he said. "Traveling in such bad weather. It caused havoc in the city; one of the trains was derailed. Fortunately, no one was seriously hurt. But I was worried about you."

"I'm grateful for your concern, but I'm fine, quite fine. Thank you." The words tumbled out coolly, much more coolly than Maura would have believed. Or intended. She watched his eyes turning colors in the firelight, dark blue to glittering black, and wondered what he was thinking. . . .

She is an ice maiden, Neil thought. He had come, as quickly as he could, half out of his mind that something might have happened to her in that storm. This was a bad time of year to travel. Why had she suddenly taken it in her head to go? Whatever the reason, it was far too early for her to be in Newport. There was a rough element on the other side of town that had always worried him. People rarely spoke about it. In truth, in season, there was little occasion to go over to the other side of town. But he, personally, had always been aware of the element. When he'd heard Maura had gone to open the house, it was the first thing that had come into his mind.

Yet looking at her now, he wondered. She had a waist so small he could span it with his hands. She had a long, slender neck, delicate features, graceful hands and feet. She looked so fragile that he'd envisioned the turbulent winds that had caused havoc last night breaking her in two. But for the first time since he'd first set eyes on her, it occurred to him that Maura was deceptive. That coolness in her voice, that look in her eye. There was steadiness and strength of will. She was far stronger than she appeared to be. An ice maiden, an iron maiden.

As the two of them stood, eyeing one another, taking each other's measure, Neil could not help realize, also, that Maura was angry. Well, if she was, she had every reason to be, he decided. . . .

"I'm sorry," he said suddenly. The words struck him, at once, as inadequate. "I am truly sorry," he repeated. "I shouldn't have barged in like this. Your instincts were right, as usual. The papers were a ruse. Ross could have signed them, of course. He has power of attorney. I'll give them to him."

Bending down, he scooped up the papers.

He's not going to leave! Maura thought. He can't come here, and then just leave like that! Perhaps he misunderstood. . . .

"Please!" Maura reached out and grasped his sleeve. The touch was light but a shock went through her, as it had that very first time they'd touched. This time, she was aware, however, from the way his eyes caught and fixed on her, that he was as affected as she.

Her hand remained on his sleeve, her eyes locked with his. She did not have the power to break away.

But he did not break away. Instead, he pulled her toward him with an urgency that surprised Maura. She staggered slightly as the weight of his body pressed against her, his mouth nestled in her hair, his hand caressed the curve of her cheek, then moved down to cup her breast. Maura could hear her own breath beginning to come in small whimpers. She was on the edge of releasing herself to him and the tiny electric sensations she felt throughout her body—

Yet in the flush of happiness and warmth, she suddenly caught herself. What kind of a woman was she? He had left her—walked out on her! He hadn't come near her once while she was having her child. She might have died then; had he ever considered that? No, all he had thought of then was his own injured pride. Because she would not accept his impossible scheme for them! And now, suddenly—on a whim of his?—he'd come up to Newport to see her. And she, like a little fool, had fallen into his arms!

"Get away from me!" It took every bit of strength in Maura's arm to shove him away from her, but she did.

"I'm not a—a plaything!" she cried. "You can't put me aside, and then pick me up again when you feel like it! No!"

He was perplexed. What had gotten into her? "Maura, I said I was sorry. I am!"

"Sorry? How easy to say. But what are words compared to long nights? Nights I waited for you. . . ." She choked suddenly, embarrassed that she should be blurting out these secrets. And why shouldn't she? And why shouldn't he know how she'd suffered, and through no fault of her own. He might have eased that suffering. But he had chosen not to.

"Maura, I understand. It was my own damnable pride. And my disappointment. Surely, you can understand that. . . ."

She shrugged. "Perhaps."

They were standing apart now, the fire gleaming on Maura's golden hair. There were tiny green and gold flecks of fire in her eyes as she remembered again the night he had left.

"It was a mistake," Neil said again. "I freely admit it. But surely you're not going to let that stand between us always? Are you?"

But as he looked into her eyes, he saw that she would. That stubborn Irish streak of her father's. Well, he was just as stubborn, he thought. She had met her match.

He pulled her toward him, not gently as he had done in the past, but with force and energy, and roughness born of his sudden, sharp anger.

"Let go of me!" she cried. "I told you no!"

"And I won't take no!" he snapped back. "You don't mean it, Maura. You know that. When I touch you—" Holding her tightly, he ran one hand along the white smoothness of her throat, then slipped it inside the low-cut gown, fondling one breast, then the other.

In spite of herself, Maura felt herself responding to him. The touch of his hand felt so good against her cool breasts. She *had* missed him. Yet again pride stopped her. Did he think she was simply his to take, to plunder?

"Leave me!" she said, wriggling free. "This is the last time I'll tell you! Otherwise, I'll scream!"

She got no further. At once, his mouth crushed down on hers, stopping any scream. His tongue, rough, like a cat's, moved over her lips. Then, to her surprise, he released her.

"I will tell you, Maura; I had thought to tell you later, actually. . . ." He paused. Would he have told her? He wasn't sure. But the way she was acting now he felt he had no choice. In any event, he was beginning to feel he owed her a bit more of an explanation.

"It wasn't just pride," he went on. "Oh, yes, it was that at first. But after a time, I began to see that you had no choice; you were doing the honorable thing. And in spite of everything, I admired you. I made up my mind I would come to you, and then something damnable happened again. It occurred to me that both of us were taking it for granted that the child would be a boy. But what if it were a girl? Then there would have been no problems, nothing to separate us. For that reason, I decided, again, to wait. I would come to you when you had your baby; we would start afresh. When I heard from Ross that the baby was a boy, I couldn't believe it. It was as though fate had dealt us a dirty trick. It was difficult to reconcile myself to it. . . ."

He paused, again. It seemed to him there was a glimmer of understanding in Maura's blue eyes. "You do understand now, don't you?" he said.

Maura was beginning to. But while her mind was making the connections, telling herself he was not to be blamed so much, after all, and that he *did* care, her body still stubbornly held back. When he pulled her toward him again, she resisted. But only for a moment. As he pulled her closer, tighter, her resistance fled.

He began to draw slow, teasing patterns with the tip of his tongue along her lips. Almost against her will, her mouth opened. His tongue was hot and sweet like honey. When that tongue began to make the same maddening patterns down her throat to her breasts, she could think of nothing but him—his mouth, his tongue. Her senses had left her; she was pure sensation. She felt wave after wave wash over her until she let go completely, sucked in and under, hardly able to distinguish reality from the fantasy world with which she had put herself to sleep with so many nights. Only when she felt him start to undo her gown did reality once again intrude on her senses.

"Not here!" she pleaded. "The servants pass by! Someone will see—" She gathered the folds of her gown modestly around her.

"I'll close the door."

"But they'll know."

"So?" With a shrug he went to close and fasten the door.

If she'd wanted to shout for the servants, for help, she might have done so then. But she simply waited for him to come back, to hold her again, to touch her.

But first, he quickly started to undo his own clothes in front of the fire. Had she forgotten how beautiful he was? His skin turned golden in the firelight, the thin down of golden hair on his chest gleaming, the chest itself broad, the muscles underneath lean and defined.

"Come here, my darling," he smiled, starting toward the green velvet couch, where she had sat down.

The word "darling," once so sweet, stung her. She realized now, from what he had told her, that he had missed her, that he had wanted to come. Yet that one word still bothered her. "No," she said, "I forbid you to call me that!"

Forbid? In his lifetime, Neil could remember only two people saying that to him: one a schoolmaster who was dismissed by the Captain when he found out about it; the second was the Captain himself. There was little Neil could do about the Captain, but he had never taken the word from anyone else. And from Maura? First, her stubborn willfulness and now this? It was the kind of thing Sarah might do, but playfully. But she and Sarah were not to be mentioned in the same breath. At least the Maura he remembered. But where was that sweet, compliant Maura?

"What has gotten into you?" he asked angrily. "Is it motherhood?"

"Perhaps." She raised her head proudly. "Perhaps having to fight for my son."

"Maybe Peter had something, in just going after virgins," he muttered, a little bitterly.

She slapped him, and the sting of her hand across his face set off his anger and his passion. He had not meant to say that; if he could have bitten off his tongue at that moment he would have. But that slap worked against all his reason.

He crushed her to him in a kiss more compelling than any he'd ever given her before. His mouth was rough and hard as it ground into hers, his hands were like steel vises as he held her to him, then with one violent yank he ripped her dress, baring her to the waist.

Maura fought him. I will not be taken this way, she told herself. Neil, who had wrestled at college and once, as a joke, did a day's work as a sparring partner with a fighter, was amazed at how strong she was. For a short time, she managed to keep him from either raising her skirts or pulling her dress off.

In the end, however, her strength was nothing compared to his. In a matter of moments, her skirt was down. He undid his trousers hastily and, bold and ready, he fell on top of her on the couch.

The weight of his body stunned Maura. She'd forgotten the feel of him, and how sweet to have his naked chest brushing against her bare breasts.

The touch of Maura's flesh also seemed to subdue him. His hand, caressing her hair, became more gentle. She heard him murmur, softly, "Maura, oh Maura!" as he entered her.

Instinctively, her body took up the rhythm of his. It was the first time he had made love to her in so long, the first time since the baby. In a sense, the baby had become her lover, nibbling at her breasts as he'd nursed, throwing his chubby arms around her neck. But the sensation now was as nothing she'd ever known. Neil's tongue teased her breasts as intensely as the urgent rhythm his body had imposed on hers. She thought she would die if he didn't stop; she thought she would die if he did.

Finally, he lifted her hips slightly. The pace and rhythm of his lovemaking quickened in intensity. She felt him shudder violently as he called out her name: "Maura!" An instant later, she began to tremble violently. "Neil!" she cried, as she buried her head on his shoulder. . . .

They slept, legs entangled, arms around one another. Maura would have thought it impossible to sleep like this, but she slept like a baby.

The late afternoon sun, warm, golden, poured into the room, waking both of them. They were tangled so that when Maura tried to move her arm, which had fallen asleep under Neil's shoulder, she let out a small cry. They both laughed, and Neil, at once, rubbed then kissed the pale white arm, the faint blue vein that throbbed through it. He thought he had never seen anything so beautiful.

The anger that had passed between them had spent itself in bed, in the release of their passion. What remained in Neil's mind was the impression that Maura, in the past year, had grown into womanhood. He desired her more now than ever, but the new independence she had flung at him earlier had given him a new respect for her.

Maura, lying next to him, had also been cleansed of anger. She did love Neil; she knew with a certainty, that he loved her. Still, she was aware that if they were to have any kind of relationship, he would have to show more respect for her, more consideration. "All men have to be taught," her mother had once said. It was one of the few sayings of Nora O'Rourke that had stuck with Maura, but she recognized the truth of it. "And no matter how brilliant, how knowing the man is," Maura added quietly to herself.

There was a soft rap on the door. Then, Abby's voice: "Mrs. Van Diver?"

"One moment," Maura said.

Hastily, she pulled up her gown. The bodice had been torn but, fortunately, she was still able to fasten it so it looked somewhat presentable.

"The door is locked," Neil reminded her. His shirt was on; he was fastening his trousers.

"I'll give you a moment more," Maura said, "before I open it." She paused. "You're leaving this afternoon?"

She hadn't realized she was holding her breath until he answered. "I think I'll wait until morning. That is—" He looked inquiringly at her.

"Oh, yes!" She gave him a radiant smile, then ran to unlock the door.

"Cook wants to know about dinner, ma'am. And Peter's been askin' for you," Abby said.

"Oh, yes. I'll see Peter shortly. As soon as I change my gown."

She glanced at Neil. A finger to the side of his patrician nose, he was eyeing one of the tapestries that had recently been steamed.

"I'll be fine," he said, glancing up. "It's a while since I've been through this house. I'll just take a look around."

Quickly, Maura changed into a pale blue gown, remembering that it was Neil's favorite color for her. When she came downstairs, he had his cloak on, which made her heart skip a beat.

"Have you changed your mind?" she asked. "Are you leaving?"

"No. I just thought it might be nice for the two of us to take a walk along the beach."

"That would be lovely. I'd thought of doing it earlier. . . ." She trailed off, turning to Abby. "Would you get my shawl, please?"

She spun back to Neil. "But first, I'd like you to meet my son."

She held her breath again, as the nanny brought in the baby. She'd been told many times that Peter was a charming baby but now, even recognizing her own prejudice, she had to admit it was true. Peter threw back his head and laughed enchantingly as he entered the room. Neil also laughed, and took him in his arms.

"Looks exactly like you, doesn't he? It's a pity he's not a girl."

He paused—and she realized, at once, what he was thinking. If Peter had been a girl. . . .

"He has a strong chin," she defended, after a moment. "He's very definitely a boy." And I'm proud of it! she thought.

"He has such masculine ways," she went on. And that chin, she thought, was not hers or Peter's. It resembled, instead, the one in the portrait over the fireplace in the library of the Fifth Avenue home.

"Yes, he has the Captain's chin," Neil confirmed. "He'll be a man to reckon with, one of these days."

He handed the baby to Maura, who kissed both cheeks and gave him back to Miss Richards.

"Now, shall we go for our walk?" Neil asked, taking her arm.

Chapter Fourteen

It was many and many a year ago
In a kingdom by the sea,
That a maiden there lived whom you
  know,
By the name of Annabel Lee;
And this maiden she lived with no other
  thought,
Than to love and be loved by me. . . .

As Neil finished this last line, he grasped
Maura's hand. They sat in silence for a moment, on the dunes, looking down the beach
and into the blue waters.

"It's so sad," Maura said, at last.

"Yes, Poe's life was sad, but glorious too. He
wrote so many beautiful things that will live
on. That's the really important thing, isn't it?"
One shaggy eyebrow cocked the question at
her.

Maura nodded, lowering her gaze.

"What are you thinking, darling?"

He'd used the endearment almost without

thinking, but now he watched to see how she would react. But she looked up, smiling.

"That this is a kingdom," she said. "All of it—the beach, so white and beautiful, that magnificent house. The wonderful way it looks down over this beach and the water. To live here is to live like a king."

"Or a queen," he smiled, "like you." He gazed down the length of the beach, then turned back to her. "In truth, there are many kingdoms along this beach—you know that, don't you? And you know"—he hesitated, wondering if he should bring it up, then deciding it was as good a time as any—"about the 'footstools?'"

"No," she said, curious. "Tell me."

"The footstools, darling, are what we"—with one sweep of his long arm he indicated the length of the beach—"the inhabitants of this kingdom call the townspeople. They're the people who've not been so fortunate to possess kingdoms, but who still feel they have a certain say in the way things are run around here. The simple fact is the footstools were here first. Though not physically *here*." He dug one finger in the sand to emphasize his point. "They've always lived on the other side of town. The point is, darling, they despise us, and we're not too fond of them."

"We?" Maura shook her head. "But not me, Neil. You're wrong there. I lived my entire life on the wrong side of town. I won't forget that soon. And I will not look down on people simply because of where they live or how they dress, or—"

"That's admirable," Neil cut in. "But I think, after you've been living in this kingdom for a while, you may begin to feel otherwise. If you go shopping in the town, for example, and you see how shabbily you are treated by the footstools. They never miss an opportunity to cheat or do you in. Hatred breeds hatred, you know. They hate us so much they charge ten, sometimes twenty times the regular, fair prices of goods. They live well, believe me, on what they make on us."

"So? What is the harm in that?" Maura replied. "We have plenty of money. Why shouldn't we share some of it with them?"

"Sharing of your own free will is one thing. Being robbed is another. The Van Divers have always been more than generous with contributions to the poor. But this gouging, this thievery—" He stopped. "I'm sorry if I'm upsetting you, Maura." He took her hand again for a moment. It seemed chilled and he rubbed it between the two of his, gently. "I'm probably going on about this in the wrong way," he apologized. "But one of the reasons I came to see you—" He paused, remembering how quickly that reason had flown out of his head, the moment he saw her. "I was concerned. There's an element in town I would rather you would avoid, particularly until the rest of the summer people come down."

"You're saying?"

"To limit your drives around town. And not to go into town, in the stores, without one of your footmen. Abby alone simply will not do."

Maura considered for a moment, then nodded.

"Good," he smiled. "That will ease my mind when I can't be here. Now, come here."

He pulled Maura to him, tenderly this time, wrapping his cloak around her, shielding her from the wind, the sharp pellets of sand that were flying around and that stung when they hit the skin.

"We should leave," he said softly, regretfully. The May sun was fading; very shortly, it would be growing cold. And yet he loved being alone with her, with not even servants to intrude.

He buried his face in her hair. It smelled of sea; her skin smelled of sea, too, so fresh and clean and soft to the touch he thought he would never get enough of it. Of her . . .

"Do you want to go back, darling?" he asked.

"No, not yet. It's too perfect." Much too perfect, she thought. Even as she did, a chill went through her. Her Irish forefathers had been skeptical of too much good luck, too much perfection, just as she was.

"What is it, darling?" he asked. She would not say, but he kissed the tiny frown between her brows until it was smooth, and the edges of her mouth until they turned up once again in a smile.

For a short while, they remained quietly on the beach. Then, Neil, fearing Maura would catch a chill, insisted they go back to the house.

Maura would remember the evening as the

most wonderful they'd ever spent with each other. The times they'd had together before the news of Peter's birth had also been wonderful, but different. She felt a greater freedom that evening with Neil than she ever had before, as though they had, at last, come to a truer understanding of one another. She reminded herself that, in truth, they had not had that much time together before the reading of the will and her discovery that she was carrying an heir. So perhaps it was only normal that they should go through this process of discovering things about one another. Even little things. She discovered, to her amazement, that Neil was one of the few people she'd ever met who did not like chocolate. He, in turn, found that her hands, which for some reason he'd never taken that much notice of before, were, in addition to being the slimmest and most graceful he'd ever seen, incredibly articulate and expressive. She used them as an accomplished actress would. Something else, Neil guessed, Maura had inherited from her late father.

They had their dinner served in the drawing room. Maura, who usually took her meals with the baby, wondered if Neil might mind, but he seemed to enjoy Peter's company as much as she. Peter liked Neil as well, Maura realized suddenly, as he did Harold. Ah, but children are fickle, she thought.

As though he'd guessed her thoughts, Neil, as the butler was pouring coffee, suddenly asked: "And how is your English friend? What is his name again?"

Maura started. "You mean Lord Parker? He's fine, I expect. He's in England at the moment."

"And he's expected to be visiting again soon?"

She flushed. "His plans are indefinite."

"You saw quite a bit of him last season, didn't you?" Neil persisted.

"Neil, this interrogation is silly." What has gotten into him? she wondered. "Really, I . . ."

But Neil was shaking his head. He'd come to the same conclusion himself. He *had* been jealous all season whenever he'd seen her on Parker's arm (and of course, he remembered his name!), but it seemed senseless to question Maura now. Maura was much too honest a person and much too innocent to allow Parker to take liberties, and then to behave with him as she had earlier. Maura was not, and thankfully would never be, another Sarah.

"I'm sorry," he said. "Let's forget I mentioned it, shall we?"

They played with the baby until at the dot of eight Miss Richards came to take him away. All evening, Neil had been longing to take Maura in his arms, but with the servants coming in, with the baby, he'd stayed in his place and kept his distance. One thing he did not want, he knew, was a replay of the morning on that narrow couch.

"Shall we go upstairs?" he said.

Maura was pleased to see her suite had been made more comfortable, less barnlike, than the night before. The drapes had been hung, along with some wall-hangings. There was a bowl of fresh flowers on one of the tables, and some fruit by the side of her bed which Maura liked if she sat up late reading.

But she would not read tonight. An instant after they arrived in the room, Neil started to undo her gown. It was a different undoing than that of the morning. Now there was a tenderness, there was care. He would stop after undoing a button to kiss her neck, the pulse that was throbbing wildly under his touch. As excited as she had been that morning, she became even more excited now. On the bed, the leisurely pace of his lovemaking made her even more impatient for him. But he would not be hurried. He took his time with her, stilling his own desires to teach her, first, about his own body. With his hand, he led her own small, graceful one over his chest, down to the hard, firm stomach, down further still to the center of his manhood.

She heard a small gasp from him and was thrilled to think that she could please him the way he did her.

Suddenly, he rolled over and kissing her, murmured: "And now, you, darling!" On his knees now, he leaned over and kissed the inside of one knee.

"No!" Maura moaned, and tried to pull away.

"Stay!" His hands held her firmly, though not roughly. With his tongue, he began to explore the entire leg, from slim ankle, to knee again, up the back of her thigh. Maura shivered and moaned, pressing her head into the pillow. She was in the most exquisite kind of pain. When she thought she could take no more, he suddenly flipped her onto her back.

He wanted her so! But he delayed a few moments longer, running his tongue over her sweet, rosebud breasts, down to her taut, quivering belly, down even lower to the secret place she tried to keep hidden by crossing her legs.

"No!" she whispered, "please!"

But he could resist her no longer. He pulled himself up, stretching his body across the length of hers. As he mounted her, her legs twined around him. Her hands clutched at his shoulders, that smooth, golden chest, as the driving motion of his body brought her to a peak of sensation. She felt him shudder violently, then a moment later, she did, feeling, for an instant, as though she was being torn apart. The exquisite pain was over, and oh the sweetness!

He held her in his arms afterward, caressing her tenderly, murmuring in her ear. More than anything, he wanted her to remember this night and to forget the morning. And all the other nights.

"This is a beginning, darling," he said. "No more surprises, no more shocks in store for us. We know who we are now. I don't ever want to be separated from you again, no!"

She went to sleep with those words in her ears. She thought they were the most beautiful she'd ever heard. . . .

* * *

Neil rose early the next morning and dressed quickly. Maura, still half asleep, lay in bed watching him, with barely open eyes. When he realized she was awake, he came and sat on the bed and kissed her.

"Don't get up," he said. "It's early."

"But I'm always up early," she insisted. "And you have to have some breakfast—"

But the words were scarcely out of her mouth when Neil started to undo his tie, take off his jacket. He reached for her and took her in his arms.

"What are you doing to me?" he murmured in her ear. "You're a little witch, you know that? You've cast a spell over me!"

"Oh, Neil . . ." she began, close to ecstasy as she realized he would not be going, at least not for a while. And then, she could not talk because of the kisses, sweet, hot, on her forehead, her throat, her breast, distracting her, disarming her, driving her out of her senses, again . . . !

He finished undressing and in one swift movement climbed on top of her and they were together. She was part of him and he, her, in the dearest, most intimate way two people can be linked together.

"Come this way, darling," he whispered and flipped her over, so that she was astride him. It was a different, curious sensation for Maura. She missed the weight of him, yet she enjoyed the feeling of strength, of power, of being in charge.

He guided her rhythm skillfully with his

hands on her buttocks. His hips arched against hers; he moved with her in strong, powerful thrusts. She closed her eyes and began to tremble.

Suddenly, he flipped her over, and again she felt his weight and his ever-present need for her in those powerful thrusts. Until neither he nor she could put off any longer, and they both exploded. . . .

Lying next to him in bed, she felt almost drowsy again. But something kept nagging at her. Finally, she realized what it was and turned to him. "I don't like to tell you, Neil—" She loathed telling him, really, but she felt it was her duty. "But you will be late getting back, if you don't get started—"

"Foolish woman." He laughed and, reaching over, ruffled the golden hair. "Did you think my plans were unaltered? Of course, I'm not going back now. Business can wait for me one more day."

"Really, Neil?" It was a surprise, one she hadn't dared hope for. She felt incredibly lucky at the moment, as though good fortune had, at last, decided to shine on her.

"I'll go back tomorrow," Neil went on. "But we'll have the day, at least, together."

"We can go to the beach, we can—" She paused in the midst of her ramblings. "What would you like to do? Oh . . ."

He was nibbling on her ear.

"No!" she laughed, and pulled away.

"Well, then," he said. "What about beginning with some breakfast?"

"Good." She kissed him quickly, then slipped on her robe and went out to see the cook. Remembering his small, hasty breakfasts in the past, she ordered only coffee and rolls. They would make up for it at lunch and dinner, she thought.

She bathed quickly; Neil used the master suite to bathe and dress again.

After breakfast, Miss Richards brought the baby in. He seemed delighted to see Neil again. While Neil played with him, he asked: "Was there anything you planned to do today, Maura?"

"Well, there were a few letters I should get out. . . ." Maura hesitated.

"Why don't you? Ross mentioned there's a set of books here. It wouldn't hurt if I took a look at them."

They went into the study. Of all the rooms in the house, it was possibly the most simply and sparingly furnished, but everything was quietly perfect from the polished wood floor to the magnificent rosette in the ceiling. The draperies were a rich rose, the chairs and secretary of dark mahogany. Mrs. George had seen to it that a fire was burning brightly in the small fireplace to take any chill off the room.

Maura fetched the books for Neil. He sat at the secretary and started to thumb through the entries.

She settled herself at the small writing desk. From time to time, she looked up from her letters to study Neil. She thought she caught him frowning several times, but she couldn't be sure. At any rate, her letters, all duty letters but which, nevertheless, must be answered, engrossed her.

It was past noon when she looked up again. "Are you hungry?" she asked. "I should see about lunch."

"I'm not quite finished," he said, without looking up.

Was it her imagination, or did he sound a little short with her? But, she reasoned quickly, most people don't like to be bothered when they're working.

"I'll go see the cook," she murmured again, and slipped out of the room.

Neil stayed at the desk, eyes focused not on the books, but on a letter that had fallen out of one of the many pigeonholes in the desk. Neil was not one to read other people's mail, but he couldn't help but notice the name and address on the flap—Lord Harold Parker, London. . . . And he could not resist.

"My dearest Maura"—it began. At once, Neil was brought up short. He tried to shrug it off, but he began to see that the letter was full of endearments. He started, almost against his will, to revise his thinking about Maura and Parker.

Was there something going on between them? As he read and reread the letter looking for clues, he began to notice something else.

Parker kept talking again and again about the "business," referring, of course, to the Van Divers' many enterprises. While Neil was not all that familiar with Parker's background, he was well aware that, in financial circles, Parker had quite a reputation as a brilliant organizer and thinker. Neil couldn't help wondering why Parker and Maura were discussing the business in such detail. He smiled ironically. Was Maura planning on replacing him with Lord Parker as head of the company—as well as in bed?

"Dinner will be served in half an hour," Maura announced cheerfully as she walked in. "Will that be all right with you? If you like, it can be later."

"That's fine." Neil had tucked the letter back in its envelope and shoved it into one of the pigeonholes. He slammed the book shut.

"Is everything all right?" Maura asked him, a little worriedly.

"Oh, fine, fine," he shrugged. "Have you ever gone through the books yourself?" he asked casually.

"No, I've been meaning to," she said truthfully, "but I haven't had the time. Harold though," she added, as she remembered, "did go over them once or twice."

"Did he?"

Neil gave her a sharp look. Maura could have bitten her tongue. She should know better than to mention Harold. For whatever reason, it seemed to upset Neil.

"Would you like to wash before lunch?" she asked a little shyly, changing the subject.

Lunch, an omelette, broiled fish and a custard for dessert, was pleasant. Maura was relieved to hear Neil laughing again at one of her jokes.

Later, when they went for their walk on the

beach, they took the baby along. Maura found a shady place beside a rock to watch the child, and settled herself in the sun. Neil sat beside her, stroking her hand.

"It's lovely, isn't it?" she said.

"Yes." But Neil wasn't interested in the weather. "Lord Parker is considered quite the financial wizard, isn't he?" he said.

"Oh, I think so," Maura answered proudly. Again, after one look at Neil, she was sorry. She should not look so proud of Harold—though, how could she help it? She was.

"Have you been studying those books on business and finance you were telling me about?" he asked.

"Oh, yes." She smiled, relieved that they were no longer discussing Harold. "I think that you would be pleased at the progress I'm making," she added.

"I'm sure," he said. He grimaced, but with his back turned to her she could not see his expression.

The rest of the afternoon and the evening went quickly, far too quickly, for Maura. Even bed and Neil's lovemaking was over much too soon. It was as wonderful, as thrilling as always, but somehow she felt he was a little distracted. And afterward, she missed the fact that he didn't hold her, but simply turned over on his side and went to sleep.

She lay awake for a while, wondering if it was her imagination that something had gone wrong between them. She decided, after worrying for a bit, that it probably was her imagination. Neil just had a guilty conscience

about taking an extra day off, she suspected.
Yes, that was it. . . .

"I'll try to arrange my work so we can spend
more time together," Neil told her in the
morning.

His hands encircled her face like a frame.
To Maura, it seemed as though he was going
away for a long time and wanted to remember
it.

"When will I see you again?" she asked,
half-frightened at what the answer might be.

"Not that long. Maybe two weeks. Will that
be all right?"

"All right," she whispered as he kissed her.
At the moment it seemed like a lifetime, but
she told herself it would pass. To be fair to
Neil, she knew it was his busy time at the
office.

He held her for another moment, while his
driver got the carriage ready. "You'll be all
right?" he asked again.

"Oh, yes."

There was a rap on the door. "Mr. Prescott's
driver is here," Abby informed them.

Neil's lips fastened on hers. Maura clung to
him for one long moment, then let go.

"Goodbye, Maura." He started toward the
door, then turned. "Remember what I told you
about the town?"

"Yes."

"Good."

Maura stood at the wide bay window, with
the baby in her arms. They both waved, and
she watched the carriage as it wound down

the road until she could see it no more. But something—why?—told her it would be a long time before that carriage made its way back and its occupant found his way to her door again. . . .

Instead of staying on the shore road, Neil's carriage turned sharply to the left and the slightly longer route that wound its way through the town. On a whim—or perhaps because it had been on his mind earlier?—Neil had decided it might not be a bad idea to drive through the town to see what the footstools were up to.

As he drove, he went over again in his mind the revelations of the day before. He was not entirely convinced that Maura and Parker were scheming against him. Yet the letter with those references—"Will check up on A&R Co."; "Perhaps I can get the figures on Cumberland . . ."—was damning. Before he would damn anyone, however, he would make inquiries about Parker when he arrived back in the city. In the meantime, he would do one thing (one *last* thing?) for Maura to set his mind at ease as to whether she was safe in her "kingdom by the sea. . . ."

Budding elms and oaks lined the road into the city. It was a pretty town, the streets narrow and winding, the houses white-washed, with filmy curtains at the windows and bright flowers lining the walks.

The stores, in the center of town, displayed their wares through sparkling windows. Only at the fringes of the town were the stores a little drab and rundown-looking. It was said that the city fathers were doing something about them, however. Neil had no doubt they would do something. Two years before, Neil remembered, the footstools had arranged for a streetcar to extend its run down Bellevue Avenue and Ocean Drive and past the splendid mansions and "kingdoms" of the wealthy. But the Astors, the Goulds and even the Van Divers, Neil recalled, had prevailed upon the city fathers to stop the streetcar. "It's an invasion of privacy!" they claimed. Shortly afterward, the streetcar's tracks were torn up.

Neil's carriage slowed down in front of one of the larger storefronts. It had been freshly painted, he noticed, in anticipation of the coming season and a new sign hung out front. "McBride's Saloon," it read. There were two saloons in town. The other, Jay's, was at the opposite end of the long street. But Neil preferred McBride's.

Jame T. McBride was a rough man, but he was also fair and, consequently, he became popular. Everyone told him their troubles. If anyone knew the gossip in town, McBride did. That was the reason Neil had sought him out.

"Ah, Mr. Prescott!" McBride cried cheerfully as Neil entered. "Can I get you a drink?"

There were only two customers at the long bar. Both of them looked as though they'd been sitting in the darkened room, which knew neither day nor night, for the past twenty-four hours.

"Sorry, no." Neil shook his head. "I just stopped in for a moment to see how you were getting along."

"Could be better. I'm lookin' forward to a good season, however." He grinned, displaying a few prominent gaps in his mouth.

"Good. How's your competition?"

McBride shrugged. His was by far the more popular of the two bars, but as each season opened, he became a little uneasy.

"I hear Jay's taken a partner," he said. The grin had faded. "Someone named Cassidy—know him? Owned a saloon on the lower East Side, I understand."

Neil frowned, trying to place him.

"Joe Cassidy?" McBride went on.

"Oh, yes," Neil said. "He was run out a while ago. He paid off Tammany, but even with payoffs, they had to get rid of him, finally. So now he's up here?"

McBride nodded. "Yeah. And he's brought an element with him. . . ." He paused.

Neil, who wasn't too fond of the element already in town, said quickly, "What do you mean?"

"Well, he claims to be more respectable than thou. He carries an ivory cane, and the way he dresses, with those fancy Prince Albert coats with poke collars! Still, I see guys hanging around—mugs, I call 'em."

McBride paused to wipe off the bar. "Anyway," he finished, "there's a bunch of 'em. A bunch too many."

Neil shrugged. "That's too bad." He put his hat on. "Well, thanks, McBride. I'll be stopping back in a few weeks. Good luck with the season."

He had not intended to make any more stops; he had a long drive ahead of him, after all. But curiosity and a nagging worry in back of his head made him stop off at Jay's at the other end of the street.

Just as he was getting out of the carriage to go into Jay's, he saw him—a light-haired, wiry mug, as McBride would have called him. Neil might have taken no notice of him, but there was something familiar about him. After a moment, he shrugged and walked on into Jay's.

Jay was a loud-mouthed braggart whom Neil had never been very fond of, but at that moment, Neil would have preferred to see him than the dandy who approached him.

"Welcome! I'm Joe Cassidy, the new owner!" He held out his hand.

As Neil shook hands with him, he noted, in the back of his mind, that Cassidy had said "owner," not "half-owner." It might have simply been bragging, or might, possibly, have been the truth; he might have bought Jay out.

"A whiskey? A Beer?" Cassidy offered. "What'll it be?"

Neil didn't want anything, but he shrugged and said, "A small whiskey."

As Cassidy turned to get the whiskey, Neil studied him. The boiled shirt, the fancy tie, the coat looked much too grand to be worn behind a bar.

"How do you like the town?" Neil asked when Cassidy served the whiskey.

"It'll be fine enough when I get settled." Cassidy grinned. "As far as I can see, whether you like the town or not depends on which side of town you're on." Cassidy winked and laughed.

The laugh rankled Neil. "And you intend to get on the right side of town, is that it?"

Cassidy grinned and downed a whiskey. "By hook or by crook, yes."

Most likely by crook, Neil thought. He pushed his untouched whiskey away. He'd had enough of Mr. Cassidy, he decided, tossing some change on the bar.

"Little too early for me, I guess," he muttered, and started out.

As the door swung behind him, he saw the mug standing by a tree. Afterward, he would wonder what made him call out, but he did.

"Hey, you there!" he cried. "I want a word with you."

The mug cocked an eyebrow. "Oh, yeah?"

Neil walked toward him and held out a thin cigar. "Like one?"

The mug shrugged and stuck the cigar in his pocket.

"You know Mr. Cassidy, I take it?" Neil began in a light, conversational tone.

Another shrug. "We've been friends for years."

"From New York, you mean?" Neil said quickly.

The mug frowned. "Yeah," he said, after a moment. "He's good people."

"Is he?"

"Yeah." The mug pulled the cigar out of his pocket, lit it and with a brief nod, walked off.

Neil was left watching him, feeling a bit perplexed. Why had he stopped the mug in the first place? Again, it was because of that resemblance to—whom? But he couldn't put his finger on it. He turned and started toward the carriage. . . .

In the shadows of a nearby store, Kevin stood, watching. He had placed Neil almost at once. Hadn't he seen him coming out of his sister's place one day? Had he been visiting again? he wondered. And what would the English gent think of that? Kevin smiled to himself. Any intrigue, or even the possibility of one, always fascinated him. . . .

Neil jumped in the carriage and started the horses off at a brief pace. He was in a hurry to get back to the city. The new people in town were not to his liking, but he told himself that Maura would be perfectly all right as long as she had the sense to obey his instructions. As far as he was concerned, he had done his duty.

And when would he see her again? He tried to put that thought out of his mind. Whether he would or not depended on the result of the inquiries he made in New York. But he couldn't help feeling—why?—it would be a long time before he would be coming back to Newport. . . .

Chapter Fifteen

"*YOU'LL FIND US ROUGH, SIR, BUT YOU'LL FIND us ready.*"

Maura rested her copy of *David Copperfield* on the coverlet. The urchins Dickens talked about reminded her of her own life on the lower East Side. Their cleverness, their wiliness! Their heroes had not been the ones they'd read about in school, like Washington, Lincoln, Grant. No, they'd been, instead, gangsters, anyone who was two steps ahead of the law. The man who could make a dollar by outsmarting a cop—*he* was a hero. There was a man called One Lung Kelly in the neighborhood, renowned because one night, when his girlfriend admired a policeman's warm coat, he blackjacked the policeman and stole the coat! Because of Kelly, a dozen women in the neighborhood had sported policemen's overcoats that winter.

Then there was the gambling. Illegal, of course, but it was everywhere. Walk into any saloon and a game of chance would be going on. On weekends, there were cockfights or, if the entrepreneurs couldn't get their hands on two cocks, two mean bulldogs would do.

The young boys became gamblers at an early age. "To strike it rich"—that was the motto they grew up on. They had watched their fathers attempting to do the same thing. Thinking about them and their fathers, Maura was reminded of Mr. Micawber in *David Copperfield:* "Make five pounds, spend four, happiness; make five pounds, spend six, misery." Yes, they were all in misery.

Of course, that's why Kevin had come to her. And how much in debt was he? she wondered. And was Cassidy involved? She had no way of knowing either, though one thing she did know: no matter how much money she'd given him, Kevin would never have been able to extricate himself. He had the taste for gambling, as other men had the taste for whiskey, for women.

Women brought Neil to mind. Maura had told herself she would never again be jealous of Neil. Yet now that they were apart, she couldn't help wondering. She kept thinking about that dark, gypsy-type woman. She kept remembering, also, how women had clamored after Neil at parties and other social events. Perhaps she might have forgotten all this if she'd heard from him.

But it was more than a week now, and she'd had only silence from Neil. Due to the storm, the phone had been out. Phones, which had come to Newport in the early 1880s to be used almost exclusively by the residents of the "kingdoms," were often put out of service by storms. But the phone was in working order now and had been for days. Still, she hadn't heard from him.

She doubted Neil had the same reservations she had about phones. The first phone she'd ever used had been shortly before her marriage. The wonder of it—that a human voice would be carried over a wire!—was something she had not yet gotten over. She still felt awkward speaking over the phone. Perhaps, she told herself, to a lesser degree Neil felt the same. Or at least he might have felt unable to express what he wanted to freely and with ease over the phone.

Of course, he might have written. That might explain the silence, she told herself. It would take time for a letter. Each day, faithfully, she waited for the mail, telling herself she would hear the next day. But the next day came, and she did not hear. . . .

She consoled herself with the thought that Neil had promised he'd see her in two weeks, and the two weeks would be up shortly. And Harold would be coming to Newport in a few days. He'd written that he was in New York and would be paying her a visit. Maura was a little anxious because of Neil, but she reasoned that Harold was a good friend and there was no reason he and Neil shouldn't also be friends.

She yawned and switched off the lamp. She had a busy day ahead of her. She would try to get some rest.

* * *

A bluebird sitting on the window ledge announced the morning. As she slipped out of bed to wash and dress, Maura began to hum.

The song was "Tim Flaherty." It was the story of a lighthearted Irish lad of eighteen and his unhappy experience as an immigrant runner. It had been a favorite of her father's; singing it made her feel closer to him.

It was a day for singing. Except for her slight uneasiness about Neil's silence, she was the happiest of creatures. Her son was growing bigger and more beautiful every day. She and Neil had reconciled and, as far as she knew, would be seeing each other shortly. And she had begun plans for her party.

Newport's glittering social season would be launched at the end of the month. Maura expected the other residents of the "kingdoms" along Ocean Drive and Bellevue Avenue to be arriving sometime next week to put their households in order for the season. Two days before, Maura had received an invitation to the first party.

Mrs. Stuyvesant Fish would be giving it in collaboration with Harry Lehr. Lehr had recently supplanted Ward McAllister as the Four Hundred's playboy. The "Beau Brummel of the Nineties," they called Lehr. He and Mrs. Astor were dubbed the "Queen and her Jester." It was said of Lehr that any party in which he'd had a hand would be a success. He was amusing, he was eccentric and he became popular not only with Mrs. Astor but with the other reigning social queens like

Mrs. Belmont, Mrs. Gould and Mrs. Fish. He had become so popular that he was generally the first to be consulted with when a party was in the planning stages.

Maura had thought about consulting Lehr for advice on her party, but she hesitated. The year before, she'd read about a party Lehr had given, called "The Dogs' Dinner." A hundred dogs and their masters had been invited. The menu had been stewed liver and rice, fricassee of bones and shredded dog biscuit. According to news reports, the dinner had been greatly appreciated; the guests ate until they could eat no more. One chubby dachshund had so overtaxed himself that he fell unconscious on his plate and, in disgrace, was carried home. The paper's report of the party was scathing. Preachers throughout the country denounced Lehr for wasting money that could have been spent to feed starving people. Lehr and society shrugged off the criticism, but it made Maura wonder if she really wanted someone so eccentric to help with her party. She didn't think so.

She had been to enough parties during the social season in New York to realize that what she did *not* want was what was called an "amusing party." Like the one Mrs. Astor had given in her barn the year before, in order to "do something different." Despite the fact that the barn had been scrubbed and scrubbed, nothing could disguise the smell of manure. Was that amusing? Maura didn't think so.

There was one kind of party she did enjoy: a masquerade ball. Mrs. Belmont had given a magnificent one the year before. It was said to have cost $250,000, more than had ever been spent in the United States for one party. The papers compared it to the feast of Alexander the Great at Babylon, to the shows put on by Cleopatra for Mark Antony and to the spectacular entertainment of Louis XIV, the Sun King.

The ball had featured a variety of fancy dress tableaux, including scenes from Fairyland, Mother Goose, the Picture Galleries, the Courts and Camps of Europe, Audubon's Birds of America, Heathen Myths and Christian Legends. All of this took place in a huge, mirrored ballroom, with baskets and urns full of hothouse roses and palm trees hung with chains of posies and peonies and pale orchids. The flowers alone were said to have cost $20,000. Their scent, Maura remembered, had been almost overpowering.

Also overpowering had been the dress of the Belmonts. Mr. Belmont had come as the Duc de Guise, Mrs. Belmont as a Venetian princess. His sisters had been, variously, a marquise, a hornet and Little Bo-Peep. All had participated in well-rehearsed quadrilles. One was a hobby-horse quadrille, for which they wore red coats and white satin skirts, while the men changed to red coats with white breeches. "All that was needed was a fox," one paper had commented.

The dramatic climax, however, had been

the late entry of Mrs. Astor. She, too, had been dressed as a Venetian princess, but she outshone Mrs. Belmont by wearing *all* of her jewels.

Maura, who'd come as Juliet in a simple white dress, had been much praised. She was sorry afterward, however, she hadn't chosen something more elaborate, like Marie Antoinette, or Madame de Pompadour or Cleopatra. It had passed through her mind that if she gave her own masquerade ball, she might be able to choose a really exciting, elaborate costume. It was a temptation. Yet, she'd decided after much deliberation, she would give the kind of party she most enjoyed going to herself: an old-fashioned grand ball.

To begin with, it suited the house. It was, without par, the most majestic house she'd ever seen. Only a grand ball, she thought, would do it justice.

But the preparations for such a ball—finding a caterer, a decorator, a florist! Hiring musicians! Seeing about, oh, the thousand and one things that must be seen to. Maura could not possibly do it all herself. She'd have to find someone to coordinate all of it. Perhaps, she thought, Neil might be able to suggest someone. Or maybe Harold, with all of his friends, might know someone. If not, she might be forced to ask Harry Lehr.

She would have to make a decision shortly. In the meantime, she decided to begin the preliminary work herself. She should have some ideas before she spoke to anyone. It was said that the florist in town was very creative and helpful. She decided she would stop in and see him this morning.

The bluebird was still singing cheerfully as she set out. Abby sat beside her in the carriage, claiming one window while Maura claimed the other. They were both excited about this first opportunity of seeing the town they'd had no chance of glimpsing during the storm.

Along Bellevue Avenue, Maura noted some of the rival kingdoms. There was Château-Sur-Mer, said to be one of the finest examples of lavish Victorian architecture in America. It had been erected in 1852 for William S. Wetmore, who had made his fortune in the China trade. There was Kingscote, a charming Victorian cottage built in 1839 by Richard Upjohn for George Noble Jones of Savannah, Georgia. The King family was living there now, Maura had been informed, which is how it had received its name. Finally, there was Rosecliff, not yet completed, but under design by Stanford White, modeled after the Grand Trianon at Versailles.

Though the other kingdoms were lovely, Maura thought (and Abby concurred) that they could not compare with the Van Diver residence. The name—"The Elms"—however, she felt did not really suit it. She would have to think of a new name, she decided. Perhaps they could christen the name at the same time she held the grand ball.

But there was plenty of time to think about both. She glanced back, forth, from her guidebook to the changing scene alongside her. She was enjoing the trip. Yet she was aware of a certain anxiety about what to expect when she reached the town. In a way, she wished Neil had not had his talk with her. At any rate, she remembered her promise to him. She would take her footman with her. So, she chided herself, there was no reason to feel anxious.

Her first impression of the town was one of compactness and of quaint and unusual charm. The old State House, at the head of Washington Square, had been built in 1739, she read in her guidebook. The gracious Colonial structure had been used as a hospital during the Revolution. She passed Touro Park, with its bronze statue of Matthew C. Perry, who negotiated the Japanese treaty of 1854. And not too far away, she saw Prescott House, named after the tyrannical British General Richard Prescott, who, during the Revolutionary War when the British occupied the city, had treated the residents with cruelty and disdain. Whenever he saw people standing together or talking or laughing, he'd cry: "Disperse, ye rebels!" Every woman was told she must bow low and every man was forced to remove his hat and remain bareheaded until the General had passed by.

"Here we are!" Abby cried.

Maura glanced up. Abby was pointing excitedly to the row of stores they were approaching.

"Yes!" she said. "Let's see. I think we'll stop at the dry-goods store first."

The driver let them off in front of a freshly white-washed shop. With John, the footman, on one side and Abby on the other, Maura entered the shop.

It was a brief stop. Maura had promised the housekeeper she would order material for new uniforms for the staff. She also picked up some light cotton to be made into suits for Peter.

"The florist isn't far," she said when they came out. "Why don't we walk?"

The florist's window, Maura was pleased to see, was simply, tastefully decorated with a lily-of-the-valley motif, and sprigs of wisteria and bunches of violets scattered about. "It's a small shop," Maura noted. "You can wait outside if you like, John, and get the air. I'll take Abby in with me."

Like the window, the interior was also in simple good taste. As Maura paused to admire, a tall, heavily built young man with close-cropped hair and spectacles hurried toward them. Maura noted that his face was attractive and shone with a natural intelligence.

"How do you do?" he greeted Maura amiably. "I'm Manny Greenberg. And you're Mrs. Van Diver, aren't you? It's a pleasure!"

"You recognized me?" Maura said, puzzled.

"From a photograph. Though I must say, it doesn't do you justice."

Usually such a remark would have made

Maura flush, but there was a frank, honest attitude about the young man she liked.

"I'll tell you why I'm here," she smiled. "I'm planning a party this season. To be frank, I've made no decisions as to when or any of the other particulars. I thought you might be able to suggest some ideas about flowers, perhaps?"

"I'd be delighted. Please sit down."

He ushered Maura and Abby into straight-backed chairs, and retrieved some paper and a pencil. "I had the privilege of seeing the Van Diver home two years ago," he said. "It's not a house you forget quickly. I have a few ideas. . . ."

Quickly, he sketched the lobby and entranceway.

"Here," he penciled in. "Perhaps some roses here. You haven't decided on a color scheme yet, I assume. I suggest white. Perhaps a few sprays of yellow-gold roses here. . . ." He penciled in the long hallway and the baskets of flowers he envisioned lining it.

As he continued, the party, just an embryo in Maura's mind until now, suddenly matured and came to life. She listened breathlessly, her eye on the quick pencil that skimmed along the paper.

When he finished, she smiled delightedly. "You're wonderful! The job is yours!" she went on impulsively. "That is," she added, "if you want it?"

He bowed his head. "I'd be honored," he said simply.

"And perhaps you'll have suggestions about some of my other problems?" She smiled again. "I'm sure you will. You'll come to the house for tea next week and we'll discuss them."

"I'd love to. I'll bring some plans with me. . . ."

He paused. As he did, Maura noted two things. First, he was wearing a close-fitting cap. Secondly, the sweep of his eyes had included, with interest, Abby. Little Abby, who was now blushing. . . .

Maura smiled and rose.

"Wait!" he said. "Just one minute."

He rushed into the other room, returning a moment or so later with a half-dozen long-stemmed roses wrapped in a pretty yellow paper.

"For you." He held out the roses to Maura, smiling. Then, turning to Abby, he gave her a single rose.

Abby flushed again.

"No visitor," Manny Greenberg explained hastily, "ever leaves empty-handed."

He was smiling, but the smile faded suddenly.

"What is it?" Maura said. Instinctively, she turned to follow his gaze.

He was staring out the window at three or four mugs who were lounging like lizards in the sun on the other side of the street. "I'll see you to your carriage," the florist said.

"Oh, there's no need," Maura said quickly. "My footman is waiting outside."

"Are you sure?" He looked concerned. "I

don't know what this town is coming to. I've had trouble before, but lately. . . ." He shrugged. "I really would feel much better if I escorted you."

"But it's not necessary," Maura insisted. "Really."

She held out her hand and he shook it briefly.

"I'll expect you about four on Monday. Is that all right?" she asked.

"Yes. And it's been a pleasure."

Maura stepped out of the shop with a light, confident air. "Do you like your flower?" she teased Abby.

"It's pretty," Abby said, shyly.

"He's a nice young man," Maura said. "What was that little cap on his head, do you know?"

"A yarmulke," Abby said. "Jewish men often wear them."

"Oh?" Maura was surprised that Abby should know. She would have questioned her further, but she suddenly stopped short.

"Where's John?"

Abby was looking around. "I don't know. Perhaps he took a walk?"

Maura said nothing. Abby knew as well as she that John was not one to disobey orders. She'd asked him to wait outside the shop; he would have waited.

"Let's walk toward the carriage," she suggested. "Maybe he's there."

They started up the street. Along the way, Maura noted that the youths they'd noticed from Manny Greenberg's window had disappeared. She wondered if Abby had also noticed. But she said nothing.

Suddenly, she jerked to a halt. There was a slight, strange sound, like a baby's cry. Maura had lived on the street all her life and she recognized danger when she heard it. She held her breath, waiting.

There was another, slightly sharper sound. This time, Maura was able to locate the direction it was coming from. At once, she started toward it.

"Where are you goin', ma'am?" Abby cried.

"You stay here," Maura told her.

But Abby hurried alongside her. She was terrified for herself, but she was more terrified for her mistress.

"Let's go back to the carriage," Abby pleaded as they turned the corner into a street so narrow it might have been an alleyway.

"Go back!" Maura told her again.

But the girl stayed stubbornly beside her. Then they both stopped short.

Maura stared. At the other end of the narrow street, they stood. How many, she wasn't sure, perhaps a half-dozen. They were standing over something—*someone*? Her heart skipped a beat. Could it be John?

Without stopping to think, she started toward them. If she had stopped, she might have realized how foolish it was. She should have gone back to get help. But her anger spurred her on.

As she grew closer, she recognized John's uniform. She heard him groan piteously as someone kicked him in the side.

"Stop it!" she cried.

They spun around. They hadn't seen her till now. Two of them stood in front of the others, grinning, and with hands on hips, waited for her.

Maura had nothing to defend herself with. All she held were the roses in her arms. When she was close enough, she threw them in a mug's face.

"Get out of here!" she ordered furiously. "I'll call the Sheriff!"

"Will ya now?" The first boy leered at her. The second youth grabbed her arm. He made the mistake, however, of grabbing it lightly. Maura yanked herself free and with all the force in her body slapped him across the face.

"Hey!" Furious now, an angry welt across his face, he stepped toward her.

Maura held her ground. She raised her fists to defend herself.

But suddenly, the boy backed away. A moment later, they all turned tail and ran.

"I knew I shouldn't let you go off alone."

Maura and Abby whirled around and saw the florist waving a menacing cane.

"Are you all right?" he asked.

"Yes. Thank you. But look at poor John!" Maura ran to him, examining him. "My poor footman! He's bleeding! Do you have a handkerchief?"

"It's not a bad cut, though." Manny Greenberg held his handkerchief to the wound. "I think he'll be all right. Can you sit up, man?"

John obliged with a small groan.

"Do you think you can stand up?" the florist went on. "Here, let me help you."

With his arm around the florist, John was able to limp back to the carriage. Besides the cut over his eye, he'd twisted his ankle when he fell. Other than that, and the fact that last week's wages were no longer in his pocket, he seemed in good condition.

"I'll see about your wages, of course," Maura said, "but I wonder if we shouldn't take you to a doctor?"

"No, I'm fine," John insisted as he climbed into the carriage.

"I wonder if you could do one more favor for me?" Maura asked Manny Greenberg. "I think John should be driven directly home. Would it be possible for you to notify the Sheriff for us?"

"I will. For all the good it will do," he added doubtfully.

Maura raised a pale brow. "What do you mean?"

"Just that the Sheriff, if past performance is any indication, won't do very much about it. Unfortunately."

"But a man's been hurt! Robbed!" Maura said, indignantly. "He must do something!"

The florist shrugged his shoulders helplessly.

"I see," Maura said. Though she did not.

"I'm sorry, Mrs. Van Diver. Here, let me help you." Manny Greenberg gave Maura, then Abby, a hand into the carriage.

"We are all in your debt," Maura told him.

"No, I am in yours. All I ask is that in the future, you do not put yourself in such danger."

"I promise. I look forward to seeing you on Monday."

He stood on the corner watching as the carriage left. Maura spun around to wave at him. Just as she was ready to sit back in her seat, she spied something that made her start again. Off in an adjoining street, she saw two more youths emerge. She was at a disadvantage, at a distance, but she could have sworn one of them was Kevin.

The carriage turned toward the shore road. Maura sat back in her seat. It had been an unsettling ending to an unsettling day.

Chapter Sixteen

MAURA'S LIFE, WHICH HAD SEEMED ON SOLID ground for a short while, suddenly began to waver, as though she were standing on a piece of marshland. Solid, dry earth, that's what she wanted. But it kept evading her. . . .

The two weeks had passed and Neil had not come. Nor had she heard from him. She was hurt as well as puzzled. After debating with herself, she'd finally put through a call to his office. "Mr. Prescott is not in," she was informed. She'd hung up hastily.

She would not call back. She consoled herself with the thought that he would call, he would come in time. He must have a reason for his silence. He must!

As perplexed and upset as she was about Neil, she was equally perplexed and upset about the incident in town. Fortunately, John was fine. According to Manny Greenberg, the Sheriff had been notified and had promised to "make an investigation."

"We shall see what kind of an investigation," the florist had shrugged doubtfully.

"Aren't you concerned?" Maura had asked. "Having a shop in the center of town?"

"Fortunately, there's very little in my shop anyone would want. And I always keep my trusty cane on hand, and lately, a handgun."

"I thought we were living in a civilized society," Maura said later, when she related the incident to Harold.

Harold had just come in from New York and would be stopping in Newport for at least two weeks, perhaps a month, he'd said, which cheered Maura. Though he himself did not look particularly cheery now.

"What got into you, Maura?" he cried angrily. "To go after those youths the way you did! You might have been seriously hurt! Did you stop to consider that?"

It was the first time Maura had seen Harold angry, but she realized it was because he was concerned. "I wasn't hurt, was I?" she said. "And besides," she reasoned, "what else could I have done, with John lying there!"

"You might have gone for help instead. That would have been the sensible thing to do."

"Ah—but by the time I'd gone for help, who knows what might have happened to him. Besides," she added, "they made me so furious."

"That was the real reason, wasn't it?" he said quickly. "Your temper."

Maura's cheeks flushed. That Irish temper. "Well, perhaps," she admitted. "But it was righteous anger. Someone had to do something about those boys."

"You are a woman, Maura, and as a

woman, you are vulnerable. You cannot place yourself in positions of danger."

"I am also a person," she said. "And I will not stand by while injustice is being done!"

Harold fell silent. He stood, then walked to the fireplace. Though the days were growing warmer, the evenings were still cool and a fire had been laid. He warmed his hands in front of it. "Tell me," he said, after a few moments, "is there something I can do?"

Maura hesitated. "It is no concern of yours, Harold."

"You are wrong. If it is your concern, it is mine." He walked toward her and sat on the edge of the couch. "Now, tell me."

"Well—" She paused an instant, then rushed on. "I would like to know a little more about this Sheriff. Who he is, why he's so lackadaisical. I'd also like to find out more about these youths. I understand they're a new element in town. Someone is bringing them in for a purpose. And I'd like to know what that purpose is."

"Suppose I ask my friends?" Harold suggested.

Maura nodded. "Thank you."

"And the fee I will extract for that," Harold went on, "is your promise not to go into town."

"Harold!"

"I mean it. I will not have you take risks."

Maura hesitated again. She was well aware that, if she so chose, she might have wrapped Harold around her little finger. But on this particular matter, he remained firm.

"I promise," she said.

He smiled. "Good. Now, shall we forget this and have another brandy? And you shall tell me about the ball we're going to tomorrow. . . ."

It was the opening dinner-dance of the summer social season. Mrs. Stuyvesant Fish was giving it in collaboration with Harry Lehr, and in honor of Prince Drago from Corsica. Maura had never heard of him, but she'd assumed Harold had. "No," he told her, and admitted he was equally curious. A Corsican prince would have excited anyone's curiosity.

On the following evening, Maura dressed in a new silk gown of pale gold. The neckline was deep and square and it was trimmed with a border of seed pearls. She wore a simple strand of pearls around her neck to match them, and carried a fox stole. Harold, wearing white dinner dress, picked her up in his gray-toned carriage.

"It's a curious thing," he commented. "But no one seems to know anything at all about this prince. I've met two Corsicans in my life and both have been extremely colorful characters. If our prince is anything like them, he'll be worth wearing this stiff collar."

Maura laughed. All she knew of Corsica was what she'd read in her books. She pictured a land of silver olive trees and green rolling hills. The prince was probably a superb horseman. Yes, it would be interesting to meet him.

When they reached the Fishes, however, they discovered that the Prince had not yet arrived, though almost everyone else had.

The highest people in society had been assembled, including many notable men in government—several ambassadors, a senator, a former vice-president. Most of the people were older than Maura; most were from the Northeast, though some came from other parts of the country, including the South and Southwest. What they all had in common, however, was the social circle they belonged to.

After paying their respects to Mrs. Fish, Maura and Harold were swept up by Harold's friends.

"Will you be coming out with us on the yacht this season?" one of the friends asked.

"Perhaps. If Mrs. Van Diver consents to come too," Harold said, with a side glance at Maura.

She smiled a little distractedly. This particular friend of Harold's could be very trying with his preoccupation with yachts. At the last party, he'd boasted about his new "floating palace," as he'd called it, with its marble dining room, its salons lined with rosewood, its red plush carpets everywhere, its half-dozen bathrooms, all with gold spigots and plumbing.

"I would be honored if Mrs. Van Diver would be my guest," he said gallantly. "You know that Morgan's bought a new yacht," he went on rapidly. "He's calling it 'Corsair.' You've heard he claims descent from Henry Morgan, the pirate."

There was a laugh all around; even Maura laughed slightly. But Harold, quick to sense her discomfort, invented an excuse and whisked her away to the terrace.

"Are you not feeling well?" he asked as she rested by the edge of the stone wall that looked out to the sea.

"No, I'm fine," she assured him. "I'm sorry if I'm not good company."

"You? You are better company than any woman I've ever known," he said.

He fell silent as he observed her. The terrace was moonlit and under it, Maura's skin turned a pure, luminous white, with her hair a golden halo. Except for one other couple, they were alone on the terrace. The setting was pure romance; yet there was an aura about Maura that seemed to say, don't touch me. And Harold understood why. . . .

"You're still thinking about him, aren't you?" he said suddenly.

Maura started, then nodded guiltily. It had occurred to her when they'd walked into the party that Neil might be here. It was a strange notion. She couldn't believe he'd come into town without calling her, seeing her, and yet—could she be so sure? His behavior had certainly been strange. . . .

"You've been seeing him, haven't you?" Harold said. "I can see it in your eyes."

"I did," Maura said. "He came to Newport at the beginning of May. We were reconciled," she finished simply.

"Well . . ." There was a pause. "I'm happy for you," Harold said, taking her hand.

Maura smiled. "Thank you. But since we've always been frank with one another, I'll tell you I haven't heard from him in a while. It worries me."

"You will hear," he said, patting her hand. "Is there anything else worrying you?"

"I suppose the situation in town. I've tried to put it out of my mind as you said, but I can't. Have you found out anything from your friends?"

"Be patient. It's a little too soon. And now—" He paused. From the ballroom, there was a sudden barrage of noises: clapping, stamping of feet, laughter.

"What do you suppose has happened?" Harold said. "Shall we investigate?"

Walking back to the room, they saw a crowd of people, with Harry Lehr in the center. It was impossible to see anything else, and Harold, holding Maura's hand, inched his way through the crowd toward Lehr.

"How do you do, Lord Parker? And Mrs. Van Diver," Lehr said, when he spotted them. "Would you like to meet the charming Prince Drago of Corsica?"

Maura gasped. A small monkey, exquisitely attired in white evening dress, stood beside Lehr.

Recovered, Maura stepped forward, smiling. "So this is the famous Prince Drago," she said. The monkey held out his hand. She shook it.

Everyone was delighted. The monkey somberly shook a few more hands, then preceded the rest of the party, as befits the guest of honor, into the dining room.

They feasted on huge prawns, rare beef

with wild mushrooms and a pink-and-white *bombe* for dessert. Prince Drago, as well as everyone else, thoroughly enjoyed himself.

The following day, however, the newspapers soundly criticized both Lehr and Mrs. Fish. "They held American society and in particular, Newport society, up to ridicule!" one paper claimed.

Mrs. Fish and Lehr, it was reported, simply laughed it off, pleased as punch with having pulled such a huge joke. But Maura, for one, found herself agreeing with the papers. The joke was on Mrs. Fish and Lehr, however, as far as she was concerned. For they were the ones who'd begun the practice of making so much of European royalty and who were, to this day, making much of them. No, their party for Prince Drago had boomeranged on themselves.

She was now very glad she'd decided to have nothing at all to do with Lehr. Manny, the florist, was coming along superbly with his plans and preparations for her ball. The one problem was that she still had not set a date. She wondered if the reason she still had not committed herself was because she wanted to set it at a time when she knew Neil would be able to come. So that she might come into the Ball on his arm? That, after all, had been part of her dream. . . .

But how foolish! She could not keep putting off the ball indefinitely. She promised Manny she would give him a definite date at the end of the week.

A few days after Mrs. Fish's party, Harold

escorted Maura to one other party, a small, quiet dinner. Other than that, Maura had seen very little of him. She was disappointed, though she told herself she couldn't blame Harold. She had been very definite about her feelings about Neil. Only afterward had she realized how painful it must have been for Harold. He was one of the people she wanted most *not* to hurt, but they had always been frank with one another. At least, she had been; she had explained her feelings from the very beginning. Perhaps, she suspected, that in spite of what she'd said, Harold had continued to harbor a secret hope. If so, it explained why, disappointed, he was neglecting her a little now.

Maura had been mistaken about Harold. He had known all along that his chances with her were slight, if any. But he had been drawn to her from the very beginning because he'd felt she needed a friend. He still felt that way. The reason for his absence was not, as Maura suspected, that he was disappointed in love, but that he was busy carrying on his own investigation of what was happening in town.

He'd learned from his friends that the Sheriff, who himself was one of the footstools, naturally favored them in any dispute. Any irregularities or small grievances, if they were committed by footstools, also tended to be overlooked.

But did the Sheriff approve of the new element in town? Of this, Harold's friends could not be sure. After all, to wink at small injustices was one thing, but to blatantly encourage thievery and—as had happened the other night—wholesale destruction by a stick of dynamite tossed in a window was another.

"It's as though the anarchist had brought his wares to Newport," one of Harold's friends said.

"Unfortunately, that may be true," Harold said, after a moment.

The more he thought about it, the more he worried about it. He would be leaving for England in just a few weeks. What might happen to Maura? Even if she kept her promise to stay out of town, she might be at a party where a bomb went off. Why, she might be maimed! Killed!

The thought unnerved him. To put his mind at ease, he declined a dinner invitation from Maura one evening and decided to take what he'd learned from his friends one step further.

All of his information pointed to Jay's Saloon as the center of whatever mischief was going on. He would go there, Harold decided. At the last moment, he asked one of his friends, Carter Jennings, an Englishman who'd relocated permanently in America, to come along.

"We're going slumming," Carter called it jokingly. Then, a little worriedly, he added: "You don't expect any trouble, do you?"

"We will make it our business to keep out of trouble," Harold assured him. "We are going to observe, that's all."

It was a Friday evening. Harold had picked

Friday since it was the night residents of Bellevue Avenue and Ocean Drive sometimes took a drive to town to visit the two saloons, "slumming." It was the safest night to go, Harold decided, since the two of them would not look too much out of place.

As they entered Jay's, a society couple from Bellevue Avenue waved. "Lord Parker!" the matron cried.

"Hello," he smiled, flushing. Drat that woman! he thought. Calling out his name had gotten everyone's attention. He was grateful to see the men turned quickly back to the bar. Harold and Carter walked past the couple, and took seats at the bar.

Harold had decided beforehand to sit at the bar. He could observe better from here, he thought. And, he might start a conversation with the bartender.

But not this bartender. He regarded Harold and Carter with a curious look. "What'll it be, gents?" he growled.

Drat that woman! Harold thought again. Well, they'd have a drink and go.

"Whiskey and soda," he told the bartender.

"The same," Carter said.

On either side of Harold and Carter were men who, for the most part, were tradesmen, merchants and fishermen. The smells of fish and sweat, cigars and whiskey, were pungent.

Harold sipped his whiskey, and tuned in to the conversation. Some of the men were laughing, more than a few were complaining.

"Business ain't what it used to be."

249

"For O'Malley, it is. Whatever his losses, he tacks it on to whatever he charges the summer people. Ha!"

There was a roar of laughter. The summer people, of course, were the residents of the kingdoms. At that moment, those residents were represented at the bar by Harold and Carter, whose presence, thanks to the woman, had not gone unnoticed.

"Maybe we should leave," Carter said, growing uneasy under the men's stares.

"Not yet," Harold insisted.

Carter groaned, but sipped his whiskey. He tuned in again.

What was it he expected to hear? Harold wasn't sure. But at that moment, both eyes and ears opened a little wider as Joe Cassidy walked in. Looking as much the dandy as ever, he took up a stance at one end of the bar. He also appeared to be observing.

Harold sipped his whiskey slowly, never taking his eyes from Cassidy. He recognized him at once from the descriptions he'd been given. If anyone held a clue to what was going on in town, it was Cassidy, Harold guessed. If he was lucky, Cassidy might lead him to something.

"How's about going?" Carter asked again. He was growing edgy.

"In a minute," Harold said. Someone had just walked up to Cassidy. No words were exchanged; there was simply a nod of the head. Then, the man turned and headed out the door.

Harold stiffened. When a moment later, Cassidy turned casually toward the door, Harold was ready.

He nudged Carter. "All right, let's go." He threw some money on the bar and started out.

Two steps outside of the saloon, Harold stayed Carter with his hand.

"Wha—?" Carter began, impatiently.

But Harold indicated with a nod of his head to be still. His instinct told him Cassidy and the other man had business they did not want to discuss in the bar. But where had they disappeared to?

The street in front of the saloon was quiet, but in the back, on the gravelly topping not yet paved, Harold heard the crunching sound of footsteps. He hurried to the corner, but when he reached it, he saw no one.

"Let's get the bloody hell out of here!" Carter said nervously.

But Harold had not gone this far to turn back. The moonlight caught a glint of steel from a closing door. A back entrance? Carefully, Harold started down the narrow path. A small portion of that path was still dirt, not gravel, and that was where he walked, as quietly as possible. Carter, muttering to himself, followed.

A few feet from the door, Harold stopped short. He heard voices.

"This is not what we agreed on!"

"I told you, Cassidy, half now, the other half when the job is done."

"But how do I know I'll be able to find you?"

"It's always me who's come looking for you, you know that, don't you? Don't worry. I'll come looking for you again."

"You ask me to take a great deal on faith, don't you?" Cassidy gave a short, harsh laugh. "This is a big one, you understand. I've got my problems. I understand the summer people are beefing up their security. That much dynamite is hard to move around. And that Belmont place has an eight-foot fence, not to mention dogs . . . !"

"Those are your problems," the other man interrupted. "All I want to know is do you want the job, or shall I find someone else?"

There was a disgusted grunt. Then, "OK."

A silence fell. Were they coming out? Harold wondered. But, at once, he heard: "Why don't we go over those plans again, Cassidy?"

Harold had just about decided to go. He'd heard more than enough. He could go to the Sheriff with this information. If the Sheriff didn't take action, he could go on to a higher authority. But with the mention of plans, Harold became greedy. Perhaps, if he waited a while longer, he might be handed a blueprint. . . .

"C'mon!" Carter whispered. "Let's get out of here!"

"Not yet," he began impatiently. Then he stopped. Did he really have the right to endanger Carter? He had enough information now.

"All right," he said. But as he turned to leave, he made a mistake and stepped on the gravelly path.

The door flew open. "Ha!" Cassidy cried. "What do we have here?"

"Cassidy, you fool!" The other man threw up his hands in front of his face. But a moment too late, for Harold had seen him. Vaguely, he recognized him, though he couldn't quite place him.

The man escaped into the darkness. A moment later, Harold felt a blinding blow on his head, and also escaped into darkness. . . .

Chapter Seventeen

Maura's Irish temper had been aroused in the past, but it had never been quite so aflame or furious as now. Because of Harold. For days, he lingered between life and death. Both he and Carter had had concussions, but Carter's was slight, and he was up and moving within twenty-four hours.

Harold was not so fortunate. Maura spent long hours by his bedside at the hospital. As she watched his pale, bandaged face, she grew angrier by the minute.

She had learned from Carter what had happened at the back door of Jay's Saloon. That one of the men had been Cassidy stunned her, but only for a moment. Cassidy had always been where there was trouble, so why not here?

Carter had gone with his information to the Sheriff, but he'd received little satisfaction. The Sheriff had advised the Belmonts to postpone their party. But, since Cassidy had vanished, the Sheriff had declined to do anything else.

"As it is," the Sheriff had told Carter, "all we have is your word that all of this transpired. It's quite possible, not having heard all, you misunderstood."

"Misunderstood? Then, what's this bump doing on my head?" Carter asked ruefully.

But the Sheriff had simply shrugged and walked off.

"What a stubborn, stupid man!" Maura had cried angrily when Carter told her. "Well, we'll just have to take things into our own hands!"

"We've done enough," Carter argued. "The Belmonts have postponed their party; we've run Cassidy out of town."

"Cassidy will be back," Maura said. "Wait and see. After a week or so has gone by, and he thinks it's safe enough, he'll be back. In the end, very little has been accomplished except to put poor Harold into a sickbed. Oh, I wish you knew who that other man was!"

"Told you, it was too dark. I never saw his face."

"Do you think Harold did?"

"Hard to say. Maybe."

If Harold had seen his face, there was no way of knowing at the moment. Maura consoled herself with the few, slight signs that said he was recovering. In the meantime, she decided after much thought that the wisest thing to do would be to form a kind of vigilante committee. Early one morning, she sat down and drafted a letter to all the residents of Bellevue Avenue and Ocean Drive, inviting them to a meeting at the Channing Memorial

Church. William Channing, pastor and head of the Unitarian Church, had graciously consented to housing the meeting.

The turnout was disappointing. To begin with, not one woman attended. About twenty men came and of these, less than half agreed with Maura that a vigilante committee should be formed. What heartened Maura, however, was that those who did agree with her were bright, stalwart men of action.

"Those young mugs should be thrown out!" George Bannister cried. Bannister was a stocky multi-millionaire who dressed eccentrically; in the past, Maura had not been especially fond of him, but she was pleased at the rapidity with which he'd backed her.

"We are in Mrs. Van Diver's debt!" he went on. "She's right! If we are to live in this town peacefully and to enjoy our summers without fear of incident or harm to our womenfolk, we will have to take matters into our own hands."

"A good start, George," William Wolf said, "would be to get rid of the Sheriff and get our own man."

"That might prove a little difficult," Bannister pointed out. "The important thing is to let him know we won't stand for any more nonsense. We will not be pushed around any longer."

"And just what will a vigilante committee do?" one disgruntled listener asked. "Will we be required to patrol our grounds? Or our neighbor's grounds?"

"We can hire guards to do that," Maura

said. "The main purpose of the committee," she went on, "should be investigative. When incidents occur, the vigilante committee should look into it at once. If we keep on top of what is going on, the Sheriff will realize he has to be more responsible."

"Very good," Bannister approved. "I do wish, however," he said, going back to his first concern, "there were some way of getting these mugs out of town."

"With Cassidy not around to pay them off, they'll probably leave of their own accord," someone suggested sagely.

And indeed, that seemed to be the case. Only a few days later, when Bannister stopped off to see Maura at the house, he reported as much.

"My son told me the other day. I pulled him on the carpet for going into town late, but he told me there's no problem. The mugs have left."

Had they? Maura wondered. When she saw the florist, she asked him.

"So it seems. And Bannister's son told him?" Manny grimaced.

"What is it?" Maura said quickly.

He shrugged. "George Bannister's a fine man. It's a shame he should be saddled with such a son."

"I don't know him," Maura said. Though, vaguely, she seemed to remember a dark, sullen-looking young boy who'd attended one of the winter balls.

"Well, the important thing," Manny continued cheerfully, "is the town is being cleaned up. I understand Mrs. Belmont has rescheduled her party. And that brings up another question."

"I know, Manny," she said with a sigh.

"Well, have you made your decision?"

She shrugged.

"I was thinking," Manny said, "the Fourth of July weekend would be ideal. How does that sound to you?"

"Well, yes . . ." Maura said at last.

Manny grinned triumphantly and Maura sighed again. But the date was set. . . .

Harold was making rapid strides. His color was back, he was eating well and though he tired easily, the doctor was releasing him from the hospital.

"But, you understand," the doctor said firmly, "you are under strict orders to rest for at least two weeks before making that arduous trip back to England."

"But I've already promised Mr. Gladstone I'll be back within the week!" Harold argued.

"Your first duty is to yourself," the doctor reminded him.

Reluctantly, Harold agreed. He would stay in Newport for two more weeks. Maura had offered the use of one of her cottages, but Harold declined. People would talk, he said. Luckily, however, a friend owned a nearby cottage. Harold made plans to stay there and to take most of his meals with Maura.

She was delighted. "You will have a wonderful rest; the cook will make all sorts of nourishing food. And we'll go to the beach. It'll be good for you."

Around noon, one sunny day, they set out for Bailey's Beach. Bailey's Beach was Newport's most exclusive recreational club. No footstool had ever bathed there; only the elite summer people were allowed. Guards were posted at intervals along the beach to protect it from interlopers. Unless they were accompanied by a club member or bore a note of introduction, they were ejected. If they liked, they might go to Easton's Beach, the common beach, where they might share the sea with the club members at Bailey's.

"It's rude, undemocratic and probably not even legal," Maura had said when she first heard the rules.

"I assure you it's perfectly legal," Harold told her. "A private club has the right to choose its own members. And while I agree with you that it's rude, there's very little we can do, Maura, about changing the world. At least in one single shot."

"I suppose so," she said. "Well, at least you," she went on, changing the subject, "look very nice."

He smiled. He was wearing the striped bathing pants and pajama-style top that were the usual bathing attire for men. "I'm not so sure about me," he said, "but you look lovely."

Maura wore, as the other women did, a full-skirted bathing costume, with long black stockings.

Only the baby wore a short bathing suit,

topped off by a floppy hat to protect him from sunburn. His mother also wore a floppy hat. Even though Harold had ordered a cabana, she kept the hat on to shade her eyes.

"It may be silly," she told Harold, "but not quite so silly as Mrs. Belmont, standing in that water, carrying a large green umbrella!"

They both laughed.

"And what about Mrs. Van Allen," Harold pointed. She was bathing, wearing a white straw hat with a monocle fixed, as usual, in her one near-sighted eye.

They laughed again.

"It's good to hear you laughing," Maura said. "There were times . . ." She did not finish.

"I know." He nodded. "Ah! If I ever get my hands on that Cassidy!"

He'd said it to provoke a laugh, but Maura only looked alarmed. "If you're ever even within breathing distance of him, I want you to turn around and run! You remember I kept my promise to you. I want you to promise me this!"

"Don't be so upset," Harold said at once. "I promise. Besides," he added, "it's an easy promise to make. We've seen and heard the last of him."

"I wonder," Maura said, half to herself. Harold had stretched out in the cabana and closed his eyes. Maura studied him for a moment. She still felt an incredible guilt that Harold should have been almost killed because of her. He had become incredibly dear to her, yet her feeling for him was as for a very sweet brother—the *sweet* brother she'd never had! In a way, it was a pity that she could not feel more, but we do not choose the ones we love, as her father used to say . . . and how unfortunate.

Harold was sleeping now, as was the baby, cuddled in his portable bed under the watchful eye of Miss Richards.

Maura yawned. The sun was climbing higher and hotter in the sky. The cool water looked inviting. She decided to take a dip.

She wore her floppy hat down to the water, tossing it on the beach as she started to wade. She was grateful, afterward, that the water was only ankle-high when she saw him. She surely would have fallen in. . . .

"Neil!" His name was out of her mouth before she could stop herself. But she was absolutely stunned at seeing him.

He stood on the edge of the beach looking, indeed, like a bronze God, Neptune, emerging from the deep sea. Maura was vaguely aware of a woman, not that dark, gypsy-type woman, but a redhead, standing off to the side. But Maura's eyes remained focused on Neil.

And his remained fixed on her. For he looked as stunned as she was feeling. A moment passed before either flicked a finger or even an eyelash.

Then Neil, without a word, started toward her. Was it something in his manner? His eyes? Maura, almost without realizing it, took a step backward, frightened.

He moved quickly then, and grabbed her, his large hands encircling her tiny waist. For one long moment, they simply stood, looking at one another. Maura had forgotten his eyes were such deep, black pools. She had forgotten, also, that they could shine with such wildness, such fire.

"What are you doing here?" she stammered at last. "Why did you stay away so long? Without calling me, without even a line . . . ?"

"Why? You ask me why?" Neil laughed, a short, harsh laugh that hurt Maura's ears. She clapped her hands over her ears and as she did, he scooped her up and carried her into the deep water with such ease that she might have been a child.

"Where are you taking me?" she cried. But still he said nothing. He was angry, that much Maura could tell, and she was afraid of that anger. And yet, she told herself, this was Neil, her love. Why should she fear him?

Suddenly, he stopped short. His lips, warm from the sun, brushed her cheek, then found her lips. The pressure of his lips drove all other thoughts from her mind. For a few brief moments, neither of them took any notice of where they were. All they were aware of at the moment was each other. Until a huge wave came, nearly drowning both of them.

"Maura?" Neil sputtered when the wave had passed, breaking further up, closer to shore. "Are you all right?" he asked.

She shook water out of her hair, her eyes. Salt water clung to her eyelashes like tears. She'd been certain she was going to drown. "Let's go back! Please, Neil!" she pleaded, frightened.

"Is that what you want?" His eyes were suddenly dark, intense pools. She could see that wild fire again. "And then, what?" he went on. "Will you go back to your fiancé? Will you?"

"Fiancé?" She frowned, trying to understand. "You mean, Lord Parker? But—but Harold is just my good friend. I don't understand."

"No." He shook his blond head impatiently. "Don't tell me that! Lord Parker"—he drew out the name, so that it sounded like an insult—"is much more than a friend."

She stared at him, puzzled.

He laughed harshly again. "You're acting as though you don't know? How like you! Always with the look of sweet innocence. Butter wouldn't melt in your mouth—would it? Would it?"

His voice grew harsher, more insistent. His grip on Maura tightened.

"Neil, you're hurting me!" she cried. "And I don't understand you! You're talking in riddles! Please—what are you trying to say?"

"You're just making it worse, Maura. Why won't you speak the truth? You know, I've checked up on your Lord Parker. He's one of the shrewdest businessmen around—and one of the most acquisitive. You couldn't have picked a better partner—for business, or love!"

"What?" She gulped, and swallowed a

mouthful of water. The waves, like small mountains, splashed and spattered against them. Maura swallowed sea water, again and again. She was becoming convinced that Neil had turned into a madman. What was he saying? She was sure she hadn't heard properly.

Now he pulled her closer. "I could drown you," he murmured.

His eyes told her that he could. "Neil!" she cried, her anger suddenly reviving itself. She loved this man, but if he'd suddenly turned crazy—that talk about Harold was crazy!— she would not allow him to drown her, not without a fight. She kicked, she punched. One hand drew blood across his cheek. Still, she could not free herself; instead of letting her go, he pulled her closer.

He kissed her again, a rough, maddening assault on her mouth. His tongue pillaged her lips, her mouth opened against her will. They both tasted of sun and sea, and Maura's cheeks tasted slightly of tears. Drained of strength, clinging to him, she was sure she was drowning—no, dead. She had one crazy image of the two of them drowned, but living together contentedly on the bottom of the sea, much as Neptune himself was reputed to live.

All at once, she felt sand and earth under her feet. They'd been swept back to shore. Sputtering and coughing, she was vaguely aware of Neil murmuring in her ear, "Goodbye, Maura."

She struggled to keep her footing. She was furious and upset, with both him and herself.

Tears mixed with salt water, blurring her vision.

Suddenly, a hand reached out to her. She grasped it and looked up into Harold's face.

"I was worried about you," he said, guiding her onto the dry sand. "What happened to you? You look like a drowned rat."

She said nothing, just clung to his arm. He'd found her floppy hat, and sat it on top of her head to hide the long clumps of wet hair.

"It was Prescott, wasn't it?" Harold guessed. "I saw him walking off the beach, looking very much like you."

"Please, Harold," she managed, after a moment. She heard him sigh, but she was grateful he did not question her further.

Guided by Harold, she limped to the cabana. She had turned her ankle somehow, and it ached; every part of her, in fact, ached. She collapsed into a chair in the cabana, gasping, taking great gulps of air. There were more tears behind her eyes, but she would not release them, not now with Harold watching.

She closed her eyes, and kept them tightly shut. Still, Neil's image pushed its way through. She saw an angry, accusatory Neil, a Neil who'd told her: "I could drown you . . . !" For an instant, she almost wished he had—that they had drowned together. At least, then, they would have been together. . . .

But how foolish! She was too much of a fighter to accept that. No, she would push him away, out of her thoughts.

Yet, try as she might, one image persisted: the image of him kissing her. She ran her tongue over her lips. She could still taste him, warm from the sun, then cool from the salt water. She wanted to forget, but she could not.

Chapter Eighteen

NEIL PRESCOTT WAS THOROUGHLY DISGUSTED with himself. Why had he come to Newport in the first place? he asked himself. Certainly there were other pleasure spots. He might have gone to Saratoga. It did not have the social life of Newport, but it had the casinos, the horses. Or, since the summer was his slow season, he might have gone to Europe, at least for part of the summer. He had many friends who spent the entire season in Europe. He was well aware that these were also the people who were afraid of being snubbed in Newport, where outsiders, no matter how wealthy, were excluded by a set of ironclad though unwritten rules.

But Neil had no such gaps in his social armor. His place was firmly established. He was an extremely eligible bachelor. He might have stayed with any number of friends in Newport and always be assured of receiving invitations to the best, most exclusive parties.

As if he cared. The parties that used to

amuse him, at least for a time, now meant nothing at all to him. Parties bored him; people bored him. If that was the case, he kept asking himself, why had he come to Newport? But it was one of those questions he could not answer. All he knew was he had tried to keep away, but like a magnet, Newport kept drawing him.

To be more honest, it was her. He knew that. He could not get her out of his mind. . . .

But why should she lie to him? Over and over, that was the question he kept asking himself. She had looked stunned when he put it to her. But he no longer trusted her looks, her expressions.

He wished he could have forgotten them and *her*, but he was beginning to fear that he never would. He knew there would never be another woman for him. . . .

The thought of Maura and Harold as lovers stung him to the core. No, he could not bear the thought of another man touching her. . . .

He thought of how she had denied it. "We are friends!" she insisted. So firmly, he almost believed her. But if so, what was he to think of the inquiries he'd made. "The man's a shark!" Neil had heard, from at least four highly respected businessmen. "He acquires businesses the way a child acquires toys. The man is ruthless—be on your guard with him!"

As a result, and coupled with what he had read in the letters, what was he to think? There had to be more than friendship involved. But were they lovers? Wasn't there some middle area? Maura was not like all the other women—like Sarah, for example—who fell into bed so easily. Or—*was she*? How could he know?

Damnit! Again, he cursed his coming to Newport. That evening he'd received an invitation to a small dinner party. He'd torn up the invitation and started to drink instead. But drinking alone was unsatisfying. He decided, after a while, to take a ride into town.

It was a foggy night, a chilly one, with a storm reportedly on the way. It kept most of the summer people and even the footstools at home. When Neil reached the main thoroughfare, the only person he found on the streets was a guard, hired by the vigilante committee to patrol the town at night.

"'Evening, Mr. Prescott." The guard recognized him and tipped his hat.

Neil nodded and headed toward McBride's. He found the bar as deserted as the street. McBride, who looked as though he was about to doze off, snapped to, cheerfully.

"Well, Mr. Prescott! I was just thinkin' of closin'. Glad I didn't. What'll you have?"

"Whiskey and soda," Neil said. "And pour one for you rself."

As McBride busied himself, Neil went on, conversationally, "What's the news? What's been happening?"

McBride looked up, frowning. "Nothin', unfortunately. The town's become a ghost town. Can't even work up a good cockfight."

"Too bad." Neil sipped his whiskey.

"You heard Cassidy's been run out of town? That's one lucky break. Saved a bit of bloodshed. But the mystery man's still on the loose."

"The mug?" Neil said. For some reason, he'd been thinking of the light-haired youth he'd met.

"What mug?" McBride looked puzzled. "No, I'm talkin' about the anarchist."

"Oh, yes. Of course." Neil nodded. Actually, he'd heard the story several times. George Bannister, one of the first to relate it, had gone on to explain about the vigilante committee and Maura's part in organizing it. "She's a wonderful woman, that Mrs. Van Diver!" Bannister had told Neil. . . .

"Another drink, Mr. Prescott?"

Neil snapped out of his reverie. "Yes," he said. "Do it again. And another for yourself. I wonder," he went on, as McBride poured the drinks, "about the mugs. Know anything about them?"

McBride shrugged. "Most of 'em have left town."

"But not all," Neil picked up, quickly. "Is that it?"

"Well, every so often, I see one of 'em. Here's lookin' at you." He raised his whiskey and downed it in one gulp.

"I see." It had just been an idle thought, Neil decided, that perhaps McBride could have put a name to that mug's face. How should he know who Neil was talking about, anyway?

"Another?" McBride asked.

Neil shook his head. He was thinking of

leaving when the doors swung open and a tall,
lone figure strode up to the bar.

"Hallo? It's like death's door in here!" the
new customer said.

"How d'ya do, Mr. Jennings?" McBride said
happily. "What'll it be?"

"A whiskey. And one for the gentleman."
He nodded at Neil. "I hate to drink alone. Say,
don't I know you? Of course." He held out his
hand. "Carter Jennings."

Neil shook hands, briefly. "Neil Prescott.
Thanks for the drink."

"My pleasure. You know how deadly it is to
drink alone. But this whole town's turned into
a morgue."

"That it has," McBride echoed sadly.

"I almost envy my friend—Lord Parker—
you know. He'll be going back to England
soon. Told myself when I left I wouldn't be
stepping foot on that turf soon. But there's got
to be more action—even at Brighton—than
here! What do you say, McBride?"

McBride laughed in answer.

"Why does Lord Parker make so many
trips?" Neil asked, as casually as possible.

"His work with Mr. Gladstone, of course.
Then, he has his own businesses there and"—
Jennings winked—"business here, too."

"Actual business?" Neil asked quickly.

Jennings shrugged. "Oh, I do think Harold
has one or two irons in the fire. Though I'm
not privy to any information, of course. And
there's his lovely friend, Mrs. Van Diver.
She's reason enough to cross the Atlantic."

"I see. And Lord Parker has told you this himself?"

Carter hesitated. He was caught between loyalty to his friend and the fact that Carter did love, above everything else, gossip. "Lord Parker and I do not discuss his business and certainly not his personal affairs. But as far as that is concerned, I can only tell you what everyone says. And that is, she would make a lovely Lady Parker."

"Ah, yes." Neil slammed his glass down on the bar with such force that McBride, who'd begun to nod off again, suddenly woke up. "I'm afraid I have to be going. Thank you for the drink, Mr. Jennings."

"My pleasure, as I said."

Neil picked up his hat. "I'll be seeing you, McBride. Thanks."

"Sure thing. If I stay open, that is. I've been thinkin' of takin' another run to the South Seas, where there's some action."

"Watch out for those cannibals, if you do," Neil called over his shoulder on the way out.

He found the street misty with fog and as deserted as before. The guard was resting under an elm tree.

"Quiet night, sir," the guard said.

"Yes." Neil climbed into his small, two-seat buggy and eased the horses down the street, toward his rented cottage. His head was beginning to ache from all the drink. From experience, he knew it would ache even more in the morning.

What bothered him even more than that

were Carter's last words, echoing in his brain: "The future Lady Parker."

Was it simply gossip, or was it true? Oh, he was sorry he had come, doubly sorry he had talked to Carter. The man's words only confirmed Neil's suspicions. Parker did have irons in the fire. Was the Van Diver business one of them? And was Maura the other . . . ?

Chapter Nineteen

MAURA HAD MADE UP HER MIND. THIS TIME, she must definitely forget Neil. She could fool herself no longer into believing he would come back. His anger, no, it was more than that—for an instant, she had felt *hatred*—was too strong.

He was mistaken, of course. Somehow, he had chosen to believe that something existed where nothing, in fact, did. Possibly, knowing Neil (at least, she'd thought she'd known him!), he'd found some sort of "evidence" that backed up the accusations he'd made. But what?

She went over and over in her mind the last time they'd been together, those two days he'd stayed at the house. Finally it came to her: the books. It was when she'd run down to the secretary to look over the books that the letter had fallen out of the pigeonhole. . . .

She'd read it several times. All the phrases seemed so innocent to her, but after the third reading, she began to see where some of them might be misleading. The ones about business, for example. But she had simply asked Harold a few questions, which he'd answered. She was continually asking Harold questions; there was so much she didn't know about the business, so much she wanted to know so she would be able, one day, to pass it on to Peter.

But perhaps, reading the letter, it hadn't seemed like a simple question-and-answer to Neil.

Yet how could he think she would scheme against him? And—what was even more incomprehensible to her—how could he believe she could lie in his arms one night and then go to another man's bed? Did he really believe her capable of such duplicity?

She didn't know. She tried to put herself in his place. Would she have reacted the same way? She was jealous of him, that much she had always known. If someone had told her Neil had been engaged to that dark, gypsy-type woman or that redhead on the beach all the time he had been making love to her, what would her reaction have been? Would she have believed the gossip?

Maura had to admit she might have been fooled. Yet if Neil had sworn there was no truth in the gossip, she still thought she would have taken his word. Though she could not be sure of that—could she? Ah, there's the rub! she thought.

Shakespeare brought her to Dickens. She remembered how Pip in *Great Expectations* had been deceived in so many ways by Estella —though that had never stopped his loving her. She wondered if, beneath his anger, Neil still loved her. But if so, he had a fine way of showing it! No, this time, she'd definitely made up her mind: she had to forget him.

She had one positive love in her life: her son. Her beautiful son. She held him close to her, to comfort her, as she made her plans.

Those plans all revolved around him. When he was a little older, she would coo to him (and he would listen, with wide eyes), they would travel. They would spend some time in England with Uncle Harold, then they would go on to the Continent. She would see France, Germany, Italy, all the countries she'd longed to visit.

Before they went, however, there were things she must do. She was more determined than ever to establish herself as a social leader, for her son's sake.

"It will be a glorious ball," she whispered to him. "I will have photographers to take pictures so that years later, you'll look through them and it'll be as though you were there and not tucked upstairs in bed."

"No, Mama." He shook his head and made a face at the mention of bed. Maura laughed.

"And what are you two whispering about?" Harold said, walking in.

"We're talking about growing up and parties!" Maura smiled.

"About parties—Gladys Van Diver, I understand, is holding a party sometime after the Belmont's party. I'm not sure of the day," Harold said. "Have you been invited?"

"No, and I don't expect to be." She

shrugged. "Oh, but I wish you could be here for mine!"

"I've already cabled Mr. Gladstone to see if it's possible to extend my stay. You know I'd like to. If not, Carter can take you in on his arm." He smiled.

Maura sighed. "A nice enough man, I suppose, but a poor substitute for you."

"As I am a poor substitute for . . . ?" He looked at her with a raised brow.

"No! Definitely no!" she said at once. "You can't believe that, Harold!" She would have gone on, but he stopped her.

"I'm sorry, Maura dear. I'm not being fair to you. . . . And where are you running off to, young man?" he asked as Peter, grinning, slipped off his lap and toddled toward his nanny.

"Let's talk of other things, Maura." Harold smiled. "Mrs. Belmont's party. I understand she's fit to be tied. After having to postpone it once, now there's a conflict with Mrs. Pendergast's party."

"Everyone will go to Mrs. Belmont's. She knows that, Harold."

"Yes, but I still sympathize with the poor lady."

The words were said tongue-in-cheek. Maura laughed, and said, "And what about poor Mrs. Pendergast?"

They both laughed now, then Maura suddenly clapped. "Oh, Harold, look at the baby!"

He'd just toddled back into the room, grinning again, and wearing a pint-sized baseball uniform. Maura, who'd never seen a game, had been given the baby's uniform by a baseball enthusiast.

"Well, now that you're dressed, let's play some catch," Harold suggested to Peter. He rolled a ball toward him.

All three spent the rest of the afternoon playing with the baby. A lovely afternoon, Maura thought, though toward the end of the day, she was a little alarmed when she noticed Harold. He looked so tired and drawn! He had not fully recovered from his illness, she decided. With the Belmonts' party just a few days away, she worried that he wasn't up to going. Knowing Harold, he would insist on appearing. Well, she would see to it he rested all day before the party.

The sky was starless, the streets covered with a thick mist. The storm that had threatened the other night and had never come was once again looming.

"Mrs. Belmont will not be pleased," Harold said.

"People will come regardless," Maura insisted.

And, of course, they did. The mammoth, lavishly decorated ballroom was filled with everyone who was anyone in the summer colony. In addition, the notable guests included a German baron who scrutinized everyone through his monocle, a handsome Polish prince with his princess, a very young princess, indeed, and a pretty one, her beauty marred only by a florid complexion improperly set off by an orange-red gown.

The gown Maura had chosen was of pale gray silk, short-waisted, trimmed with fine French lace and girdled with a ribbon just below the breast.

"You look ravishing," Harold had said, more than once.

He, Maura was happy to see, was looking rested and much better than he had been. He was obviously enjoying the party. There were at least a dozen or more Anglophiles present. One couple had recently returned from England and was entertaining everyone with the latest gossip. They talked of *The Mikado,* which had taken London by storm. The Music Halls—like the Pavilion, the Oxford, the Alhambra, the Empire—were thriving. Comic men in loud check suits danced their way across the stages, while stout corseted ladies displaying ample bosoms and legs sang. The popular songs of the day were Florrie Forde's "Waltz Me Around Again, Willie," and Vesa Victoria's "Our Lodger's Such A Nice Young Man." Marie Lloyd, much admired by the Prince of Wales, was making a current hit of "Oh, Mr. Porter!" And there was a young comedian named Charles Chaplin, whose small son bore his name (and would one day be famous), singing ballads about Gay Paree.

Maura danced a slow, pretty waltz with Mr. Belmont, a stout, amiable man, who stepped on her toes a half-dozen times. She was glad to exchange partners. Harold and she danced a quadrille. She was enjoying herself until, near the end of the dance, she saw a curious look pass over Harold's face.

"What is it?" she asked, alarmed. "Are you all right, Harold?"

"Yes, fine. Fine," he assured her. But the moment the quadrille was over, he drew her off to the side.

"Who is that man with George Bannister?" he asked.

Maura glanced around the room. Toward the entrance, she saw George with a tall, thin young man, with a dark, sallow face above a stiff white collar. "Why, that's his son," she said.

"I thought so." Harold nodded. "He's the one."

"What one?"

"The one I saw with Cassidy the night at the saloon."

Maura stared. "Are you sure?" She could not believe it.

But Harold nodded. "Yes, I'm certain of it. He's the one."

Maura looked at him with growing alarm. His face was flushed; there were tiny beads of perspiration on his forehead. "Harold," she said, gently. "Why don't we sit down for a minute and talk about this?"

"Stop treating me like a child, Maura," he said at once. "Something must be done about him!"

"Something will be done," she agreed, "but I want you to sit down first."

Firmly, she guided him to a chair. "I'll get someone to take care of it. I promise."

"Wait." Harold had allowed himself to be led to a chair; he did, in fact, looked relieved to be sitting down and at rest. But he kept a firm hold of Maura's hand.

"Tell me," he began now, "who are you going to with this information? I want to be sure it's handled properly."

She paused. But there could be only one person. "Neil Prescott," she said.

Harold released her hand. "He'll be fine," he said.

As Maura left him, her heart began to beat so wildly she was sure it could be heard. Foolish! she told herself as she started slowly toward the other end of the room where Neil stood.

She had noticed him the instant he'd come in. Fortunately, she'd been off at one end of the room, and he at the other, so neither had had to take any official notice of the other. But from time to time, she had caught herself turning in his direction, only to find, invariably, his eyes on her. Both of them, each time, had quickly turned away.

It's a child's game we're playing with one another, she thought. And how could she ever put him out of her mind if, at each function she attended, he was always there? But her stronger self counseled: it might take time, but she would learn to steel her heart. She must.

Now, as she approached him, her steps

grew shorter, as though to delay the moment when she must face him. She tried to think of an alternate plan. But she could not. Neil would know what to do. He and Bannister were friends. Perhaps he could break the news to him. . . .

She held out her hand. "How do you do, Mr. Prescott?"

There was a rosy flush under the tan skin. He had not expected this. Not at all. He took her hand, almost as he had that first evening. "It's good to see you, Mrs. Van Diver," he said, a little stiffly. "And how are you?"

"Thank you, very well . . ." Her words drifted off as she noticed the petite blonde by his side. Maura was almost certain Neil had come in alone. At some time during the evening, however, the blonde had flown to Neil's side. At the moment, she seemed to be edging closer to him, as though establishing proprietary rights.

Quickly, Maura put an end to it. "Would you dance with me?" she asked.

There was a strained moment while she held her breath, thinking: what if he refuses? She had a sudden, wild desire to laugh. She knew now how a beau must feel when he worries if his lady will turn him down.

But she needn't have worried. The next moment, Neil had taken her arm and was waltzing her around the floor.

"This is, indeed, a surprise as well as an honor," he said, in a half-mocking tone.

"You needn't play your gallant self with me," she said curtly. She was anxious to put things right, at once. "I did not ask you to dance for your good looks or your charm. Though I'm sure *she* thinks they're both considerable." Maura tossed her head in the blonde's direction.

"I asked you to dance for one reason," she went on. "To talk without any curious ears. Actually, I did it for Harold's sake."

She felt his arm stiffen around her; his jaw tightened. It occurred to her she could have been a little less curt and abrupt.

"Oh?" he said, coolly.

"Yes," she hurried on, almost angry with herself. "He's not well and I'm anxious that he not overexert himself. The only reason I sought you out is I know you know George Bannister well."

His brows knitted together; his dark eyes bore into her. "Exactly," he began, coolly again, "what has Bannister to do with this?"

"Not Bannister exactly, but his son. Harold recognizes him from that night at Jay's Saloon. What I'm saying is," she continued, "Bannister's son—is his name Fred?—is the anarchist."

Neil's eyes deepened; she saw little glints of fire. Was he listening? Was he flirting with her? Why had she ever thought she'd understood this man?

But he'd been listening. "Is Harold certain of that?" he questioned.

"Yes."

For the first time, Neil's eyes left her to travel around the room. "I don't see Bannister now. What exactly is it you want me to do?"

"I'm not sure. I thought perhaps you could speak to George. . . ."

"What makes you think he'll take my word against his son's?"

"Well . . ." Maura paused. She had not thought of it that way.

"There must be more proof."

"Harold is proof. I believe him. Don't you?"

"Still, it was night. . . ." He hesitated, then nodded. "Yes, I believe him. But let me think."

Without talking, they waltzed across the floor. As they dipped and whirled, it seemed to Maura that their bodies were one. Almost against her will, she thought of that first dance she had had with him at the Plaza, when Peter had still been alive. It all seemed centuries ago. . . .

He was pulling her closer; she felt as though she were drowning again. Waves sweeping her under, the taste of salt water, his lips. . . .

She pushed him away. She could not think with him so close. "I think you should act. Now. Before something happens. But first—" She paused. It had occurred to her suddenly that if she were ever going to set things straight with Neil, now was the time. Perhaps she would never have another.

"I want you to know about Harold and me. You are wrong if you think we were conspiring against you. My interest in the business is simply that I wanted to have some knowledge of its workings. Harold was kind enough to explain some things. He is very kind and sweet and brotherly. And that explains our relationship—totally. Whether or not you choose to believe—"

Maura paused again. The way he was looking at her! She had never been able to read those dark eyes, but now she was almost certain of what she saw: disbelief.

But before she could protest, she felt a tremor underneath her feet. Like an earthquake—

"Dynamite!" someone yelled as glass shattered across the room. The broken glass splattered against a man's forehead and cheek, while his wife cried: "You're bleeding!"

The room was cloudy with smoke, noisy with the shrieks of women, the demands of men wanting to know what was going on. In the center of the room, Neil stood with Maura. His arms had not released her from the dance. He held her, ready to push her to safety. But which way was safety?

Suddenly, a high-pitched voice rose above the clamor and the settling smoke.

"Silence! Do you hear me! I have something to say!"

All heads turned in the direction of the voice. There were a few small gasps when they saw the speaker.

It was Fred Bannister, his dinner jacket off, his hair unruly. His dark face, which had always borne a sullen expression, was curiously lit up. Every muscle of his face seemed aquiver with excitement; the light in his pale eyes was so bright that it frightened Maura even more than whatever it was he was waving in his hand.

"An explosive," he explained. "Not dynamite, but an easier-to-carry cousin. But it's as lethal as dynamite, I assure you. All I would have to do is—" He paused, waving the small stick in his hand toward the flickering light of a candle.

"No!" someone shrieked.

He laughed wickedly. "Well, you see. But never fear. I'm not going to do that, at least, not at the moment."

His bright eyes roamed the room. "You!" He shook his head disgustedly. "I had thought, at first, to remain hidden, anonymous. I felt the more discreet I was, the more I could accomplish. But I can no longer remain incognito. You people have made me furious!"

Under his gaze, his captive audience shifted nervously.

"Look at you!" he cried. "How much did you spend for this party, Mrs. Belmont?" He pointed at her. "I'm asking you a question!"

The poor woman looked as though she might have an apoplectic fit. "I—I don't know," she stammered.

"You don't know," he repeated, mimicking her. "Why don't I tell you, then? I'll guess you spent about $100,000, if not more. $100,000! Do you know what that money could mean to the poor? Money that was thrown away, wasted, on flowers, food, decorations, servants! Do you know people are starving? That most of this food, which could feed hun-

gry children, will be thrown out? Look at it!"
He waved a hand at the buffet table, where
mounds of pâté in the shape of swans, caviar
piled high as a small mountain stood.

"Pâté, caviar!" he cried. "Only the best!
The most expensive to line your fat bellies!
And all of it going to ruin!"

He ran a hand through his unruly hair,
keeping his stick of explosive aloft and dan-
gerously close to the candle. Maura's eyes
traveled from the candle back to his eyes,
bright and furtive as an animal's.

"Oh, how the footstools would love some of
that food!" he cried now. "And who was the
first person who coined that phrase? Do you
remember? Wasn't it you, Mr. Astor?"

He spun toward a white-haired, heavyset
man whose face grew red under his white
muttonchops.

"One of Mr. Astor's brighter sayings," Bannister went on. "'Our footstools'—that was
the complete phrase. Neat, eh? To turn another human being into your footstool! What
right have we, tell me! What right has any
human being!" he raved on.

And now, Maura was aware of a hand slipping away from around her. She turned, as
Neil put a finger to his lips, to stop any in-
quiry. Silently, she watched as he slipped
away through the crowd.

"What right?" Bannister went on. "We had
a revolution in this country to free ourselves
from tyranny, but will there ever be a release
from what is even a more insidious kind of
tyranny? The rich over the poor! What right

have you"—he pointed to one of the more portly guests—"to fill your big belly while he"— Bannister's finger waved toward a rather undernourished-looking waiter—"starves? Tell me!"

The man flushed, then stammered, at last. "Ah—no right. No right!"

"Good. You're learning. And you, with those jewels . . ." His finger wagged at a heavily bejeweled matron. "Do you read? I mean, something other than the society page?"

The matron flushed as he went on: "Have you ever heard of Reverend Tucker and his Gospel of Wealth? Well, you're just the kind of person Tucker's talking about!"

He went on, while the poor woman, looking as if she were about to faint, was visibly held up by her husband.

"Fred, please!" It was George Bannister. He was out of breath, as though he'd been off in one of the rooms, playing billiards, and had just been alerted. "What are you doing? Sit down, for God's sakes!"

"No, *you* sit down, Father!" Fred snapped back. "Sit or else!" He waved the stick of explosive. George Bannister shrank back into the crowd.

Oh, where had Neil gone? Maura wondered. She had lost sight of him in the crowd. Suddenly, she spotted him. He had made his way cautiously around the room, edging nearer and nearer to Bannister. But Fred, wise in his madness, had stationed himself in front of the door, giving himself a wide berth between himself and his audience. There was no way Neil could get near him, without Bannister spotting him first.

Unless? Maura thought quickly, then suddenly spoke up: "I know of Reverend Tucker, Mr. Bannister."

Fred Bannister whirled toward her. "Who is that?" he asked angrily. "Oh yes, it's you, Mrs. Van Diver."

"Reverend Tucker," Maura went on, "speaks against laissez-faire and for improvement of the conditions of the poor. All of which I applaud. But nowhere have I read that Reverend Tucker approves of violence."

Bannister flushed angrily. "And what makes you an authority? What interest is it of yours, anyway, with all your furs, your jewels?"

"Because I didn't always have furs and jewels." She raised her head proudly. "Unlike you, Mr. Bannister, I come from the poor."

This did not sit well with Bannister. "Then you should applaud what I'm doing!" he snapped back angrily.

"Applaud belittling people?" She frowned. "Embarrassing them, frightening them to death?"

"If it's the only way!" he cried. "Why not? Why not?"

Once again, he waved his explosive toward the candle. Maura's reply lay unspoken on her lips. She was getting him angrier; she would have to be careful. Still, his attention was on her, which was the important thing, as Neil crept around in back of him. In another moment or so, he would be there. . . .

"Why?" she continued. "Why violence? When there are a dozen peaceful ways you haven't tried?"

"I know what you're leading up to—charity! But that doesn't work! We've seen that!"

He shook his head angrily and at that moment, Neil grabbed him.

They struggled together, in an almost silent scuffle, while everyone in the room held his breath. Fred was young and strong; Neil, slightly older, was, however, stronger. He finally wrestled the explosive away from Fred. In the process, he loosened his hold on Bannister.

Fred turned and dashed out the door.

"Come back!" George Bannister cried and rushed after his son. Several men, including Neil, joined him in the chase.

In the ballroom, there were audible sighs of relief after the long ordeal. Women who had held back tears now let them flow freely.

Maura ran to find Harold. He was struggling through the crowd, toward her.

"You foolish girl!" he cried, when he saw her. But he hugged her to him. "Getting up like that! Oh, you were wonderful, dear Maura!"

"Wasn't she?" Several couples stopped to praise her.

Maura flushed under their admiring eyes. "Thank you," she murmured, then turned to Harold. "I think it's best we leave. You need your rest." And I want to get away! she thought.

They started toward the doors that Fred Bannister had flung open. Suddenly, from the street, they heard a terrible shriek, a neighing of horses, then a cry: "Oh, my God! My God!"

Maura recognized George Bannister's voice. "What happened?" she cried, as a man rushed back from the street.

But he would not say. "Stay back!" he warned her and the rest of the crowd.

Maura found a seat and waited patiently with Harold while the man guarded the door. They did not have long to wait.

Neil had come back. He whispered a few words to the man at the door, then held up his hand for silence.

"Fred Bannister is dead," he said slowly. "In the fog, a team of horses ran over him. His body is being removed now. You may go."

There were murmurs of dismay, and some of approval.

"Served him right!" someone said.

"Poor George Bannister!" someone else sympathized.

Neil had disappeared into the fog again. Two by two, the guests started to leave. Tired, distraught, Maura and Harold also left.

"Poor George!" Harold murmured.

"Yes," Maura agreed. But how strange that not one person had said: "Poor Fred!" Did no one feel a touch of pity for that crazy but unhappy boy? Well, she did. . . .

As they climbed into their carriage, Maura spotted Neil, walking with George Bannister. For one moment, Neil's eyes strayed to her. Their eyes locked for an instant, then he turned to George again.

Maura and Harold drove off into the fog. . . .

Chapter Twenty

THE FOLLOWING DAY, THE PAPERS, AFTER praising the colorful, unusual flower schemes and decorations, the gowns and the numerous, noteworthy guests, only briefly mentioned the frightening incident. After discussing the explosives, Fred Bannister's tragic death took up only a short line, as an unpleasant addendum to the evening.

At first, Maura could not believe that it could be shrugged off so easily, so heartlessly. But in the next few days, as she saw no further mention, she came to believe it was so.

"If there's been any change at all," Manny, the florist, informed her, "it's simply that people are relieved. The anarchist is dead; the mugs are gone. There's no more threat to themselves and their good times. And so, life goes on."

"While a life has been lost," Maura reminded him.

"Fred Bannister would never have amounted to very much, no matter what."

"But his cause was a good one," Maura said defensively. "So much waste is irresponsible in the face of poverty."

"I agree with that," Manny said. "But I don't sympathize with Fred Bannister and his like. He was a cause-seeker. In another time, he would have had a different cause, simply as an excuse to rebel against society. Don't waste your tears on him."

Maura fell silent for a moment. She was helping Manny arrange the seating chart for the supper following the ball. She pushed a few name-cards into place, then observed quietly: "He was a human being, Manny, and a young one. I myself will never be the same again, because of him. No dinner, nothing, in fact, that transpires in this house will be wasteful. I've given the servants strict orders and I'll see that they're carried out."

"You're a good woman," Manny observed. "I wish there were more like you."

Something in his voice made Maura stop and look hard at him. "Have you been bothered again?"

"Oh, no. Now that the hoodlums are gone, everything's been fine."

"But you are still on edge?" she guessed.

"I am a Jew, after all," he answered simply. "We live that way."

"Oh, Manny!" She sighed. "You know," she went on, after a moment, "you have never told me your story. I know that you are a Jew, that you are a clever man as well as an exceedingly gentle one. But that is all I know."

He shrugged. "I do not have that much of a story, but if you would like to hear it?"

"Oh, yes!"

Manny continued to write out the place-cards and to hand them to Maura, one by one, as he talked.

"My ancestors came from Spain in 1745, driven out by the Spanish Inquisition. One of my forefathers is credited with beginning the spermacetti industry in the United States. Are you familiar with that?"

Maura shook her head.

"In the whale," Manny explained, "there is a white, waxlike substance which is useful in making cosmetics, healing ointments, candles. My forefathers, actually distant cousins, learned to produce this and sell it in huge quantities."

"I see."

"It is quite a profitable industry," Manny continued, "and they flourished until the American Revolution. But the British occupation of the city ruined commerce. My relatives left, many going south and settling in Georgia and Tennessee.

"After the Revolution, however, my great-grandfather, Zeke, came back. He had only been a boy when his family had been forced to leave, but he had loved the climate of the city, the freshness of the sea.

"Zeke found the city different, however, from the one he remembered. The British, followed by the French occupation, had killed commerce, and the once prosperous city. Population had decreased to four thousand. The colony of Jews was gone; only one or two families remained. Ironically enough, these families had come to Newport to escape persecution. But where they'd been tolerated in a prosperous society, they found, in a failing one, they were unwanted again.

"My great-grandfather might have left. Surely, that would have been the wisest thing to do. But two things stopped him: first, as I've said, he liked the climate. Secondly, he fell in love with the daughter of one of the Jewish families.

"She was a lovely, red-haired young girl. Zeke was a handsome young buck and she also fell in love. They were married and Zeke joined her father in business. The man had a small grocery store that was twice burned and twice erected again, first by Zeke and his father-in-law, later by Zeke and his own son, my grandfather.

"My own father rebelled at the thought of working in the store. He would not stay in a town where he was not wanted, he told my grandfather. When my grandfather died, my father sold the store and went off to join his richer relatives in the South. He did well, but he made the mistake of bringing me up here one year, on vacation. . . ."

"And you came back to start your own business?" Maura finished.

"Yes. And, in my great-grandfather's tradition, I have also fallen in love with a lovely Jewish girl."

For one moment, Maura was taken back.

"You mean Abby? But I always think of her as Irish."

"And one-half Jew," he reminded her. "That's the important part," he smiled.

Maura nodded. She and Abby had had a long talk the other day. Abby explained about her parents. Her mother had been a Jew. Abby had never known her, but her mother had been desperately in love with her father, and had been forbidden to marry him by her father. Abby's mother had borne her in sorrow and desperation, only to die shortly afterward. Abby had been raised by her father's sister, a spinster.

"I found a picture of my mother," Abby had confessed. "She was so beautiful! I began to read everything I could about the Jews, how they'd been oppressed and persecuted over the centuries. I learned as much as I could about their religion. But it was something I could never talk about with my aunt. . . ."

"You know," Manny said now, "there is no one else I can ask for Abby's hand, so I am asking you."

Maura smiled softly. "I think you will make a lovely couple. Only I will miss Abby," she added.

"It will be some time, yet," he assured her. "Actually I hadn't planned to say anything for a while. I want to build a house first. My rooms are not big enough to house a family—"

He broke off as Abby entered.

"Come here, Abby!" Maura cried at once. "Let me kiss you. Manny has just told me."

Abby ran to her, flushing, and Maura kissed her.

"I didn't want him to say anything yet, ma'am," Abby began.

"Oh, I'm glad he did! I'm so happy for you!"

"Thank you, ma'am." Abby beamed. She looked almost beautiful as she stood clasping and unclasping her hands. "Oh, I almost forgot. Miss Richards wants to see you about Peter."

Maura stood. "I'll go up right now."

"She said she'll be down, ma'am."

"That's all right. I can run up. Why don't you stay? And order some tea for three."

She left the loving couple alone, and proceeded up the long staircase. She took her time, in order to give Manny and Abby a few more minutes with each other. She was happy for them, even though she was sad that Abby would eventually be leaving. But loved ones leave, she reminded herself. She was happy that Abby would be making a good life for herself. She would always be her friend, as Manny would.

"Did Abby misunderstand me?" Miss Richards said, alarmed, when Maura greeted her in the hallway outside of the baby's door. "I told her I wished to speak to you, but I was coming downstairs. There was no need for you to come here, ma'am!"

"That's all right." Maura smiled. "What is it? A problem with Peter?"

"Oh, no, he's fine. It's—it's my vacation. I wondered . . ." She paused, a little uncertainly. "I would like to take it sooner than we'd planned, if possible. You see, my mother is not feeling well. . . ."

"Oh, I'm sorry. Well, of course," Maura said. "When would you like to go?"

"Well, she's very sick, ma'am. Maybe—if you could get someone—I'd like to leave by the end of the week."

"You can go tomorrow. Abby and I can look after Peter."

"Oh, that would be wonderful! Thank you so much, ma'am!" Miss Richards bent down and kissed Maura's hand in relief.

There was a sudden wail from inside the room. Miss Richards straightened up at once. "Peter's waking up. Excuse me, ma'am."

She slipped inside the door. Maura might have followed, but the parlor maid suddenly appeared.

"It's Lord Parker, ma'am. I showed him into the drawing room."

"Lord Parker?" she repeated, puzzled. "Thank you." She started toward the stairs, wondering why Harold was here. She was expecting him for dinner, but it was much too early for that. And it wasn't like Harold to drop in unexpectedly.

"Did I disturb you, Maura dear?" Harold asked as she walked into the small drawing room.

"You never disturb me. How are you feeling?"

"Fine, dear. I must apologize, however. I can't make dinner. I've just received a cable from Mr. Gladstone. I'm afraid I have to start back."

"Oh, Harold! When?"

"Tonight, dear. There's a ship sailing at eight. I was lucky to get passage. If not, I'd have to wait until Tuesday."

Maura sat down at once. "That means I won't be seeing you for a while."

"I'm afraid not. I am sorry I won't be here for your ball. But I've already phoned Carter; he will make a proper escort."

"Yes. Thank you."

"And I will be there in spirit," Harold added.

She laughed suddenly. "It would be oh so much better if you could be here in person! But I understand. It's only . . ."

"What is it?" Harold asked at once.

"Oh, Harold." She shook her head. "It's nothing. You're busy. You have packing to do. . . ."

"Nonsense. It can wait. Tell me what is troubling you."

"I . . ." She looked up into his dear face. She had never really explained about Neil to him—or anyone, for that matter. All this time, she had carried her thoughts, her worries, inside her. She felt the sudden need to unburden herself. . . .

"My dear friend, thank you. I'll try to make this brief. It's so kind of you to listen.

"I'm one of those creatures, I think, who falls in love only once and is doomed, fated to live without their love. My husband and I, as you must have guessed, were never a love match. I fell in love on my wedding day, at first sight—as they say—with Neil. Do you think me a foolish maiden? I don't blame you. I've told myself that many and many a time. But we can't choose whom we love. If we *could* choose—ah! How much simpler life would be!

"I, fortunately or unfortunately as it's turned out, fell in love with Neil. But through misunderstanding, bad timing, ill luck, each time it seemed as though we might be able to have a life together, something, someone, came between us.

"At first, it was the will. Neil begged me to marry him and give up the inheritance. How I was tempted! But I could not give up my son's birthright—you see that, don't you? Then, after Peter's birth, when it seemed as though Neil and I might be reconciled again, we had another misunderstanding. He"—here Maura faltered, slightly—"read a letter you had written and completely misinterpreted our relationship. He thought we were planning to join hands in business and turn him out.

"He also thought"—here, Maura's voice lowered, a trifle embarrassed—"you and I were more than friends. . . ," She drifted off.

"Ah, how I wish that were true!" Harold said in a low voice. He seized Maura's hand. "I'm so sorry, m'dear. To see you in pain like this is painful to me. Is there anything I can do?"

"No." Maura looked up into his gray eyes. "I

shouldn't have unburdened myself like this. I did tell him, you know, the night of the Belmont party, about us."

"And what did he say?"

She shrugged. "Nothing," she said hopelessly.

"The fool!" There was anger in Harold's voice. "I shall talk to him!"

"No, don't!" Maura cried at once. "I don't want you to, Harold. Please! You must promise me!"

"Maura—" He looked at her helplessly. He could see she meant what she said.

"Promise," she repeated.

"All right," he said, against his will.

"And you'd better be going. Although I hate to see you go, Harold, dear. But I know you must have a million things to do."

"I do," he admitted as he stood.

"You will write?"

"Every day. Now, give me a kiss."

She kissed both cheeks, and hugged him to her for a long moment. Then he picked up his hat and hurried out.

She stood at the window with a heavy heart, watching him leave. She would miss him terribly. She guessed that it would be a while before she would see him again. It was rumored that Mr. Gladstone would be forming a new government. If so, Harold would be at the center of it. He would have no time to fritter away on trips from England to America.

She turned away from the window. She had the strange feeling that suddenly everyone—

Abby, Miss Richards, and now, Harold—was deserting her. . . .

Two nights later, standing on her terrace, she felt even more deserted, more alone. The night was unusually clear and in the distance, tier upon tier of windows alit, and sparkling like a magnificent castle on the Rhine was the estate of Gladys Van Diver. Carriage after carriage lined up in front of the estate, as their passengers climbed out on their way to Gladys's house.

The night before, Gladys's husband had stopped off at Maura's house to personally extend his invitation to the party.

"The entire town is talking about how marvelous you were at the Belmonts'," Thomas said. "The family is proud of you! It would be an honor to have you," he told her.

"It's very sweet of you to say so," Maura said. "I'm thrilled that you should ask me. . . ." She'd hesitated. It was on the tip of her tongue to say it would have been a great deal sweeter if Gladys herself had come by to extend the invitation.

That was not the reason Maura declined, however. She simply was not up to going. Her own ball would be the following evening.

The fear she'd had that no one would come, that she would be snubbed, had gone. If all went well—and with Manny's wonderful creative help and advice, it should—the ball would be a huge success. She would achieve, at last, what she'd set out to do.

Yet, if it would be a triumph, it would not be

quite the triumph Maura had envisioned. She would be alone, without Neil. She tried to tell herself it didn't matter, yet deep within herself, she knew it did. And she wondered. . . .

What she knew of marriage and love she had learned through her mother and father. There was one incident that stuck in her mind. Once, backstage at the theater, she'd caught her father kissing the young girl singer. Maura had not been a child; she'd realized what was going on. She'd walked off in a huff. When her father had caught up with her, he'd tried to explain.

"She means nothing to me, Maura," he'd said. "But you don't understand how it is between your mother and me. . . ." He'd paused then, and broken off a twig from a tree, with a sprig of flowers, pink and budding, still on the end. "It's alive, but it will die," her father pointed out. "Once it does, it can never be revived."

Was love really like that twig, as her father had tried to say? And was it the same between Neil and her . . . ?

"Will you say goodnight to Peter, ma'am?"

Maura looked up, startled. "Yes."

Peter ran in and Maura hugged him to her. A child is the most precious thing in the world, she thought. Yet as she held her child, she shivered slightly. Those dreams of evil to come had been haunting her for the past few nights. Perhaps Fred Bannister's death had triggered them; she wasn't sure. But something was going to happen. She felt it in her Irish bones. . . .

"Come now," Abby called.

Peter ran off, leaving Maura alone again. How quiet the house was! She'd given most of the servants the night off, since they would all be on duty the following evening.

She stood, her eyes fixed on Gladys's house. It occurred to her that, except for the lights flashing on and off, there was no sign of another human being. It was so quiet! Just the sound of the crickets chirping.

She shivered again. Not with the breeze, but with a sudden premonition. . . .

She heard a light step on the terrace and turned, expecting Abby.

"Hi, sis."

He laughed at her shocked expression. "Tell the help to close some of the windows if you don't want visitors."

"I told you once before," she said, composed again, but angry, "never to come here."

"Well, ain't that something!" He wagged a finger at her. "The day I take my orders from you, that'll be the day."

He walked around the wide terrace that was the size of a living room, observing, admiring. "Boy, you really fell into it, didn't you? And why are you so selfish with me?"

He shook his finger again, angrily. "It's because of the likes of you that my livelihood's destroyed. And from what I hear, you personally had a hand in it."

"You mean Fred Bannister?"

"Yes, Fred. And your friend—" He leered. "The one who ran Cassidy out!"

"Cassidy deserved to be run out!"

"Did he now!" Kevin snapped back. "What if I told you Cassidy will be doin' just fine. It'll just be a matter of time until he sets up business again."

"The Cassidys of this world will always survive," Maura said grimly.

"And prosper! Don't forget that, sis! Prosper!" he cried. "But until he starts goin' again," he went on, "I'm goin' to need some money—" He broke off. "Where are you goin'?"

He blocked her way, grabbing her.

"Stay away—" She jerked away. "I'm going to the phone. I will not put up with this anymore."

But he grabbed her again, digging his fingers into her arm.

She thought of the servants—if any were around? But she doubted it. If she shouted, Abby might hear. But she didn't want to take the chance of frightening Peter. Abby would be tucking him in now.

"You're not goin' anywhere." Kevin grinned wickedly.

She stared at him stonily.

"Ain't it a shame that a pretty little Miss like you doesn't have a fella?" He laughed. "I saw the dunking you got at Bailey Beach. By that Prescott." He laughed again. "And now your English gent's left too. . . ."

"What business is it of yours?" she snapped.

His eyes turned steely.

"But this is gettin' us nowhere. I told ya I want money. And a lot. No two-bit necklace this time. I'm clearin' out. And if I get any trouble from you—" He paused. His fingers were still digging like claws into her arms. Suddenly, she saw a flash in his eyes, as though he'd just thought of something.

He started to drag her toward the edge of the terrace.

"What are you doing?" she cried.

"Why?" he said, grinning. "You afraid? Afraid I might push you over? And why shouldn't I? Who needs you? I don't see any fella around," he taunted. "Who would care if you went over the edge?"

She knew he was capable of it. She had to break away. But he was holding her so tightly. . . .

She tried her best to wriggle free. If she could just get enough leeway to shove him—

At the corner of the terrace, there was an extra inch of space. She moved slightly in, then quickly brought her leg up and kneed him, catching him in the groin.

"Ow!" he cried, and let go of her.

She ran toward the door. She almost made it, but she was not quite quick enough.

"You!" He grabbed her by her long hair, and twisted it back between his fingers. She felt as though her hair were being raised from her scalp. It hurt so! But she would not give him the satisfaction of crying out.

"Hurts, huh?"

His face was contorted in an ugly rage. He grabbed her and pulled her again toward the edge. She knew now there was no getting away from him.

Still she fought. She would not be pushed over without a fight. While there was still a chance, she would try. For her son's sake, she pleaded: "Please!" There must be some feeling in him. "We are brother and sister, Kevin!"

"Ha. When it suits you." He laughed. "Now, shut up! Shut up!" Grabbing her hair, he yanked her head back, then fastened his fingers around her throat. "Now you'll shut up!"

She felt herself losing consciousness. . . .

Was she dreaming? Dead? She heard Neil's voice. Angry, shouting: "What do you think you're doing? You!"

She opened her eyes. It was Neil. He had pulled Kevin off her. The two of them were struggling at the other end of the terrace.

Suddenly, she saw the glitter of a knife in Kevin's hand.

"No, Kevin!" she cried.

He turned toward her, surprised, and Neil grabbed for the knife. But with a cry, Kevin spun back and slashed at Neil.

Maura saw Neil flinch. Her heart stopped. Had Kevin wounded him?

"No!" she cried, and rushed toward them.

Halfway there, she saw Kevin leap on top of the parapet in triumph. Neil was holding his arm in agony.

"Ha!" Kevin cried.

Suddenly, a look of terror crossed his face. Maura realized, at once, what it was. He'd lost his balance.

"Help me!" he pleaded.

Neil reached for him with his good arm and at the same time, Maura ran to grab him. She caught a piece of his jacket, but it ripped off in her hand as he fell down three stories to the jagged rocks below.

"Kevin!" she screamed.

"Don't look!" Neil warned.

But Maura had already seen the broken, twisted form on the rocks below.

"It's horrible!" She buried her head on Neil's shoulder.

"I know. But it could have been you on those rocks, and he wouldn't have reached out to help you. You know that's true. . . ." Neil paused. "He was your brother, wasn't he?" he added, finally making the connection.

She nodded.

"I saw the resemblance at once. And yet you're so different." He flinched suddenly, as she touched his arm.

"Are you hurt?" she cried, alarmed. "Let me get Abby."

"I'm all right—just let me hold you for a minute. Oh, Maura!" He pressed her close. "I've been such a damn fool! Harold told me—"

"Harold! But he promised!"

"He told me to tell you this is the one and only promise he will ever break to you. But he had to. And I, for one, am grateful he did."

"Oh, Neil." She closed her eyes and rested against him. Neither said anything for a moment. There was no talk about plans for the future, no promises of things to come. It was not the time or the place. But Maura knew, with a certainty, that both the time and place would come.

Chapter Twenty-one

FEATHERY OSTRICH PLUMES GILDED THE EN-
trance, bright with candles, fragrant with
flowers.

Aristocrats, sportsmen, dowagers, Russian
nobility, titled English—they were all there!
Included among them were the cream of
Newport society, waiting in the ballroom with
its dazzling crystal chandeliers, its huge,
bronze columns supporting an ornate gilded
dome, circled with delicious, small murals of
cavorting pink nymphs. At the far end, the
glass doors opened onto the terrace overlooking the sea.

A cool breeze stirred the candles as everyone waited.

Upstairs, Maura took a final turn in front of
the mirror. White, Manny had suggested for
the gown. And she had taken the suggestion.
The finest Irish lace, the softest, silkiest
French satin, all fitted and snug around her
slim figure.

"Wait!" Abby said. Quickly, she adjusted
the diamond tiara on Maura's head.

There was a knock on the door.

"I'm ready," Maura said.

Do I look all right? she wondered. She turned and saw the answer in Neil's eyes.

"Turn around," he smiled. He fastened a diamond necklace around her slim neck. Then he bent and brushed his lips against her hair. "You look beautiful," he whispered.

Arm in arm, they started down the stairs. The orchestra started to play a gay Merry Widow waltz. But the tune was drowned out by the sound of applause.

"Bravo! Bravo!" everyone cried.

Maura bowed, like a diva, accepting her applause. Then, with Neil's arms around her, and the sound of clapping hands ringing in her ears, she began slowly to circle the floor.

JOY GARDNER is the pseudonym of a full-time writer who has published articles in numerous national magazines. She is the author of three previous books and lives in New York City, where she is at work on a new novel.

Tapestry

HISTORICAL ROMANCES

Breathtaking New Tales

of love and adventure set against
history's most exciting time and
places. Featuring two novels by the
finest authors in the field of romantic fiction—every <u>month</u>.

Next Month From Tapestry Romances

IRON LACE
by Lorena Dureau

LYSETTE
by Ena Halliday

POCKET BOOKS